D0796760

THE GLASS COFFIN

A Joanne Kilbourn Mystery

GAIL BOWEN

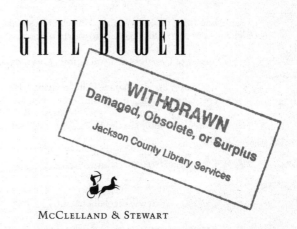

McClelland & Stewart

Library and Archives Canada Cataloguing in Publication

Bowen, Gail, 1942-
The glass coffin : a Joanne Kilbourn mystery / Gail Bowen.

ISBN 978-0-7710-1305-8

1. Title.

PS8553.08995G53 2011   C813'.54   C2011-900311-2

We acknowledge the financial support of the Government of Canada
through the Book Publishing Industry Development Program and that
of the Government of Ontario through the Ontario Media Development
Corporation's Ontario Book Initiative. We further acknowledge the
support of the Canada Council for the Arts and the Ontario Arts
Council for our publishing program.

Published simultaneously in the United States of America by
McClelland & Stewart Ltd., P.O. Box 1030, Plattsburgh, New York 12901

Library of Congress Control Number: 2011925605

Cover art: © Guarant | Dreamstime.com
This book was produced using recycled materials.
Typeset in Trump Mediaeval by M&S, Toronto
Printed and bound in the United States of America

McClelland & Stewart Ltd.
75 Sherbourne Street
Toronto, Ontario
M5A 2P9
www.mcclelland.com

1 2 3 4 5   15 14 13 12 11

For my agent, Bella Pomer,
and
my husband, Ted Bowen,
with love

Thanks to Helen Rogge, who taught me how to make a marzi-
pan pig with soul; to Joan Baldwin, the best family physician
any family could hope for; and to the Saskatchewan Indian
Federated College for a golden sabbatical year.

THE
GLASS
COFFIN

CHAPTER

1

If ever in her short life Linn Brokenshire had prayed for a good death, God hadn't been listening. When she leapt from the top floor of Hart House on a bright October afternoon, bystanders said that midway into her plunge she seemed to change her mind, screaming the word "No" as she plummeted through the gold autumn air. No one who witnessed Linn's fall would ever forget the anguish of that single word; nor would they forget how, hands clutching her worn copy of the New Testament, body trim in college-girl tartan, Linn had smashed into the pavement below. At her funeral, a lifelong friend eulogized her as a girl whose mind had broken when she couldn't reconcile what university taught her with what she had learned in Sunday school. The eulogist was a simple man whose eyes welled when he said that Linn was the gentlest, most considerate girl he had ever known and that if she had ever imagined her death would hurt so many people it would have killed her.

Seven years later, Annie Lowell met death in a manner that also seemed unnaturally cruel. Her life had been an act of defiance, a middle finger raised at the black spikes and slow waves that characterized the brainwave pattern she shared with Dostoevsky, Van Gogh, Napoleon, and millions of other epileptics. Wild at the post-production party of a film that later proved to be her breakthrough as an actor, she had pocketed the keys of a fellow guest, slipped down to the parking garage, and driven his Porsche at a speed the police clocked at 200 clicks before she ploughed into an oncoming semi and was decapitated. Free at last of the endless procession of doctors who had peered over her electroencephalograms and grimly pronounced her fate.

Linked by the tragedy of dying young, Linn and Annie shared another bond. Both had been married to the same man, a filmmaker named Evan MacLeish. When the first two Mrs. MacLeishes had departed this world at an age well short of their Biblical allotment of three score and ten, Evan hadn't wasted any time shaking a fist at the heavens; instead, he had kept his video camera rolling. The artist as alchemist, he had transferred his video to film and in so doing transformed the tragedy of his double loss into the gold of career-building movies.

As I flicked off the VCR in my family room that chilly December morning, I had to admit the movies were brilliant. My admiration for the work did not extend to its maker. In my opinion, Evan MacLeish was a scumbag who, in violating the trust of two women who had loved him, had established himself as the lousiest choice for a life partner since Bluebeard.

But my friend Jill Osiowy hadn't asked my opinion. In thirty-six hours, barring cosmic catastrophe, she would become the third Mrs. Evan MacLeish. I am by nature an optimistic woman, but I wasn't counting on a shower of meteorites.

When it came to men, there had never been any happily-ever-afters for Jill. She was a terrific woman: loyal, generous, honest, and, like Winnie the Pooh, unobtrusively at your side when you needed her. She was also a consummate professional who for twenty-five years had succeeded in the air-kissing, daggers-drawn, axe-grinding, ego-driven world of network television without sacrificing either her sense of humour or her integrity. Simply put, she was amazing, but her built-in radar for bullshit flamed out as soon as a man came into her life. The best of Jill's men were stud-muffins, big, tall pieces of man-candy whose Speedos were better filled than their noggins; the worst were drinkers, slackers, stoners, gamblers, liars, and, during one of the darkest periods of both our lives, a sociopath who abused her trust and her body. When she analyzed her history of romantic disasters, Jill had 20:20 vision. She had, she would sigh, been dumber than dirt. Those of us who cared for her sipped deeply from whatever we were sipping and remained silent. There was no point in arguing with the truth. Now Jill was in love again, and this time she was apparently convinced that the object of her affection was not just Mr. Right Now but Mr. Right.

To be fair, the rest of the world would have seen Evan MacLeish as the answer to a maiden's prayer. His documentaries drove critics to cringe-making clichés like "darkly nuanced" and "soul-shatteringly intimate." Serious film fans deconstructed his oeuvre in earnest Internet chat rooms. Most importantly, he was on the A-list of every agency that cut the cheques that make movie production possible.

No doubt about it, Evan's future was, in the words of the hit song, so bright, you had to wear shades, yet when Jill had called from Toronto, where she'd been working as an independent producer, to announce her surprise engagement, she had been oddly reticent about the man she was going to marry. As she discussed her plans for a wedding in Regina with all her friends around her, she had fizzed with enthusiasm about Evan's seventeen-year-old daughter, Bryn, but when I'd pressed her for details about Bryn's father, she'd stonewalled, finally e-mailing me an interview with Evan MacLeish that had appeared in the *New York Times*. The writer, himself a young filmmaker, had clearly been awe-struck in the presence of the great man. The toughest of his questions were soft lobs, and Evan hit them out of the ball-park. As he discussed an upcoming retrospective of his work, Evan was thoughtful and articulate. He was also, if the tiny photo on my computer screen was to be believed, as craggily handsome as the hero of a Harlequin romance. Looking at him, I could almost understand how Jill had convinced herself that she had caught the brass ring; what I couldn't understand was how she could have missed the smear of blood on her shining prize.

The *Times* article had been hagiography, but the subtext of the dead wives alarmed me enough to phone Jill back and ask if Evan's track record didn't raise any red flags for her. She'd dodged the question. "Just be happy for me," she said.

"Then give me a break," I said. "Fill me in on the man who's going to be guiding your hand as you slice into the wedding cake."

"If you want to know about Evan, look at his movies," she said.

I'd come up empty at our local video stores, but I found a distributor on the Internet who promised to rush order the two films I was keen to see: *Leap of Faith*, Evan's documentary about the life and death of his first wife, and *Black Spikes and Slow Waves*, Annie Lowell's story. The distributor's definition of "rush order" apparently gave him a lot of wiggle room. The videos hadn't arrived until the day before Jill's wedding, but despite the fact that I had beds to make and bathrooms to clean, I'd hunkered down to watch.

It had been a mistake. There was no disputing the value

of the movies as art. Evan MacLeish had been a graduate student when he made *Leap of Faith*, and it was clear from the grainy images and jerky transitions between scenes that the movie had been shot on the fly and on the cheap. That said, it was a coolly professional piece of work without a single extraneous frame or moment of self-indulgence. Evan's portrait of a woman whose mind had shattered when it collided with rationalist teachings inimical to her faith was the work of a mature artist who set his sights on a target and hit it.

But the very assurance of the film raised an unsettling question about Evan's relationship with his subject. In theory, his was the camera's eye, unblinking, dispassionate, yet Linn continually addressed the man behind the camera, pleading with him, arguing with him, begging him to see her truth. In the scene before her suicide, she stared directly into the camera's lens and sang the children's hymn, "Jesus Bids Us Shine," which ends with the image of a personal saviour who wants nothing more than to look down from heaven and see his followers shine "you in your small corner, and I in mine." Eyes red from weeping, Linn begged her young husband for something to replace the Jesus who had been ripped from her heart. Evan didn't even offer her a tissue. To my mind, that suggested a detachment bordering on the monstrous.

Evan MacLeish's film about the life and death of his second wife was the work of a man at the top of his game. He had learned many lessons in the decade between *Leap of Faith* and *Black Spikes and Slow Waves*, but apparently he hadn't mastered compassion. Annie Lowell was an actor by profession and she clearly knew her way around a camera, but Evan's betrayal of her was as complete as his betrayal of her sweet-faced predecessor. As I watched his meticulous recording of Annie's attempt to embrace all of life pleasures before the screen faded to black, I wondered how the film-maker could have subsumed the husband so completely. Annie was clearly a woman bent on self-destruction. Why hadn't the man who loved her stopped her?

I had tried all day to banish the images of Evan MacLeish's wives by busying myself with the Mrs. Dalloway rounds of a woman planning a party, but the agony of these two very different women had burned itself into me. As I stood by the front door waiting to meet Jill and the man whose camera had captured those images, I had moved beyond concern to dread.

It was the night before the winter solstice. When I had offered to hold the rehearsal dinner at our house, my eigh-teen-year-old son, Angus, who was habitually short of cash but long on inspiration, put himself in charge of producing a seriously great event. It had taken him many hours at the computer to ferret out traditions that weren't flaky, but as I watched him sprint down the walk in his cut-offs and Mr. Bill sweatshirt, igniting the pine tar and paraffin torches that he had wrapped and hand-dipped, I knew that at least one of his decisions was a knockout. Within seconds, a dozen flames licked hungrily at the thin winter air and the scents of smouldering pine tar and peat smoke drifted towards us.

My eight-year-old daughter leaned over the porch rail to watch the flames. "Angus says people used to build bonfires and light torches on the longest night of the year, so the spirits of the dead would stay away and the sun would remember to come back, but Mr. Kaufman says the dead don't have spirits and the sun just *appears* to come back because the earth starts to tilt the right way."

"What do you think?" I asked.

Taylor traced a pattern with her toe in the skiff of snow on our front porch. "I kind of like Angus's story better," she said.

"So do I," I said. "But, of course, I still believe in gnomes and pixies."

Taylor grinned. "Is that why you stayed in the garage with Angus when he was making his torches?"

I drew her close. "Nope," I said. "I just wanted to make sure there was someone there to drag him out if that tar and paraffin he was heating exploded."

"I heard that!" Angus twirled his torch triumphantly in the air. "As you can see, I'm still here. You worry too much, Mum."

"Just about the people I love."

"And that includes Jill," Angus said. He peered down the street. "Hey, there are two taxis headed our way. This party is finally ready to rock and roll."

"Not without me, it isn't." Taylor jumped off the porch and ran down the walk. I followed her.

As the first cab pulled up, Angus gave me a searching look. "You could try smiling," he said. "You're so weird about this wedding. Is there something the matter with this Evan guy?"

"I hope not."

"Give him a chance. That's what you always tell us."

"Okay," I said. "I'll keep an open mind." But the power of positive thinking was no match for the lingering intensity of the images captured by Evan MacLeish. Clearly, he was one hell of a filmmaker. As the second taxi slowed in front of my house, I knew in my bones that neither science nor dancing flames would keep the spirits of Linn Brokenshire and Annie Lowell from the party celebrating the marriage of one of my oldest friends to the man who had once been their husband.

As Evan MacLeish eased out of the taxi, I felt my nerves twang. There was no denying the fact that he was a stunningly attractive man, but he had the kind of physical presence that intimidates. He was tall, well over six feet, with a

body so powerful that the exquisite tailoring of his handsome winter coat couldn't disguise it. He bent to help Jill out
of the car, then stepped towards me. His mane of greying
hair curled onto his collar, a Samson image of potency, and
his features were strong: heavy eyebrows, a large nose, full
almost feminine lips, a cleft in his chin. For a beat, he looked
around, taking in the scene, then his gaze settled on me.
He had a sentry's eyes, icy and observant. "The matron of
honour," he said, and he opened his arms to me.

My response was atavistic and unforgivable. I froze,
drawing my arms against my sides like a child steeling
herself against the embrace of a loathsome relative. It was a
gesture of stunning rudeness; one of those jaw-dropping
episodes that offers no possibility of a graceful recovery.

Evan raised an eyebrow. "Fearful of the villain's clutches?"
he said.

I was fumbling for an answer when Jill joined us. Tall and
lithe, Jill was born to wear clothes well. She was not a clas-
sical beauty. Her hazel eyes were a touch too close together,
and her smile was endearingly crooked, but that night, in her
full-length hooded cloak, she had the timeless elegance of
the heroine in a medieval romance.

Her face glowing with cold and excitement, she threw her
arms around me. "Jo, it is *so* good to see you. And look at
those torches! Absolutely spectacular!"

"You're looking pretty spectacular yourself," I said
shakily. "That cloak didn't come from Value Village."

"My soul is still Value Village, but this is a gift from my
mother-in-law-to-be. She wore it to her wedding."

"A woman who appreciates you," I said. "I can hardly wait
to meet her."

"Maybe some day," Jill averted her eyes.

"She's not coming?"

"She doesn't travel," Jill said.

"Not even for her son's wedding?"

"Caroline MacLeish is a complicated woman," Jill said. "But let's not talk about her now. I just want to enjoy being here in Regina with you and your family. I know you must be swamped this close to Christmas."

"That's why I stepped in," Angus said airily. "So Mum could just do all that cooking and stuff she likes to do at Christmas."

Jill rested a hand on each of his shoulders and gave him an assessing look. "You know when you were a kid, you were a wild man, but you're improving with age."

"How about me?" Taylor said.

"Still a question mark," Jill said with mock gravity, "but definitely showing promise. Now, let me introduce you to *my* prize." Jill brushed past her husband-to-be and held out her hand to the girl still waiting inside the taxi. "This is Bryn MacLeish," she said.

I was watching my son's face as Bryn got out of the car, and I knew that while the calendar might say we were on the cusp of winter, Angus had just been struck by the summer lightning of love at first sight. At seventeen, Bryn made the cut when it came to the criteria for junior goddess: shoulder-length raven hair, centre-parted, pale translucent skin, huge watchful eyes, wide generous mouth. She was wearing a vintage A-line coat, claret with a black Persian lamb collar – demure, yet sexy, the kind of outfit Audrey Hepburn might have worn in *Roman Holiday*.

Jill touched my arm. "Wasn't she worth waiting for?"

I was surprised at the tenderness in her voice. "Discovering the joys of motherhood?" I asked.

Evan MacLeish answered for her. "As if she'd invented it," he said. "But to get the child, Jill must take the father." His tone was matter of fact, that of a man stating a simple equation.

The three other members of the wedding party had sent off their cab and trailed over to the sidewalk, waiting to be introduced. Jill was oblivious. Her eyes hadn't left Bryn's face. "She's worth it," she said. "In twenty-four hours, I'll have a daughter."

Jill's intensity about Bryn unnerved me, and I tried to lighten the moment. "Without stretch marks, labour pains, or jeopardizing your status as a size six," I said.

For a split second, the mask of the radiant bride slipped. "Nothing good is free, Jo. You know that." Jill gave me a thin smile, straightened her shoulders, and turned to the other members of her wedding party. "Time to get festive," she said. "Everybody has to meet everybody else, and given what's ahead, we could all use a drink."

Angus, who had never made a halfway commitment to anything in his life, had transformed our house into an oasis of New Age serenity: yellow and white candles dispelled darkness and promised new beginnings; pine and cedar boughs filled the air with the sharp green scent of renewal; crystal bowls glittered with chips of quartz for courage and chunks of rich blue sodalite for old knowledge. Taylor, a skilled artist and a romantic, had made place cards in which exotic birds carried laurel wedding crowns in their beaks. My contribution to the bliss had been Bill Evans's *Moonbeams*, my personal conduit to transcendence. As far as I could tell, we had made all the right choices, but five minutes into the party I didn't need Angus's Enlightened Web sites to tell me the energy in the room was spirit-suckingly negative.

Our party was small, just six people besides my family. There had been a mix-up about luggage at the airport, and Felix Schiff, Jill's business partner, had stayed behind to clear up the tangle. As I was hanging up coats and ushering people into the living room, Jill introduced me to Evan's sister,

Claudia; his second wife's twin sister, Tracy Lowell; and the best man, Gabe Leventhal. One way or another, they shared a lot of history, and if the emotional undercurrents that eddied around us were any indication, there was nothing in that history to inspire a Hallmark card.

Most of the tension in the room sprang from Tracy Lowell. My throat had tightened when I saw her in the light of the front hall. Her resemblance to her twin was uncanny: the same dark bangs, artfully fringed over the high forehead; the same spiky-lashed round eyes and spoiled cherub's mouth. There was, however, a significant difference. In *Black Spikes and Slow Waves*, Annie Lowell was luminous with the glow of youth; time had drained the lustre from her sister's face. Both women were as frenetically fragile as hummingbirds, but unlike her twin, Tracy had lived to reap what she had sown.

With her sequinned white shirt, Manolo Blahnik strappy sandals, fluttering hands, and hard-edged trilling laugh, she had the mark of a woman who would become dangerous with drink. I was relieved when she rejected liquor in favour of good old Colombian coffee. But as she knocked back cup after cup, I began to wish she'd switch to Jack Daniel's. Halfway through the cocktail hour, Tracy had enough caffeine in her to jump-start a Buick.

Taylor was wired too, but her adrenaline rush came from the purest of sources. She was wearing a swooshy dress; she was going to be up long after bedtime; and the next day she was going to get her hair styled by a real hairdresser and be the flower girl in a wedding. She had also discovered that passing around the canapés gave her an excuse to get up-close-and-personal with everyone else at the party. She'd already swung by to report that Jill and Claudia were on the back deck smoking cigarettes; that Mr. MacLeish and Mr. Leventhal were arguing; that when Mr. Leventhal talked, he sounded like Columbo on A&E; that Bryn was super-shy; and that Angus was acting like a total dweeb trying to make her like him. By the time my daughter swept through with the smoked trout rolls, she had stumbled upon some really big news. "You know what?" she stage-whispered. "That lady with the sparkly top is on TV. She's the Broken Wand Fairy on 'Magictown.'"

I took a second look at Tracy. "I didn't recognize her without her tutu and her orange sneakers," I said. "But I think you're right."

"I knew it!" Taylor whooped with delight, tilting her plate and sending a dozen canapés to the floor. Our Bouvier, Willie, bent his head to investigate, but Taylor's recovery was laser-quick. In the blink of an eye, she'd grabbed the errant trout rolls, flicked off the dog hair, and rearranged them on the plate.

"Nobody will ever know," she said.

"*We'll know*," I said. "Taylor, you're going to have to scrape those into the garbage and start again."

"They're too good to throw out," she said. "I'm going to eat them."

"Me too," Claudia MacLeish, an athletic blonde in a navy V-necked cardigan, extended a freckled hand and snagged some trout. "If dog hair could kill you, I'd have been dead long ago. I own a pair of Rottweilers."

Taylor's head shot up. "I *love* Rottweilers. Jo says people aren't fair about them – they're really nice dogs unless they have bad owners."

Claudia licked her fingers contentedly. "Jo's very astute," she said. "With Rotties, it's all in how you handle them. They need to recognize the pack leader – same as people." Claudia glanced across the room at Tracy Lowell, whose zoned-out smile suggested she was headed for trouble. "A case for alpha intervention if ever I saw one," Claudia said, popping another trout roll in her mouth. "Time to remind Tracy who's boss."

Claudia gave Willie a final pat, walked over to the fireplace, and murmured a few words in the ear of the woman who had once been her sister-in-law. Whatever she said appeared to do the trick. The chords in Tracy's neck showed the strain, but her all-Canadian smile was dazzling. By the time the best man stepped forward to propose a toast, the Broken Wand Fairy from "Magictown" was delivering a socko performance.

Stocky, swarthy, seriously in need of a haircut, and dressed in a suit that hadn't been pressed since "Columbo" was in first run, Gabe Leventhal was hardly a casting director's idea of either a best man or a pre-eminent film critic, but he was both. When Jill told me that Gabe was coming west for the wedding, I'd felt a schoolgirl flutter. I'd been reading his column, "Leventhal on Film," since university days. Unlike Shakespeare's Leontes, Gabe Leventhal was not "a feather for each wind that blows." He loved movies, and he had enough respect for the people who plunked down hard coin on the basis of his opinions to maintain stringent standards. More than once I had left the paper folded at "Leventhal on Film" beside Angus's breakfast plate. Angus believed newspapers had as much relevance to his life as eight-track cassette players, but he thought Gabe Leventhal was cool. That night as Gabe put down his unlit cigar and raised his glass to Jill, Angus paid him the ultimate tribute: he stopped mooning over Bryn and snapped to.

"Before today," Gabe said, "my only knowledge of Saskatchewan came from a movie."

Jill winced. "A *godawful* movie. I'd almost managed to delete it from my memory bank." She turned to Bryn. "It was called *Saskatchewan*, and it was about a Mountie who courageously drove a Sioux war party out of here and back to the U.S.A."

"Talk about unenlightened," Angus said, glancing at his young goddess to make sure she was on side.

"Two mitigating factors," Jill said. "It was made in 1954, and Alan Ladd played the Mountie."

Gabe looked at her with real interest. "You're a fan?"

"From the moment I saw *Shane*."

"I own every movie Alan Ladd ever made," Gabe said. "If you're ever in New York, you've got a standing invitation . . ."

Bryn hadn't murmured more than a pleasantry all evening, but Gabe's words ignited her. "We're *moving* to New York," she said. "All of us. Jill's show's going to be syndicated."

Bryn's gaze shifted to her aunts. If she was hoping for a reaction, she got it. Tracy Lowell's rictus grin freeze-dried, and Claudia scowled. The smile Bryn gave them was winning, but a sliver of malice undercut its Pre-Raphaelite perfection. "I thought you'd be happy for us," she said sulkily.

Tracy's behaviour so far hadn't earned her a place on my Christmas card list, but I winced at her words to Evan MacLeish. "You promised that everything would stay the same," she said.

"Let's keep our private lives private." Claudia's tone was brusque. More tough love, but this time Tracy wasn't buying.

Quivering with rage, she balled her small hands into fists. "I believed you," she hissed at Evan. "Nothing was supposed to change. That was the agreement."

"Nothing has to change," Evan said quietly.

"Watch your step," Tracy said. "Your mother's not going to be any happier about this than I am, Evan. Ignoring what the rest of us want will be a big mistake."

"I'll take my chances," Evan said.

"You'll regret it," Tracy said. "I've always been the third

rail in your life. The only way you've stayed safe until now is by being very careful around me."

Evan swept the room with his cool sentry gaze. "We're wrecking the party," he said. "Why don't we finish this in private?"

After the double doors to the dining room clicked shut behind Tracy and Evan, there was a moment of agonizing awkwardness, followed by a flurry of attempts to restore equilibrium. Jill and Angus hovered over Bryn, reassuring her that nothing that had or ever would go wrong was her fault. Taylor, the queen of diversion, invited Claudia to come up to her room to visit her cats. That left Gabe Leventhal and me.

He waved his cigar. "I wouldn't mind lighting this."

"You're my guest," I said.

Gabe put a match to his cigar. "Bolivar Corona Gigantes. One of Cuba's best," he said. "And I bought it at your airport. This party just keeps getting better and better." He inhaled happily. "Now tell me, what the hell does Tracy Lowell have on Evan?"

I shrugged. "Your guess is as good as mine. I just met her tonight."

"Then my guess is better than yours," he said. "Tracy and I had a romance."

"How long did the romance last?"

"Forty-five minutes," he said. "It began in a hotel room before I went to the preview of a film in which she was the fifth lead and ended the next morning when my review appeared."

"She didn't care for the review?"

"She stalked me for three weeks, kept leaving noxious notes and other little nasties in my mailbox. I escaped, but if the affair had continued, she would have killed me. I'm paid to tell the truth, and Tracy was never much of an actor." He gazed thoughtfully at the lengthening ash on his cigar. "Her sister was good – always interesting to watch, but Tracy was just a dewy bloom in the hero's lapel."

"Do you think it's possible she spent some time in Evan MacLeish's lapel?"

"Could be," Gabe said, flicking ash into his open palm. "Tracy bloomed for a lot of men."

I handed him an abandoned plate. "Thanks," he said, dumping the ashes carefully. "I'd be interested to know what she's doing now."

"She's on a kids' show here in Canada," I said. "She plays a character called the Broken Wand Fairy. Some evil wizard snapped her wand, so none of her magic works any more."

Gabe raised an eyebrow. "Block that metaphor."

I sipped my drink. "She hasn't totally lost her touch. Jill mentioned that Evan wanted her here for the wedding."

"He wanted me here too, and there's not a lot of magic between us. I've known him since he was married to Annie, but it would be a stretch to describe us as 'close.'"

"Still, you must have some idea about what makes him tick."

Gabe's mouth twitched with amusement. "Don't tell me you're a groupie – trying to get the skinny on the Great Filmmaker."

"No," I said. "I just want to know if he's a good man."

Gabe's smile vanished. "I'm not an ethicist, Joanne. I write about movies."

"Then I'll ask you a movie question," I said. "This morning I watched *Leap of Faith* and *Black Spikes and Slow Waves*. Do you believe a decent human being could use people who loved him as material?"

"At least they were adults," Gabe said.

"Meaning?"

"Meaning, I find those movies less problematic than I find Evan's film about his daughter."

I felt a chill. "They didn't mention that one in the *New York Times*."

"Not many people know about it." Gabe stuck the cigar back in his mouth. "He's been shooting footage of Bryn since she was born. I think the plan is to create the film equivalent of a *roman-fleuve*."

"How does Bryn feel about having her life turned into a movie?"

Gabe shrugged. "I don't imagine that's an issue for Evan. He sees it as his life's work. He's shown me some rough cuts. It's going to be sensational."

"And that exonerates him?"

Gabe squinted at me through the screen of smoke. "Do you know who you remind me of, Joanne?"

I shook my head.

"Sam Waterston," he said.

"Is that line supposed to make me blush and go weak in the knees?"

"You didn't let me finish. I was *going* to say you remind me of Sam Waterston in *The Great Gatsby*."

"When he played Nick Carraway."

"Right," Gabe said approvingly. "The young man who wanted the world to stand at moral attention. You've got more than a little of Nick Carraway in you, Joanne, and that line *is* intended to please you. Moralists raise interesting questions." He looked at me hard. "Now I have a question for you. Are you romantically entangled?"

I tried to stay cool. "In the process of becoming unentangled," I said.

"What happened?

"Taylor would say that he just found somebody he liked better."

"He must be a jerk."

"Thanks," I said. There was a catch in my voice that

seemed to surprise us both.

Gabe reached out and touched my cheek. "Maybe I can help," he said.

It was a moment pregnant with possibilities that my son aborted by roaring into the room and slamming on the brakes like a cartoon character. "Sorry," he said, "but you asked me to remind you to take the meat out at twenty after."

Gabe shook his head in mock dismay. "First time I've made a pass in five years, and it's intercepted."

"Come help me rescue dinner," I said. "Heroes' journeys are filled with detours."

When Gabe and I walked into my kitchen, I knew we'd taken a detour that had led us into a danger zone. Tracy had backed Evan into the sideboard. She was pressed against him, her body taut, her hands splayed over his thighs. It was a scene from John Updike: two handsome people, restive with the longings of mid-life, anxious to grab a quickie before old age made *carpe diem* a joke. But this encounter wasn't about lust.

As Tracy leaned into Evan, her voice was as hushed as a lover's but the words dripped venom. "I could fucking kill you," she said.

Evan placed his hands on her shoulders and pushed her back gently. "Stand in line," he said. "No one's raising the roof beams about this marriage, but it would be easier for you if you accept the fact that it's inevitable."

"And it would be easier for everybody if you just backed out." Tracy rubbed at the places where Evan's hands had touched her.

"I'm not going to," Evan said mildly. "Jill and I are both committed to this marriage."

"Till death do you part," Tracy said. "You're one evil son of a bitch, Evan." As she stomped out of the room, her stiletto heels tapped the hardwood like hammer blows.

"Great exit line," Gabe said admiringly. He turned to me. "And to show you how seriously I take my duties as best man, I am going to tame the virago. I'm assuming there'll be a reward."

"If you can save this dinner party, you can name your price," I said.

"Now that's an offer I can't refuse," Gabe replied.

After he left, I opened the oven to take out the venison.

"Anything I can do?" Evan asked.

"I'm fine," I said, putting the pan on the counter.

"No, you're not," Evan said. "I saw your face when I got out of that taxi tonight. You'd made up your mind about me before you met me."

"Jill suggested I watch your movies," I said. "So I did – at least two of them."

He sighed. "I can guess which two." He stepped close, put his hand under my chin, and lifted it so I had to meet his gaze. "I'm not a monster, Joanne. I didn't kill my wives."

"You didn't save them," I said.

"They were beyond my reach." Evan's eyes bored into me. "I thought I was past the point where people could disappoint me, but you disappoint me, Joanne."

Suddenly, I was furious. "What are you talking about? Why would you have any expectations about me one way or the other?"

"Because you sent Jill the illumination of that text by Philo of Alexandria."

A flush of shame rose from my neck to my face. Evan's lips curved in a smile. He had me. "I was looking forward to meeting the woman who believed those were words to live by." He took a step towards me. "You do remember the words."

Suddenly, I felt light-headed. I closed my eyes and nodded.

"Say them." Evan's tone was commanding.

"'Be kind,'" I said mechanically, "'for everyone you meet is fighting a great battle.'"

"Good," he said approvingly. "Now why don't you make some effort to understand the battles I'm fighting."

CHAPTER

2

From the moment I'd read the article in the *New York Times*, I'd suspected Evan MacLeish was the wrong man for Jill. Now I was dead certain, and time was running out.

In our house, the dinner table had always been the place where people came to learn things. That night, as we gathered in the candlelight, I was desperate to learn something that would penetrate Jill's wilful blindness about the man she was about to marry. Discovering who among my guests had the silver bullet would be problem enough. Convincing myself that I had the right to use it would be even more difficult. Jill was an intelligent woman who had assessed a complex situation and made a decision. It was going to be a stretch coming up with a rationale for interfering in her life.

I was glad Felix Schiff had sorted out the luggage problems and joined the party. He was an appealing guest, affable and fine-tuned to nuance. Like many men who work in media, Felix had adopted the man-boy costume of leather jacket and blue jeans, and the combination worked well for him. Looking at his unruly shock of chestnut hair and anxious grey eyes, it was easy to see the tightly wound child he had been. Industry colleagues knew Felix to be one tough cookie, but that night his sensitivity was apparent. He prided himself on being, in a phrase from his native Germany, *ein prakiter Mensch*. Faced with a party ripped by tension, the practical man ratcheted up the charm. Radiating the innocent shine of a Norman Rockwell schoolboy with a frog in his pocket, he surveyed the table.

"And to think, none of us would be here tonight if it weren't for a water-skiing squirrel," he said, eyeing his fellow guests to see if he'd hooked his audience. He had, and as people leaned forward with expectant half-smiles, eager to follow the anecdote, I felt my nerves unknot.

Noticing that a tiny frown was crimping Bryn's forehead, Felix whispered confidingly, "You'll have to forgive Jill for holding out on you. I'm sure she simply wanted to protect you from the knowledge that she's anti-squirrel."

"Hang on," Jill said. "This is my party, and I'll tell my own story. And in my version, I behave valiantly. Here's what really happened, Bryn. Felix and I were working on a show called 'Canada Tonight.' He was the executive producer in Toronto, and I was the network producer here in Regina. Everything was cool, including the ratings, so, of course, NationTV decided it needed a saviour."

"A twenty-seven-year-old saviour," Felix said. "Still paying off his student loans, and they put him in charge of the network's news division. A wunderkind, they said. Some wunderkind. We'd been hearing the same mantra for ten years. Appeal to a new demographic: younger, edgier, more urban, more buzz."

Jill rolled her eyes. ". . . shorter segments, less analysis, more happy talk . . ."

"And," Felix intoned gravely, "more squirrels."

"Right," Jill sipped her wine. "More squirrels. Somehow our young genius in Toronto got wind of the fact that a cottager out here had taught a squirrel to water-ski. Now clearly the cottager was a baguette short of a picnic, but the wunderkind was enchanted. He ordered me to replace two minutes of our political panel with squirrel footage, and I refused."

"Squirrel against woman," Angus said.

"Right," Jill said. "And no possibility of rapprochement. The squirrel was out on Echo Lake slapping the waves with his little custom-made skiis, and I was here in Regina clinging to my standards."

"And you lost," Taylor said.

Jill nodded in agreement. "And our twenty-seven-year-old genius meted out the worst punishment he could think of . . ."

"He banished you to Toronto!" Angus said.

"Precisely," Jill said. "With the kind of task evil fairies hand out in fairy tales. He gave me six weeks to create a cheap, ethnically diverse, spiritually neutral show that would get a 7.8 share on Sunday mornings."

"Absolutely impossible," Felix said. "It was a matter of principle. Jill quit, and so did I."

Jill dipped her index finger into the water in her glass and passed it through the flame of the candle in front of her. "Luckily, Felix and I are not risk-averse. And we were both dying to show that little snot-nose what talent and experience could do."

"Thus, after only a dozen or so false starts, 'Comforts of the Sun' came into being." Felix bowed his head modestly. "A simple premise but brilliantly executed."

We all laughed, but the truth of the matter was the premise behind "Comforts of the Sun" was simple: Jill and a small film crew followed ordinary people as they revelled in the pleasures of their Sunday morning. The show cast its net broadly: an all-girl skateboarders' club in Sault Ste. Marie; a rafter-rattling gospel choir in Halifax; the owners of a trendy lesbian eatery called Tomboy who opened their doors on

Sunday mornings to the homeless of Winnipeg; a Tai Chi group who, for three generations, had been harmonizing their minds and bodies in a Vancouver park; an octogenarian Anglican minister who, accompanied by his bulldog Balthazar, drove up and down the Sunshine Coast delivering thumping good sermons to anyone who was of a mind to sit still and listen.

As we passed the wild rice, we talked about why the show had struck a chord with so many people. "I'll bet most people are like me," I said. "We watch 'Comforts of the Sun' because it makes us feel good."

Felix furrowed his brow. "Feel good is yesterday, Jo. When I was pitching the show in NYC, I talked about urban alienation, fragmentation, and the human need for connection and affirmation."

Claudia snapped her fingers at an imaginary waiter. "Another order of bullshit for the gent here at table three," she said, and her laughter was full-bodied and infectious.

Felix was serene. "Manure has its uses," he said.

"You bet it does," Jill said. "Thanks to Felix's judicious spreading, our little family will be in Times Square New Year's Eve." She hugged herself. "This show has made so many things possible. It's an uphill battle not to get cynical in hard news. You're always trying to get past what people want to reveal so you can shed a little light on what they're trying to conceal. But 'Comforts of the Sun' makes watching the human comedy fun again. Everybody we talk to is pleased as punch to reveal everything."

Throughout dinner, Bryn and Angus had been so tenderly absorbed in one another that it seemed the rest of us were just a backdrop, but Jill's words caught Bryn's attention.

Achingly beautiful, she leaned across the table. "But those people *chose* to let you in, Jill. It's different when the camera invades your life."

Evan shifted in his chair. "A camera doesn't 'invade' your life, Bryn," he said. "It's just there."

"A camera is *not* 'just there,'" Bryn's eyes bored into her father. "There's a person behind it, changing the lens, making sure the shot's in focus, deciding how far to go."

Evan speared a morsel of venison. "People who step in front of the camera aren't victims. They're willing accomplices. They can always walk away."

"Not if they trust the person behind the camera," his daughter said. Her skin had the pale lustre of the white tulips in the centrepiece.

Jill reached across the flowers and took Bryn's hand. "We have so much to look forward to," she said. "Sometimes it's best just to forgive and forget."

"Great advice, stepmum-to-be." Tracy's voice was jagged. "Except where do you draw the line after you pardon scavengers who pick the flesh from other people's bones?"

Ever the conciliator, Felix jumped in. "Aren't you being a little unfair, Tracy? We're not talking about 'Jerry Springer.' We're talking about our show, and we have nothing to be ashamed of. As Jill said, people who step in front of our cameras *want* to reveal themselves. We give them a legacy – something they can slip into their VCRs to prove their lives have meaning."

Tracy's blue eyes glittered with unshed tears. "And that's why they count on you not to lie, not to distort, not to seduce them into giving up things that are sacred." She turned miserably to her brother-in-law. "Some of us counted on you for that too, Evan."

Taylor had stopped eating. She loved venison and she was, as a rule, a trencherwoman, but the sight of the Broken Wand Fairy having a tantrum obviously knocked her off game.

"Counted on me for what?" Evan asked. "Tracy, the scenes you're part of in *Black Spikes and Slow Waves* show you at a time when you were more alive than you'll ever be again. No matter what happens to you, that woman will still exist. What else could you ask?"

"To be treated as a human being," Tracy snapped.

Evan shrugged. "It's an old argument: what matters more, art or life? Thomas Mann said that as he watched his young daughter die, he couldn't stop himself from framing the scene to use in a novel. He gave that child immortality."

"Is he your role model, Daddy?" Bryn's voice was bleak, and Jill drew her close.

Claudia mouthed the favourite obscenity of the frustrated, then tapped her wineglass with her knife. "May I make a modest suggestion?" she asked. "Why don't we all just shut up and eat."

It was a small window of opportunity, but I squeezed through. "There's more of everything," I said. "But leave room for dessert. It's my daughter Mieka's recipe."

Jill brightened. "The lemon pudding cake with raspberries?"

"You've got it," I said. "The Queen of Comfort Foods."

Gabe drained his glass. "Bring it on," he said to no one in particular. "We have become a party sorely in need of comfort."

Taylor picked up her fork. "And joy," she said. "Don't forget the joy."

As we walked from the parking lot to the MacKenzie Art Gallery for the wedding rehearsal, snowflakes fell on a world silvered by a winter palette. It was a Currier & Ives evening, but we were an Alex Colville crowd, our alienation as knife-edged as our emotions. We had paired off idiosyncratically. Angus had deep-sixed his Mr. Bill sweatshirt and cut-offs in favour of pressed slacks, a blue button-down, and a solicitousness towards Bryn that would have been appropriate if he were rescuing her from the gulag, but seemed excessive for a wedding rehearsal in Regina. Claudia, her feet squarely planted in sensible Sorels, had taken on the task of her sister-in-law's keeper and was frog-marching the skittish, bare-legged Tracy towards the warmth of the gallery. Surprisingly, Jill was walking not with her fiancé but with Felix Schiff. Heads together, their whispered discussion grew so heated that Felix finally strode ahead to catch up with Claudia and Tracy, and Jill dropped back to join the two other odd couples: Taylor and Evan, and Gabe Leventhal and me.

Taylor was pointing out the snow maze that the gallery employees and the kids who studied art at the MacKenzie had constructed on the east lawn. It was a serious effort with six-foot walls of packed ice-snow and enough branches and forks to give the maze real complexity. Bathed in moonlight, it had an otherworldly glow.

"Straight out of the Ice Planet Hoth," Gabe said, shaking his head. "You really could get lost in there."

"You could," Taylor agreed, "but I know the secret of how not to."

"A golden thread," Gabe said.

Taylor wiped her nose on the sleeve of her coat. "That would probably work," she said. "But I was talking about the right-hand trick. As long as you keep your right hand against the wall, there's no way you can't get out."

"Nice to have at least one guarantee when you're stepping into an uncertain world," Jill said.

"Do you consider marriage an uncertain world?" Evan asked.

Jill's smile was enigmatic. "I don't know," she said. "Can you guarantee that if I keep my right hand on the wall, I'll get out safely?"

Gabe led our small group through the maze. In his ancient coat, toe rubbers, and striped muffler, he seemed an unlikely guide, but when he announced that, grateful as he was for Taylor's tip, he planned to find the goal by letting go of his conscious self and stretching out his feeling, we cheered. There was a goofiness about his allusion to *Star Wars* that lightened our spirits and made it seem possible that the Force was with us after all.

We walked single file between walls of ice not much more than three feet apart, along ground that was worn treacherously smooth. Above us stars splattered the sky with an ancient pattern, and as we shuffled along, making mistakes, taking wrong turns, our breath rose in puffs, like incense. Our silence was broken only once, when Evan, who was behind me, asked. "What's at the end?"

"A surprise," Taylor said.

"As long as it's not the Minotaur," Evan said.

I looked over my shoulder at him. "Closer than you think," I said.

"Really?"

"Stay tuned."

We turned a final corner and found ourselves in the square that enclosed the goal. Instinctively, we flattened against the walls to improve our view of the snow sculpture at the centre of the tiny enclosure.

Gabe was the first to speak. "Worth the trip," he said. "But what the hell is it?"

Taylor took his hand in hers. "You can look closer," she said. "Have you ever heard of Jacques Lipchitz?"

"One of the great sculptors of the twentieth century? I didn't just fall off the turnip truck, young woman."

Taylor rewarded him with a smile. "Our gallery has a bronze sculpture that Jacques Lipchitz made. It's called *Mother and Child II*. During the war, Jacques Lipchitz saw a Russian lady with no legs. She was singing so he made this sculpture of her. You can see it two ways: as a mother with her child or as the head of a bull."

"Love or war," Gabe said.

"That's right," Taylor said approvingly. "Anyway, the sculpture is sort of the trademark of the MacKenzie Gallery, so that's why we made a snow one for the end of the maze. Neat, eh?"

Gabriel moved closer to the piece. "Yeah," he said. "It really is neat."

"I wish Bryn had come out here with us," Jill said. "Speaking of . . . we should get back. They must be wondering where we are."

"I know the way," Taylor said. She hiked up her swooshy dress and headed back through the maze. Jill and Gabe were not far behind. I started after them, then I realized Evan wasn't with us. When I turned I saw that he was still gazing at *Mother and Child II*. His head was slightly bowed and his hands were crossed in front of him, like a man worshipping or paying his respects at a funeral. His face was unguarded, suffused with a look that I could only describe as longing.

When he saw me watching him, he stiffened. "My mother says this is my natural habitat," he said.

"A maze?" I said.

"No," he said. "Snow. She calls me the snowman. She says I have a mind of winter. It's a line from Wallace Stevens. I assume Jill told you my mother is a scholar of sorts."

"She didn't mention it," I said.

Pain flashed across Evan's face, but the moment was brief, quickly replaced by an ironic smile. "There's not much about me that Jill believes is worthy of mention."

My mind was reeling, but I didn't want the connection between us to break. "What does your mother mean by saying you have 'a mind of winter'?"

"That I'm detached from humanity, unable to love."

"Are you?"

Two words, but they were a body blow. Evan slumped. "You've seen my life. Judge for yourself." He reached out a gloved hand and caressed the icy contours of *Mother and Child*. "Time to go inside," he said. "The others will be waiting."

Numbed by this insight into the battles Evan MacLeish was fighting, I followed him out of the maze. As we trudged between the hard-packed walls, my thoughts drifted from Evan to Caroline MacLeish. Evan had described her as a scholar, and I wondered if, in the course of her studies, she'd come upon Philip Larkin's poem "This Be the Verse" with its astringent opening lines: "They fuck you up, your mum and dad,/They may not mean to, but they do."

During the rehearsal, Evan was composed. Not surprisingly, his delivery of the familiar words of the marriage ceremony was flawless. The mask had slipped back into place, and I was left trying to imagine what kind of catalyzing trauma could sever a man from his emotions. But if Evan's mention of his mother raised one question, it answered another. As Jill lifted her face to be kissed, I sensed for the first time why she had been drawn to this painfully detached man. She was a good person who, despite a lifetime of evidence to the contrary, still believed that a human being could be salvaged by love.

And, of course, there was Bryn. As I looked at the wedding party, I realized that with the exception of Gabe Leventhal and me, everyone was shooting anxious glances her way. She didn't seem in imminent danger. The judge, a silvery-haired, preening gnome of a man who worked his hands together when he spoke, was explaining the ceremony, and Bryn's face showed nothing. She was a spectacularly self-possessed adolescent, and the possibility crossed my mind that her outburst at dinner had been strategic, a way of stirring the pot.

It seemed that Gabe's reading of the scene and mine had been the same. When the judge finally wound up his instructions, Gabe put his lips next to my ear. "If she's that powerful at seventeen, she'll be causing wars by the time she's twenty-one," he whispered.

"Mothers, lock up your sons," I said. "Mine is certainly no match for her. Until tonight, he's bounced through life on charm, a good throwing arm, and the philosophy of John Madden."

Gabe raised an eyebrow. "Hard to imagine a life situation not covered by John Madden's wit and wisdom. I met him once, you know. We were in the green room of a TV show. He let me try on his Super Bowl ring." Gabe flexed his fingers. "It was massive and it was cheesy, but the memory of seeing it on my hand still gives me goosebumps."

"If you told Angus that story, he'd build a shrine for you," I said.

"I'll hold that information in reserve. Some day I may just need your son's approval." Gabe glanced around the gallery. "We seem to be just about finished here. Can I buy you a drink?"

"I'd love one, but I'll have to take a rain check," I said. "I left a serious mess at the house."

Angus was at my elbow. "I'll clean up," he said.

"Out of the goodness of your heart?"

"I've been thinking it might be nice if I got Bryn something – kind of an early Christmas present. They've got some cool stuff downstairs at the gallery shop."

"Cool . . . and pricey," I said.

"That's where you come in," he said.

"It always is." I handed him my credit card. "Be prudent."
I turned to Gabe. "We could have that drink at my house.
Since Angus has volunteered for scullery duty, all I have to
do is put Taylor to bed."

The family room was relatively untouched, so I led Gabe in
there and took his order: tea – nothing fancy, just plain hot
tea with lots of sugar and milk. When I came in with the
tray, he held out the videos of *Leap of Faith* and *Black Spikes
and Slow Waves* and looked at me quizzically. "Homage to
our friend Evan?"

I put the tray on the coffee table. "Less homage than
homework," I said. "I was trying to get acquainted with Jill's
beloved."

"Bad call," he said. "The movies are brilliant – not many
filmmakers can convey human loneliness with that kind of
intensity – but there's no doubt that they're troubling."

"Evan MacLeish is a troubling man," I said. "There are
moments when I understand why Jill is drawn to him, but I
can't get past his history. And that scene we walked in on in
the kitchen didn't help."

Gabe was silent, absorbed in his private thoughts. When
finally he spoke, his words seemed a non sequitur. "Would
you mind if we watched the ending of *Black Spikes*?"

"Your turn for an homage?" I said.

Gabe poured the tea. "Nope. Same as you, just doing my
homework."

I put the tape in the VCR and fast-forwarded to the party
scene. The screen was filled with dazzling disjointed images:
Annie in a fuchsia halter top, caught like a bird in flight
against the brilliant frolic of a Joan Miro painting; Annie
slithering playfully through a nightmare melee of women
with too thin bodies and too tight faces; Annie throwing her

arms around a man whose back was to the camera and kissing him passionately, eyes wide open, watching the camera watching her.

Finally, she broke from the embrace, exposing the man she'd been kissing. When I saw his face, the breath caught in my throat. It was Felix Schiff.

"I missed this part this morning," I said. "Willie was barking to be let out."

"I imagine Felix wishes everyone had missed it," Gabe said dryly. "This footage was shot at the Toronto Film Festival the year everyone discovered ecstasy. Most of us just dabbled, but Felix was convinced he'd found the Holy Grail. That night, he was deep into his journey towards chemical enlightenment."

"You were at that party?"

Gabe nodded. "I even have a cameo in this movie. My appearance comes just about . . . now!"

The image of Gabe was fleeting. The camera moved in on his face, then the shot went jerky as if Gabe had been trying to wrest the camera from the man holding it. Apparently, Evan broke free because the next shots were of Annie running down the hall, punching the elevator button, and stepping inside. Just before the doors closed, she gave her husband a mocking wave.

Scenes from a marriage.

And then the final scene – this one set in the weird hallucinatory dream world of a traffic accident. Marrow-freezing sounds of sirens and screams; lights as pitiless as the glare on a film set; professionals working silently to extract a body from a twist of metal. Then a man's voice, rough-edged with fatigue and emotion, "Got her," as a fuchsia rag is pulled from the wreckage. The camera zooms in hungrily, but Gabe Leventhal shuffles out of the darkness and throws his jacket over the body, denying Annie Lowell's husband the chance to get his money shot. Then darkness, and the sound of a woman moaning.

Gabe leaned forward. The TV screen filled with images of the final moments of a childbirth. The baby's head crowns; its shoulders emerge, hands reach down to pull the baby from its mother's body. Oddly, the camera doesn't linger on the newborn. The focus is on the child's mother. When the baby is given to her, she turns away, lifts a slender arm, and pulls the surgical sheet over her head, shutting out the kitten-like cries of the newborn, denying motherhood.

Gabe was staring at the screen like a man who had never seen pictures move.

I was the one who broke the silence. "Evan told me tonight he couldn't save Annie because she was beyond his reach. I didn't believe him. I thought he was just making excuses, but a mother who rejects her newborn *is* beyond reach. Poor Annie," I said. The penny dropped. "Poor Bryn – having irrefutable proof that her mother never wanted her."

"Bryn was able to spare herself that particular trauma," Gabe said. "She flatly refuses to watch any of her father's films. A very sensible decision, in my opinion."

"I agree," I said. "She certainly didn't need to see that scene at the party." I turned to Gabe. "You were trying to get Evan to stop filming his wife."

"She was out of control," he said dully. "Annie never met a drug, a drink, a fast car, or a man she didn't like. After Bryn was born, it got worse, but the night she died Annie was beyond wild – it was as if she could hear the clock ticking and she wanted to experience everything before it stopped."

"And you were trying to keep Evan from making a permanent record."

"There was Bryn to consider – not that either of them ever

did. Annie seemed to be taunting Evan that night, trying to provoke him."

"Why?"

Gabe locked his hands around his cup. "I have no idea. Annie was beautiful and talented and she'd just delivered a dynamite performance in a film everyone knew was going to be a hit. She was on her way . . . but you know, Joanne, when the phone rang that night and Evan's answering service said Annie had been in an accident, I wasn't surprised. Somehow, I had the sense that he wasn't either.

"I drove him to the accident scene. Annie hadn't gotten far, but it was the longest drive of my life. As soon as I saw the state of the Porsche, I knew she was dead. There was no way she could have lived. But Evan walked over to one of the cops, introduced himself, and took out his video camera. For all the emotion he showed, he could have been filming a family reunion."

"The snowman," I said. "Evan told me tonight that's what his mother calls him, because he's doesn't feel what other people feel."

Gabe slumped. "Poor bastard," he said. "Maybe that's why he's always been drawn to women with such hot emotional lives."

"Very Jungian," I said. "Also very smart for a filmmaker. You get to record the mess other people make of their lives with a clear eye."

Gabe looked startled. "The ending." He turned to me. "What did you make of the way Evan juxtaposed Annie's death and Bryn's birth?"

"Maybe he was saying that no matter what happens to the individual, life continues."

"So by reconstructing what we know of reality and time, Evan shows a greater reality?" Gabe's gaze was piercing: the professor pressing for an answer from a promising student. Unfortunately, the student's promise was limited.

"I'm out of my depth here," I said. "I was the only girl in my dorm who didn't understand *Last Year at Marienbad*."

Gabe put down his tea and looked at me curiously. "That's an interesting connection."

"Especially since I haven't thought about that movie in twenty-five years. But just now, when we watched the ending of *Black Spikes*, I felt the same sense of manipulation – as if the filmmaker deliberately made me lose my bearings."

"'Always walls, always corridors, always doors – and on the other side, still more walls.'" Gabe's voice was a murmur. Seeing the concern in my eyes, he shook off his reverie and reached out and took my hand. "So what's been going on in your life since *Last Year at Marienbad*?"

The grandmother clock in the dining room had just struck eleven when we said goodnight. Neither of us wanted the evening to end. Admitting that my relationship with my former lover, Alex Kequahtooway, was over was proving so painful that I'd pretty well decided there were worse options than going it alone. But Gabe and I had connected with the kind of pizza and Chianti intimacy I hadn't experienced since college. We had leapt over the mundane to attack the big topics: love, loss, and – the inevitable for anyone in their fifties – death. Gabe read widely and thought deeply. His conversation was shot through with allusions, but when he spoke about death his words were simple. "I don't fear it, but I hate the idea that everything I've ever been will be over. You were smart to have kids."

"Continuance," I said.

"An appealing thought," he said. "Especially for a man without a family." He put his arm around me and we walked to the door. To an outsider, we would have been nothing extraordinary: two people in late middle age, sagging after a long day. But Gabe and I felt the possibilities, and as we watched his taxi crawl through the ruts towards my house, he turned to me. "So what do you think of our chances?"

"I'd say that so far we're doing fine," I said.

"Dashiell Hammett would say that fine is too big a word. We're just doing better than most people."

The kiss he gave me was deep and passionate.

"The wedding isn't till three," I said. "We could take a walk in the snow."

"I'll need your number," Gabe said. He fumbled in his pockets. "No pen," he said.

I found pencil and paper in the drawer of the hall table and wrote down my cell and home numbers. Gabe took the paper, slid it into his inside breast pocket, and patted it. "Tomorrow, we get to work on 'fine,'" he said. "Wouldn't it be ironic if this wedding was the start of a real love affair?" Then he kissed me again.

The day had been jam-packed, but I was asleep as soon as my head hit the pillow. When Jill touched my shoulder and called my name, I had to swim up from the depths.

Her face was close to mine. "Can I borrow your car?" she said. "I tried to get a cab, but the snow's really coming down, and the dispatcher said she couldn't promise anything for at least an hour."

"Of course you can borrow the car," I said. I squinted at the clock. "Jill, it's 1:30. Can't it wait?"

"No," she said. "It can't."

"The keys are over there in my bag," I said. "Do you want to tell me what this is all about?"

"No," she said. "I don't. It probably won't amount to anything, and there's no need for both of us to lose sleep."

I watched at the window till Jill pulled out of the driveway. Angus's magnificent torches had been reduced to
scorched stumps. Their pagan protection was gone, and as
the Volvo disappeared down the deserted street, I felt a stab
of anxiety that was as intense as it was irrational. Jill was an
adult. If she needed me, all she had to do was pick up the
cellphone. I went back upstairs, checked on the kids, reassured Willie that all was well, plumped my pillows, and
crawled back between the sheets. After half an hour, I knew
it was hopeless. The sandman wasn't coming back to my
house. I rearranged the pillows and picked up the remote
control.

On "All in the Family," Gloria and Mike were getting
married. Weddings all around. I had seen the episode at least
five times, and the familiarity lulled me. I woke to a staticky
screen and the heart-pounding sense of disorientation that
comes in the small hours. Remembering the immediate
cause of my insomnia, I walked down the hall to the guest
room. Jill was sitting on the edge of the bed. She was wearing
a pair of panties and Angus's Mr. Bill sweatshirt.

"Is that part of your trousseau?" I asked.

"No, but at the moment, it's the perfect choice," Jill gri-
maced. "Like Mr. Bill, I am Dismembered, Squashed, and
Melted Down."

"I take it this has something to do with your quixotic
midnight ride."

Jill ran her fingers through her hair. "*Quixotic* is good,"
she said. "*Moronic* would be even better. After you went to
bed, Gabe called and said he'd just found out something I
should know before the wedding. He didn't want to talk
about it on the phone, so I went charging off into the night.
The roads were a mess and on the way downtown I hit a
patch of ice and ended up in a snowbank. Of course, at that
hour, Good Samaritans were in even shorter supply than

usual, so I had to dig myself out. The Volvo is fine, inciden-
tally, but by the time I got to the hotel I must have looked
like something Willie dragged in. The prim little gent behind
the reception desk was so horrified, I almost had to body
slam him before he'd even ring Gabe's room for me. Big surprise – there was no answer. Gabe had obviously given up on
me and gone to bed."

"And you have no idea what he wanted to talk about?"

"No, and you know what, Jo? I should have realized it was
a fool's errand. There's nothing about Evan's life that I don't
already know. That particular Pandora's box has been open
for a long time. By now, everything has flown out but Hope,
and that's what I'm hanging on to."

I put my arms around her. "You deserve better than this."

"Maybe so, but I'm forty-five years old, and I'm tired of
waiting." Jill's smile was weary. "Is there a fairy tale about a
girl who has to sleep with every loser on the planet before
she finally gets her happily ever after?"

"Maybe an X-rated one," I said, smoothing her hair.

"Not much fun being stuck in an X-rated fairy tale when
everybody else is falling into these great love stories," she
said. "This is as close as I'm going to come, Jo, and I'm going
to do whatever it takes to make it work."

CHAPTER

3

It was still dark the next morning when Taylor crawled in beside me, and Willie lumbered up after her.

"I couldn't sleep," my daughter said. "I'm too excited."

"What time is it?"

"Time to get up. Besides Willie wants out."

"Willie always wants out." I drew Taylor close, loving the gust of girl warmth as she snuggled in. "But he's a reasonable dog. He'll give us a break this morning." Ever obliging, Willie inched up the bed, closer to the centre of power. "So what's on our agenda?" I said.

Taylor propped herself up on her elbow. "First we eat breakfast and have a bath so Rapti can do our hair before she goes to work, then we go to the mall to get that garter."

My daughter scratched Willie's head absently. "Why does Jill need a blue garter?"

"To bring her luck," I said. "Brides are always supposed to have something old, something new, something borrowed, and something blue."

"Does Jill know she's supposed to have all that stuff?"

"I'm sure she's heard rumours," I said.

"Good," Taylor said. "Anyway, after we come back from the mall, we eat lunch and put on our dresses so the photographer can take our pictures." She stretched luxuriously. "My hair is going to be soooo good."

"Still committed to the ringlets?" I asked.

"Why wouldn't I be? The flower girl in that bride's magazine looked so neat." She cocked her head. "Didn't you think she looked pretty?"

"Sure," I ran my hair through Taylor's straight, dark hair. "I guess I just think you're beautiful the way you are."

"Wait till you see me with ringlets," Taylor said.

On our way down to breakfast, I stuck my head in the guest room, and was relieved to see Jill sleeping. Angus took Willie for his run while I made oatmeal and toast. After we'd eaten, I poured a mug of coffee and took it up to Jill. "Rise and shine," I said.

"Just ten more minutes," she mumbled.

"Not for the bride," I said.

Jill sat up and took the mug gratefully. "You're a lifesaver," she said.

"Proud to be your java-enabler," I said. "Rapti's coming by in twenty minutes to work her magic."

Jill got out of bed, walked over to the mirror, and squinted at herself. "I hope she's bringing some industrial-strength MAC concealer. She's got serious work ahead."

Rapti Lustig didn't reach for the MAC III, but she did make judicious use of the skills she'd acquired during her ten years as a makeup person at NationTV. She gave Jill and me facials that left us dewy-skinned, and smoothed our deep-conditioned hair into styles that were as elegant as they were understated.

There was nothing subtle about my daughter's 'do. Using the photo clipped from the magazine as her guide, Rapti spray-gelled and dry-rolled Taylor's hair into a medusa explosion of ringlets that was nothing short of spectacular. Taylor usually displayed a healthy lack of interest in her appearance, but that morning, she couldn't take her eyes off herself. As soon as the last spritz of hairspray kissed her curls, she leapt out of the chair. "Okay," she said, grabbing my hand, "let's hit the mall."

Despite my concern about Jill's marriage, Taylor's buoyancy was infectious, and I had my own private source of pleasure. A permanent relationship with Gabe Leventhal was out of the question. He and I lived in parallel universes, but, at fifty-five, I was old enough to know that *carpe diem* wasn't just a phrase from Latin class. A walk in the snow with a man who could make me laugh was nothing to sneeze at, so I left the house carrying the tool prized by those who know the value of seizing the moment: a cellphone.

Taylor loves malls, and that day I did too. The holiday decorations, the lights, the contact buzz that came from jostling shoppers giddy with impossible last-minute quests, and – a bonus – the chance to scope out the trees that were being raffled off for the symphony's year-end fundraiser. I was a fan of the symphony, and Taylor was a fan of glitz, so we had bought a dozen tickets. The Scotch pine in our living room was, in my daughter's opinion, okay but boring, and for two weeks she had fantasized about winning a second more spectacular tree. She had savoured some seductive possibilities before she settled on a feathery confection titled Snowfall at Swan Lake. The draw was that afternoon, so between stops in front of mirrors to verify that her curls were still sizzling, Taylor scrutinized her favourite, while I reminded her that the symphony had sold hundreds of tickets and that winners were promised *a* tree but not necessarily the tree of their choice. She listened politely, then pointed out that if we moved the parson's bench and the grandmother clock out of the front hall, there would be a ton of room for Snowfall at

Swan Lake. As I checked our home voice mail again to see if there was a message from Gabe, I knew Taylor wasn't the only one betting against the spread.

The man in the specialty shop gift-wrapped Jill's garter gratis and gave Taylor a sprig of real holly tied with a tartan bow for her hair, so we were heading home in high spirits when we ran into Danny Jacobs, Taylor's arch-enemy from grade three. The attack was swift and lethal. Danny took in Taylor's curls and snorted. "You know what you look like? One of those Chia Pets. You know – like on TV – Ch-Chi-Ch-Chia."

Taylor's eyes widened in horror, then she raced through the mall doors to the parking lot. On the way home, she slumped miserably in the passenger seat, and as soon as we pulled up in front of the house, she ripped the holly out of her hair and bolted. By the time I got inside, she had disappeared, and Angus was standing at the foot of the stairs, shaking his head. "What's with Taylor? She blazed by me without saying anything. She didn't even take off her jacket and boots."

"We ran into Danny Jacobs in the mall," I said. "He told your sister her new hairstyle made her look like a Chia Pet."

The corners of Angus's mouth twitched.

"If you're going to laugh, go outside," I said. "Taylor's already suffered enough."

When I heard the sound of the shower, I started upstairs. "I'd better see how she's doing," I said. "By the way, were there any calls when we were out?"

"A couple for Jill. She seemed kind of upset."

"Did she say why?"

"Nope. She just said she needed some fresh air. She put Willie on his leash and took off for the park." Angus lowered his voice. "Do you know what I think? I think she may have changed her mind about getting married."

My pulse quickened. "What makes you say that?"

"Last night, Bryn told me Jill and her father aren't in love."

"Does Bryn think they shouldn't get married?"

Angus shrugged. "I don't think she cares. The only thing Bryn's interested in is moving to New York."

Remembering how Jill glowed when she talked about having a daughter, my heart sank. Last night Evan had said Jill had to take the father to get the daughter. Now it seemed the daughter had to take Jill to get her New York Moment. Expediency all around. In my opinion, it was a hell of a way to start a new life.

The bathroom door was shut, but unlocked. I rapped a couple of times and when there was no answer, I walked in, sat down on the toilet seat, and waited for Taylor to emerge from the steam. When, finally, she stepped out of the shower stall, her skin was scarlet, her hair dripping, and her lower lip quivering. She thrust her head towards me. "Is it normal now?" she asked.

I picked up a towel and began to dry her hair. "It's normal," I said. "After a while, I can do it in French braids if you want."

The sound she made was somewhere between a snort and a sob. "That'd be okay," she said, then she streaked to her room. I went downstairs, put on some soup for lunch, and tried not to stare at the phone. By the time Taylor came down, the phone still hadn't rung. We ate a bowl of chicken with stars and made French braids. When Jill and Willie got back, my daughter was sitting at the kitchen table drawing a cartoon of Danny Jacobs with a thatch of hair that looked as if it had been attacked by termites. Jill glanced at Taylor's braids and then at me.

"Change of plans," I said.

Jill poured herself a cup of coffee. "It seems to be the day for it," she said. "Our judge called this morning. He has the flu, so he's sending a replacement."

"We can live with that," I said. "That little man's fatuous level was off the charts."

Jill sat down at the table. "I don't think you're going to be so breezy about the next change. Gabe had to go back to New York. Felix is our new best man."

I felt a flare of panic. "Is everything all right?"

"Apparently, Gabe had a heart flutter," Jill said tightly. "Evan says he's a real hypochondriac. Anyway, he went back to New York to be close to his doctor." Jill rubbed her temples with her fingertips. "Do you think there's a significant pattern here?"

My mind was racing. "In what way?"

"First the judge, then the best man. I can't see everything going wrong on the day of my wedding without believing that someone is trying to tell me something. 'From shadows and symbols into truth.' That's what Cardinal Newman said."

"Where did Cardinal Newman come from?" I asked. "I thought you had fallen away."

Jill rolled her eyes. "Fallen away, yes, but not unmarked. A Catholic education is like stigmata, perpetually suppurating. It's been thirty-five years since Sister Phyllis Mary filled me in on what boys want from girls, but I still can't sit next to a man in a car without remembering that I should leave room for the hips of the Virgin between me and my date."

Despite everything, I smiled. Jill caught my response. "I know it sounds crazy, but the Church was right about a lot of things. My sex life wouldn't have been such a disaster if I'd left room for the hips of the Virgin between me and most of the men I've known. And you and I are both old enough to know that Cardinal Newman was right about shadows and symbols. Sometimes, no matter how much you want something, it's suicide not to read the signs."

As the hour for the wedding grew near, I didn't need to be a Prince of the Church to know that the gods were not smiling. The box from the florist arrived, but the spray of creamy camellias Jill had ordered to tuck in her hair had been mysteriously replaced by a candy-cane nightmare of spruce cuttings and red and white carnations. Rapti's attempt to fashion a replacement spray by cutting camellias from the bridal bouquet ended when the Swiss Army knife she was using slipped and sliced her finger so badly that only Angus's first-aid training saved us from a trip to the medi-centre. As I held the petals under the tap to rinse the blood off, I was shaking.

When the phone rang, I dropped the flowers in the sink and raced to it. From the moment Jill told me that Gabe had bowed out of the wedding, I had been spinning a theory that Gabe's illness was subterfuge and that somehow he had stumbled upon information that needed to be verified before he could stop a marriage that clearly shouldn't take place. Considering that we had known each other for only six hours, my faith in him might have seemed bizarre, but I felt that Gabe and I had made a connection that went beyond the tectonic-plate-shifting power of sexual attraction. I hadn't yet learned the name of his favourite string quartet or how he liked his eggs in the morning, but the night before he had promised to take a walk in the snow with me, and I knew at my core that a fluttering pulse wouldn't have kept him from honouring his promise.

When I picked up the receiver, I was so prepared to hear Gabe's Columbo growl that my daughter Mieka's voice was a shock. She was calling from Davidson, a town halfway between her home in Saskatoon and mine in Regina. The snow had grown so heavy that highway driving was treach-erous, and she and her husband had decided to turn back. Mieka loved Jill, and I knew how much she had looked forward to being at the wedding and meeting Jill's new family. I could hear the disappointment in her voice. I was disappointed too, but as I hung up, I felt an unexpected wash of relief. The omens were not good, and I was glad Mieka and her family would be out of harm's way.

I'd just finished dressing when Claudia and Bryn arrived. They were alone.

"No Tracy?" I asked, as I helped them off with their coats.

Claudia shook her head. "The older she gets, the longer it takes her to get ready, but she'll be along." Claudia locked eyes with me. "Nothing is going to go wrong with this wedding. I want you to know that." It was impossible to tell from her tone if her words were intended as reassurance or warning. In her champagne silk jacket and skirt, Claudia was a figure of head-turning elegance, but there was steel in her manner. It wasn't much of a stretch to imagine her pinning her Rottweiler puppies on the ground, showing them that the sooner they recognized she was dominant, the better it would be for everyone.

By the time Gaia Powell, the photographer, arrived, we had our masks in place. Inwardly, the members of Jill's wedding party might be racked by panic, uncertainty, fury, jealousy, hatred, or terror, but outwardly we were picture perfect. Gaia, a lanky young woman in overalls, gave us the once over and announced that this shoot was going to be a breeze. Jill was clearly not a Bridezilla who obsessed about every detail, and we had a seriously edgy look going for us.

It was the year of the strapless dress, and Jill's was an exquisite, classic cream satin that brought out the warmth of her skin and the highlights in her sleeked-back auburn hair. The blood had left a faint pink stain on the camellias, but Rapti had tucked the flowers behind Jill's ear so skilfully that the imperfect petals were hidden. The dresses for Jill's attendants were black, Bryn's choice. I'd been dubious about a colour I'd always associated with funerals, but the gowns were stunning. Bryn's and mine were strapless sheaths with matching stoles lined in cream; Taylor's dress had a simple cream top and a full black satin skirt. Urban chic.

For the first ten minutes, Gaia praised the practised ease with which we moved in and out of our poses, but when Tracy Lowell came through the front door, our poise shattered. Bryn and Taylor were oblivious, but the rest of us suddenly became as tentative as people who had been blindfolded and told to walk over a floor littered with razor blades.

From the outset, Tracy's behaviour was bizarre. She was wearing an outfit that could only be described as bridal: a simple white silk shift, matching pumps, pearls, and, in case anyone had missed the intent, a white-lace mantilla draped artfully over her dark hair. Claudia took one look at her sister-in-law and growled, "What the hell are you doing? Get back to the hotel and change. I mean it."

Tracy dimpled innocently. "I thought I'd bring the happy couple luck by wearing something old."

"You must be insane," Claudia said.

I tried to lower the emotional thermostat. "It's a lovely dress," I said, "but the mantilla might be prettier draped around your shoulders."

Claudia glared at me. "She could drape it around her ass, and she'd still be wearing the dress Annie wore when she married Evan."

My heart sank. Tracy *must* be crazy. I shot a quick glance at Jill to see her reaction. Predictably, she had rushed to Bryn, who was standing in front of the pier glass between the long windows in the hall, wholly absorbed in her mirror image.

"I'm sure Tracy would change if you asked her to," Jill said gently.

"It's just a dress," Bryn said tonelessly to her reflection. Her gaze shifted to her aunt. "But, Tracy, I wish you'd let me have those pearls. I like having things that belong to people. Not just material things – secrets too."

Without hesitation, Tracy undid the clasp of her necklace and handed the pearls to her niece.

Bryn held the necklace against her throat. "Perfect," she said. Jill moved behind her stepdaughter-to-be and fastened the pearls. As she checked the mirror to make sure that the effect was indeed perfect, Jill's hands dropped to Bryn's shoulders. The gesture was one of such unaffected tenderness that Gaia Powell was beaming as she snapped the shot. Mother Love.

I turned away. I'd spent a lifetime watching Jill squander her emotional capital. Now she was turning her life inside out for a girl who didn't give a rat's ass for her. Suddenly, I was sick of the whole thing. The hours before the ceremony were now down to single digits. My fantasy that Gabe Leventhal was going to rescue the situation was looking more and more like the plotline for a B movie. In all likelihood, the cold light of day had brought Gabe fresh perspective and he'd decided he didn't want any part of the wedding or of me and hit the road.

When Gaia called me over to join Jill for the traditional photos of the bride and her matron of honour, my legs were leaden. As I smoothed an indiscernible wrinkle in one of the panels that formed Jill's sculptured bodice, I tried a smile.

Gaia shook her curls impatiently. "Come on, Joanne, your friend is getting married, not drawn and quartered."

I took another crack at it, but Gaia's grimace made it clear I was still short of the mark. "AA's got a great expression," she said. " 'Fake it until you make it.' How about a nice fake smile, Joanne?"

Jill raised her hand in a halt gesture. "Maybe just give us a moment, Gaia," she said. "Why don't you get some pictures of the kids with the dog?"

"You're paying the bill," Gaia said, and she wandered off with her camera.

As soon as we were alone, Jill turned to me. "Jo, I need you to help me get through this. I know this isn't a great romance. I even know that Bryn has certain . . . ," she averted her eyes, "certain gaps in her emotional makeup. But you're the one who told me that in every relationship there has to be a gardener and a flower. I'm prepared to be the gardener here. Bryn hasn't had an easy life. She deserves a chance to be hopeful and young."

"All I've ever wanted is for you to be happy," I said.

"Then let me help Bryn," Jill said. She slid her arms around me, and a flash exploded.

Gaia cheered. "That's the shot I was going for," she said. "Only three more Very Special Moments, and we're out of here."

We drove to the gallery under a dark and threatening sky. As we passed through the familiar streets, I stared out the window, feeling thoroughly miserable. Jill didn't seem to be doing much better. Surrounded by the soft folds of her dark green hood, her face appeared pale and tense. "Hey," I said, "remember 'Fake it until you make it'?"

"Easier said than done," Jill said, continuing to stare straight ahead.

Tracy had insisted that Bryn ride with her and Claudia. In Bryn's absence, Angus reverted to his usual raucous self, and he was amusing his sister by devising a series of inventive and excruciating tortures for Danny Jacobs. It was hard not to be drawn into their fun, but Jill's smile was remote, like that of someone suffering from an illness. I patted her hand and turned away, relieved the drive to the gallery was a short one.

Felix Schiff was waiting for us under the portico. He was holding an umbrella, and as soon as he spotted our limo, he sprinted towards us. When the limo driver opened the passenger door, Felix positioned the umbrella carefully. "I thought this might keep the snow off your hair," he said.

"You're a good soul," Jill said.

Felix's expression was wistful. "Maybe once upon a time," he said. Then he offered Jill his hand. "Time to go," he said.

Dizzy with the adventure of it all, Taylor raced ahead into the building and Angus plodded after her. I stayed in the limo, wondering and delaying the inevitable. When Felix came back for me, I motioned him inside. He closed the umbrella, slid in, and crouched on one of the jump seats.

"Is there a problem?" he asked.

"I think there may be," I said. "Have you heard from Gabe?"

Felix gazed out the window of the limo. "Why would he call me?"

"Because you two go way back. Gabe and I watched the ending of *Black Spikes and Slow Waves* together last night. I saw you in your flaming youth."

"That particular time in my life is nothing to joke about," Felix said stiffly.

"Then fill me in," I said. "Felix, you're the only person I trust who has a link to Gabe. This just doesn't make sense. According to Evan, Gabe has bowed out of the wedding because he's a hypochondriac. He's supposed to be so fearful that he flew home to New York to be with his doctor, yet last night he was the poster boy for living with gusto: smoking cigars, enjoying his wine, making plans for the future. You saw him. Do you believe he panicked and left town because he had a flutter?"

Felix's voice was gentle. "Don't ask a question when the answer can only cause you pain, Joanne."

"Are you saying that Gabe left town because of me?"

He looked away. "I'm saying that Jill's wedding is scheduled to begin in twenty minutes, and you might be wise to let this go."

"I'll let it go," I said. "But only for the time being."

"Fair enough," Felix said. "The time being is all we have."

Angus had already taken Taylor to the room where the wedding was being held, but Jill had waited, and we took the elevator to the second floor together. When the doors opened, Evan, like some apparition from a Gothic novel, was facing us.

I could hear Jill's intake of breath. "So much for the idea that it's bad luck to see the bride before the wedding," she said.

"Like all superstitions, that one is nonsense," Evan said. "You look beautiful, Jill." He nodded to me. "Your dress is lovely too, Joanne."

Jill and I are both on the tall side of average, but Evan dwarfed us. It wasn't just his height; he exerted a powerful undertow that seemed to draw those around him into his sphere. In his cutaway, striped trousers, pearl grey waistcoat, and grey-and-black-striped four-in-hand, he had the larger than life quality of a stage actor, but there were two jarring notes. Ms. Manners would have approved of his gloves, but every man I knew would have stuffed the gloves in a pocket until the last minute, and Evan was wearing his. He was also wearing makeup of the heavy-duty concealer type about which Jill and I had joked earlier.

When he caught me eyeing his face, Evan's response was a preemptive strike. "Bridegroom's jitters," he said. "Surely even you can't see anything Machiavellian in the fact that I nicked myself shaving, Joanne."

"Of course not," I said, but I kept looking. His jaw was slightly swollen and even beneath the makeup I could see discolouration.

Jill stepped closer to examine the bruising. "That must be painful," she said.

Evan raised his hand to cover the area. "It's nothing," he said.

"How does the other guy look?" I asked.

Evan's eyes widened. Clearly, I'd shaken him. "There was no other guy," he said. "I told you I cut myself shaving."

"That's right," I said. "You did." I touched Jill's arm. "We should go in now. It's almost time."

Once, during the early years of my marriage, I saw a production of *Richard III* in London. The designer had created a stage world as bloodless as a chess game: the actors were costumed in sculptured robes of white or black and the set was a series of harshly geometric metal backdrops. Until Clarence was beheaded, we were in the stark, greyscale universe of absolutes, but the beheading introduced a new element. The trough that caught Clarence's head filled quickly with blood, and the bleeding never stopped. As Richard's brutal march to power continued, the blood poured unabated. By the time the final curtain fell, the stage dripped red.

The memory of that production washed over me as we walked down the aisle towards the place where Jill's husband-to-be and his best man stood waiting. The wedding guests, shimmering in their bright outfits, fell silent as they took in our austere monochromatic gowns. It was a dramatic moment, made even more dramatic by the setting. Jill and Evan would be exchanging their vows in front of the floor-to-ceiling windows that comprised the west wall of the gallery. Jill had hoped for a pretty snowfall or for the soft glow of a late-winter afternoon, but the light that seeped through the glass had the dull sheen of pewter. The only splash of colour in the area came from the cranberry miniskirt of the replacement judge, Rexella Sweeney. Rexella's words would set the action in motion. Like the characters in that long-ago production of *Richard III*, the members of Jill and Evan's wedding party seemed to be chess pieces moving inexorably towards an endgame of sacrifice and checkmate.

Rexella, a sixtyish blonde with a whisky rasp, dagger acrylic nails, and legs that wouldn't quit, was an unlikely catalyst for tragedy. Earlier, when she introduced herself to Jill and me, she sensed Jill's tension and wheezed, "Relax. This won't hurt half as much as a Brazilian bikini wax."

The moment came for Evan and Jill to exchange rings, and I knew that, worldly as Rexella was, she was wrong about the Brazilian bikini wax. When she pronounced that Evan and Jill were now husband and wife, tears stung my eyes. Watching my friend enter into a disastrous marriage was more painful by far than anything a cosmetician at The Sweet Hairafter had ever done to me.

Felix and I walked back down the aisle arm in arm, each of us grateful for the other's presence. "Keep smiling," Felix said through gritted teeth, "it's almost over."

But there was still the reception. While the caterers set up the tables for the buffet, we gathered in the crush area outside the gallery. Servers with trays of champagne circulated, fostering cheer. Felix handed me a glass. "Flawless performance," he said. "Did you know that bridesmaids were originally intended as decoys to lure evil spirits away from the bride?"

"Finally, an explanation for all those hideous dresses," I said.

We exchanged smiles and raised our glasses. The Cuvee Paradis Brut was everything champagne that cost eighty-five dollars a bottle U.S. should be – light, crisp, and astonishingly good, but only a magic elixir could have lifted me above the sticky mud of anxiety and trepidation that had been dragging me down all day. As I looked at my fluted glass, I knew I had two options: keep the champagne coming until I had blotted out the memory of a shambling man with a taste for strong tea and morality or find out what had happened to him. The decision was easy. No other man had ever compared me to Sam Waterston.

I surveyed the room to check on the kids. Taylor was chatting happily with Rapti Lustig's son, a ten-year-old named Sam who was too kind and too suave to ever compare a young woman to a Chia Pet. Angus and Bryn were silhouetted against the window, holding hands, watching the storm that had begun to rage outside with a force almost as powerful as the hormones of the young. Safe as churches.

There was a pay telephone in the lobby. I took the elevator down, found a quarter in the mad-money pocket of my evening bag, and dialled home.

For the first time that day, there was a new message, but the voice on the other end was not one I wanted to hear. Alex Kequahtooway had been my lover for three years, and to paraphrase the nursery rhyme: when our relationship had been good it was very, very good, but when it went bad, it was horrid.

Alex had always distrusted words, and his telephone message was succinct: he had to talk to me, and I knew his number. I did know his number. I also had no intention of calling it.

Then, as if I needed further proof that when man makes decisions, God laughs, Alex himself walked through the front door of the Mackenzie Gallery. As he stood in the foyer, stamping the snow off his boots, surveying the scene, my mind raced through the kaleidoscope of possibilities that might have brought him out in a blizzard. None of them was good. When his eyes found me, they betrayed nothing, and as he walked towards me, my heart began to pound. "Has something happened to one of the kids?" I asked.

Alex's obsidian eyes were warm. "No. Your family's fine, Jo. This is about another matter." He gestured to a stone bench in the lobby. "Let's sit down."

The gallery had a number of benches upon which the weary could share space with a sculptured figure that, reflecting our politically sensitive times, represented the full spectrum of our citizens: male, female, young, old, aboriginal, non-aboriginal, executive, worker. Alex had pointed to my favourite, a pregnant woman in a sundress and sandals, reading a book. He knew that particular bench reminded me of a good time in my own life, but his first words made it clear that chance not memory had determined his choice.

"About an hour ago, we had a call," he said. "Someone trying to deliver a meat order to the Hotel Saskatchewan ran over a man's body. In the blizzard, the driver didn't recognize what he saw as human – he thought it was just a snowbank."

My nerves tightened. "What's the connection with me?"

"The deceased had the numbers for both your home and your cell in his pocket, Jo. They were the only local tie-in, so it seemed logical to start with you."

A flash. Gabe smiling. *Wouldn't it be ironic if this wedding was the start of a real love affair?* I covered my face with my hands.

Alex swallowed hard. "So you do know the man."

"His name is Gabriel Leventhal. He was supposed to be the best man at Jill's wedding today. He told the groom he was going back to New York City."

"He didn't make it," Alex said stiffly.

"How did he die?"

"They don't know. The blizzard will make determining the time of death a little tricky, and, of course, the truck driving over him wasn't exactly a lucky break."

"For you," I said furiously. "Not great for him either, but that's not your concern, is it?"

Alex ignored my outburst. "Were you intimate?'

"Yes," I said, "but not in any way you'd understand." I regretted the words immediately, not just because they were intended to wound, but because they were untrue. When I began to weep, Alex rubbed the back of my neck in a gesture of intimacy that evoked times when his touch was all I needed to restore me. More coals heaped upon my head.

CHAPTER

4

When I stopped crying, Alex waited for a moment, then offered me a tissue. Beside me, the stone pregnant woman with her secret knowing smile read on, tranquil and impervious. "I'm sorry," I said. "It's just – this is such a shock. Last night Gabe was so alive, full of plans." I met his eyes. "How many times have you heard someone say that?"

"It doesn't make it any less true." Alex held my gaze. "We don't know what's ahead, Jo. That's how we manage to get up in the morning." He ran his hand through his hair to comb out the melting snow. "Let's stick to business. The next of kin need to be notified. Does Mr. Leventhal have any relatives in Regina?"

I shook my head. "No," I said. "He's an American – from New York City."

"Then I'm going to have to ask you to make the ID." Alex eyed my gown. "Your neighbour told me you were here for a wedding. How long do you think you'll be?"

"The formal part of the reception doesn't take long: just a few toasts and the cake cutting. I can be out of here in half an hour." My response sounded confident, but my body felt boneless. I closed my eyes and tried to breathe deeply, but the image of me walking into the morgue and seeing Gabe's body was too much. "I can't do it, Alex," I said. "I'm not even the logical person to ask. I just met Gabe last night at the rehearsal dinner; Evan's known him for years."

Alex's eyes grew hard. "But you said you and Mr. Leventhal were intimate."

"I just meant we clicked. We enjoyed one another's company; we planned to get together today, but I really don't know that much about him. I don't think there are next of kin. Evan will know."

"Fair enough," Alex said. "But asking a groom to identify the body of his best man on his wedding day seems a bit harsh."

"Evan's very controlled."

"Good," Alex said. "Given the condition of his friend, he'll need to be."

Alex and I walked into a party mellowed by hot jazz, great food, smart talk, and servers who had been instructed to allow no glass to remain empty for longer than ten seconds. The room couldn't have been more welcoming, but I felt Alex grow tense beside me. He could have faced a firing squad without flinching, but social situations were agony for him. Out of habit, I squeezed his arm; then, suddenly feeling awkward, I withdrew my hand and, anxious for a purpose, searched the crowd until I found Evan. He and Jill were making the rounds, accepting congratulations.

For the first time that day, Jill seemed genuinely happy, her face flushed with the pleasure of being with friends again. When she spotted Alex, she gave me an impish smile. After my relationship with him had come to an end, Jill had called from Toronto every night for a month. She was the only one who knew how deeply Alex's brief affair with another woman had wounded me, and that night she couldn't hide her pleasure at seeing us together again.

As soon as she and Evan came over, she held out her arms to Alex. "It's so good to see you," she said. "I don't need to hear the details. I'm just glad you're here." Jill turned to her new husband, "Evan, this is Alex Kequahtooway – Inspector Alex Kequahtooway of the Regina Police Force. Alex, Evan MacLeish."

Alex offered his hand. "Congratulations," he said.

"Thanks." Evan was tight-jawed as he took Alex's measure. "Am I wrong in assuming there's more on your mind than wishing us well?"

Alex didn't falter. "No, I'm here on police business." His eyes met Jill's. "I'm sorry, Jill. I really was hoping I could talk to Mr. MacLeish alone."

"We seemed to have closed that option," Evan said.

"I guess we have," Alex replied. "So here's the situation. A man's body was found behind the Hotel Saskatchewan this afternoon. We have reason to believe the deceased is Gabriel Leventhal."

Jill's face grew dangerously pale. "Was it his heart?" she asked.

Alex took out his notepad. "Did Mr. Leventhal have a history of heart problems?"

Evan answered for her. "He had a history of hypochondria. Last night he thought he had an angina attack. He said it was mild, but it was obvious he was shaken."

"When did this happen?" Alex had his pencil poised.

Evan looked away. "I don't know. Sometime in the night. Gabe's room at the hotel was across from mine. I was asleep. I heard a knock at my door, and it was Gabe. He said he was experiencing some pain in his shoulder and he thought he should go back to New York and consult his doctor."

"Did you suggest he see a doctor here?" Alex asked.

"Why would I? He was a hypochondriac. A hundred doctors could have told him his heart was sound and it wouldn't have changed anything." Evan's tone was flat, the way his daughter's had been when Jill asked Bryn if she'd been disturbed by seeing her aunt wear Annie Lowell's wedding dress.

Evan's lack of emotion goaded me. "What happened to 'Be kind. Everyone you meet is fighting a great battle'? You knew what kind of battle Gabe was fighting, why didn't you check to see if he was all right?"

"Jo, I'm attempting to get some answers here." Alex's warning was clear, but I ignored it.

"So am I," I said. "I want to know why a man I cared about froze to death in the snow and was run over like an animal."

"Then let me do my job," Alex said. He turned back to Evan. "You were saying that it was midnight when you last saw Mr. Leventhal alive."

"I can help with the time," Jill said. She looked stunned, but she knew how to follow a story. "I was staying at Joanne's, and Gabe phoned me there – it was around one-thirty when he called. He said he needed to see me. I had some problems getting downtown, so by the time I arrived, he'd already gone to bed. The man on the graveyard shift at the front desk called Gabe's room for me, but he didn't answer. You can check with the desk clerk about the exact time."

"I'll talk to him," Alex said. He turned back to Evan. "Mr. MacLeish, why didn't you call your fiancée last night to tell her that your best man was withdrawing."

For the first time, there was a note of asperity in Evan's voice. "Because there was no point in disturbing her. It was late. I couldn't justify waking Jill up the night before our wedding because the best man was having a panic attack and wanted his doctor."

"It appears Mr. Leventhal suffered something more medically threatening than a panic attack," Alex said coolly.

"I had no way of knowing that," Evan said. "All I knew was that Jill and I were getting married the next day, and I wanted our wedding to be a happy occasion."

"I still want that," Jill said quietly. "We all do." She was not a woman who asked favours, but she was asking for one now. "Alex, can't this wait? I feel sick about Gabe – I really do, but this is supposed to be a celebration. My stepdaughter has looked forward to this day for so long. Give us a chance to start our life together with some good memories."

"My wife has a point," Evan said. "No one here has done anything wrong. And once the reception's over, I'm at your disposal. We can meet back at the hotel. I can change and check my notebook. I'm almost certain Gabe left me a couple of contact numbers in New York when we were making our plans to come out here."

Alex darted a quick glance at Jill. Something in her face seemed to decide the matter for him. "You have two hours," he said finally. "Where are you staying?"

"The Hotel Saskatchewan," Evan said. "The Bridal Suite."

"Very romantic," Alex said. "So when's the honeymoon?"

"We're flying to New York tomorrow," Jill said.

Alex glanced at the swirling vortex of snow outside the window. "Hope you make it," he said.

Jill's laugh was shaky. "So do I," she said.

Traditionally, the first toast at a wedding is to the health of the bride and groom and comes from the bride's father. Since Jill's last memory of her father was of him drunkenly picking up the tablecloth at her fourth birthday party and throwing everything – presents, plates, glasses, and cake – into the garbage can in the back alley, I'd been rung in as his replacement. Proposing a drink to the health of the bride and groom seemed such a no-brainer that I hadn't bothered to check out any of the Web sites Angus recommended. That afternoon, as I stood dry-mouthed and blank-brained before the wedding guests, I longed for the wisdom of heartfelt.com that promised words to live by and tips on body language and humour guaranteed to bring down the house.

I didn't bring down the house, but I did manage to stumble out a few coherent sentences. When Jill stood up to respond, she flashed me an understanding smile and thanked me for being her pilot light of optimism through more dark times than she cared to count.

It was a touching moment, and when Felix pushed back his chair and stood, his eyes were misty. He wasn't scheduled to speak until later, so I assumed Jill's words had stirred something in him. It turned out they had.

"I have a message from another woman who has illuminated the lives of those who know her. Caroline MacLeish sent me the following note for her new daughter-in-law." Felix took out his Palm Pilot and read, " 'I woke this morning thinking of you drawing the velvet cape around your shoulders as you went off to begin your new life. When I drew that same cape around my shoulders and left for my wedding, I knew very little. There's much that I still don't understand, but here is one true thing: Nietzsche tells us that human beings must accept the fact that pleasure and pain are inextricably linked and that a life without pain would be a life with a limited capacity for joy. Embrace the pain in your life, Jill. It will lead you to unimaginable joy.' "

When Felix fell silent, there was a smattering of desultory applause, but he didn't pick up on the hint that his moment in the spotlight was over and it was time to cede the floor. He seemed mesmerized by his Palm Pilot, staring at it, as if for comfort or advice. The silence became awkward, and Jill went over, whispered something in his ear, and guided him gently down into his seat.

The next speaker was Evan, and when he stood up, the stagy tan of his MAC concealer and his movie-star larger-than-life quality caused even the servers to stop and stare. As he raised his glass, I sensed a consummate actor was about to take us all on a journey, and I wasn't wrong.

"Thank you, Felix, for bringing Caroline MacLeish to the wedding. Not many women would have sent the gift of Nietzsche to a new bride but, as you say, my mother is exceptional. Apparently, she is also prescient. Caroline's is the only gift Jill and I can put to immediate use." Guests leaned forward in their seats, anticipating some drama. Evan didn't disappoint. "A few minutes ago, we learned that our dear friend, Gabe Leventhal, who came here from New York to be part of our wedding, died of a heart attack early this morning. We're shaken, in pain, but mindful of Nietzsche's lesson, I ask that you join me in drinking a toast that encompasses pain at the death of a friend and joy at the birth of a marriage."

The silence in the room was rooted more in awkwardness than grief. Most of the guests had never met Gabe Leventhal, but as I took in the reactions of those who had, there were a few surprises. Taylor, who was sitting beside me, was stunned into silence. "Are you okay?" I asked.

"I just don't understand," she said. "How could he be at our house having fun last night, then be dead today?"

My only answer was to pull her close. Angus was watching Bryn intently, ready to catch the pieces when she shattered, but after a beat, she opened her evening bag, pulled out a mirror, and checked her lip gloss. Tracy had begun to cry, copiously and theatrically. Claudia handed her a glass of champagne, told her to smarten up, then turned her attention to saving the party. "Time for the cake," she said. "And time to applaud the man who created the cake."

The name of the man who created the cake was Kevin Hynd, and he had a history. He was by training a corporate lawyer and, like Jill, he was a passionate Deadhead. When Jerry Garcia died, Kevin had been rocked by the revelation that life was transitory. He walked away from his six-figure income and started doing pro bono work that he underwrote with the earnings from his new business: a bakery devoted to creating edible monuments to hip excess. The wedding cake was his gift to Jill, and as the guests gathered around, it was clear that Kevin had surpassed himself. He'd created a four-tiered marvel covered in Swiss meringue butter cream, encircled by a soaring fondant ribbon bearing the legend "Let there be songs to fill the air . . ." and topped with marzipan renderings of the Rainbow Dancers, those high-stepping, multi-coloured, top-hatted skeletons who were the emblem of one of the Grateful Dead's greatest tours. The creation was slick enough for a magazine cover, but funky as the cake was, it was the knife Jill and Evan were using that drew my eye.

It was an ulu, the crescent-shaped knife Inuit women use to cut up seal meat and dress skins. The women of Baker Lake had given it to Jill after she spent a summer there doing a story about their lives and their art. At her farewell party, the women told her the knife was a vital survival tool for a woman; then they had covered their mouths to hide their laughter at the idea that Jill would need an ulu to survive in the civilized world of network television.

After Jill and Evan cut the ceremonial first piece of cake, there was the usual applause and clinking of glasses, and for a while, the room hummed with talk of the beauty of the wedding and shared memories of the Grateful Dead. Still, it wasn't long before people began exchanging holiday wishes and heading for the elevators. Clearly that night the number-one song on everyone's chart of the Dead's greatest hits was "Gentlemen, Start Your Engines."

I was counting the minutes till I could leave too. The reality of Gabe's death was beginning to sink in, and I was in desperate need of a hot bath, a pair of flannelette pyjamas, and a chance to sit in front of the fire and ponder what might have been.

I found Taylor chatting with Kevin as he cut and boxed the rest of the cake. She was a sheltered eight-year-old, and Kevin was a grizzled survivor, but they were on the same wavelength.

"So if I sleep with this cake under my pillow, I'm supposed to dream about the boy I'll marry," Taylor said sceptically.

"Sounds like a load of crap to me too," Kevin said, "but that's the tradition."

Taylor cocked her head. "What if I start dreaming about a boy I totally hate."

"Flush the cake down the john, go back to bed, and call me for a replacement in the morning," Kevin said and threw his head back with a laugh that was so infectious people standing around them smiled.

"Sorry to break this up," I said. "But I really have had enough fun, Taylor."

Usually it took dynamite to blast Taylor loose when she was having a good time, but after a quick glance at my face, she was surprisingly agreeable. "I guess we should go home," she said to Kevin. "Every time we stay out too long, our animals knock the Christmas tree down."

"Then you're wise to make tracks," Kevin said. He handed us each a tiny box tied with ribbon printed with images of the Rainbow Dancers. "Don't forget your cake," he said. "And don't forget to dream."

Felix and Jill were sitting an abandoned table, heads close, conversation heated. Felix mumbled something I couldn't hear, then he raised his voice. "And honour doesn't mean anything?" At that point, Jill noticed me and gestured to Felix, who turned to me with a strained smile. "Creative differences." Felix's German accent became stronger when he was upset, and now, when he said, "Whenever we're together, we seem to end up talking shop," all the w's turned into v's.

"I won't intrude," I said. "I just wanted to tell you the kids and I are taking off."

I was surprised that Jill looked so stricken. "Can I come by tomorrow for a quick visit before we leave?"

"Of course." I looked at her closely. "Jill, is anything wrong?"

She chewed her lip in a gesture of anxiety I knew too well. "A lot of things are wrong, Jo. Where are the grown-ups now that we need them?"

"In the mirror," I said. "We're it, Jill."

"For better or for worse," she said. She turned to Felix. "Why don't you get us all a drink – a real drink – something with plenty of alcohol and no bubbles. It would be nice to have a moment together before . . ."

"Before you begin married life?" Evan seemed to have appeared out of nowhere. When he brushed Jill's arm, she stiffened. It did not seem an auspicious beginning for a marriage. Neither did the fact that Evan had applied fresh concealer to what was now clearly a deep and painful bruise on his jawline. The tension at the table was palpable, and I wasn't keen to add to the angst.

"Why don't you stop by the house tomorrow? We can talk then," I said.

"Am I included in the invitation?" Evan asked.

"Of course," I said.

He held out his hand to me, then immediately withdrew it. "Thanks," he said. He locked his hands behind his back. "I promise to keep my distance."

I found Angus and Bryn standing by the piano, flanked by her aunts. Surprisingly, when I said we were leaving, Angus didn't complain. In fact, he seemed almost relieved.

"I'll see if I can score a cab for us," he said.

Claudia pointed towards the driveway. "The limo driver's down there, cooling his heels. Ask him to give you a ride. We're going to be stuck here till the last varmint is hung."

Angus gave Bryn an awkward wave.

"Call me tonight before you go to sleep," she said.

He smiled, but he didn't make any promises before he took off.

Bryn offered me a cheek, cool as marble, to kiss. Tracy offered nothing. After the river of tears when the news came about Gabe, she had withdrawn into a stillness that bordered on the catatonic. Her virginal dress, her white-lace mantilla, and her five-mile stare made her look as forlorn as an abandoned bride. I touched her hand. "Take care of yourself," I said.

"She's in good hands." In a gesture that was surprisingly matey, Claudia draped her arm around her sister-in-law's shoulder. "You've been skimming the trees for a while, kiddo," she said. "It was only a matter of time before you crashed. It'll be better now that the wedding's over."

"It will never be better," Tracy said flatly.

Claudia rolled her eyes. "Of course it will. Nothing is forever, although I must admit it wouldn't take too many days like this to make a dozen. Xanax moments from dawn till dusk."

My family's ride home was another Xanax moment. The snow was heavy enough to make me grateful that a professional driver was at the wheel, but the novelty of riding in a limo had passed for my children, and as we approached our street, the air was heavy with things unsaid. Taylor broke the silence with an utterance that, even for her, was cryptic. "I eat my peas with honey," she said. "I've done it all my life. It makes the peas taste funny, but it keeps them on my knife." Her brother, who was obviously dealing with some major personal issues, glared at her.

Taylor ignored him. "Last night at dinner I dropped a forkful of peas on the floor, and Mr. Leventhal said that poem – I guess he wanted to make me feel better."

"That was kind," I said mechanically.

"I liked him a lot." Taylor was earnest. "He was . . ." As she searched for *le mot juste* we turned onto our street. There was a delivery truck in front of our house and as soon as Taylor spotted it, her elegy for Gabe short-circuited. "Look at that," she said pointing to the towering plastic-shrouded tree the driver was attempting to prop against the door. "We won, Jo! You didn't think we had a chance, but we did."

"You're a lucky girl," the limo driver said.

"I know it," Taylor said. "Do you want to come in and see it without the bag?"

"I'd better stay on the job," he said. "But thanks. You have a happy holiday now."

"Oh we will," Taylor said.

Angus and the delivery man wrestled the tree into the house. It was huge, and the moment Angus ripped the plastic away, I knew that God was a Monty Python fan. My daughter's dream had almost, but not quite, come true. Snowfall at Swan Lake had gone to another lucky home; our win was a flocked plantation pine whose boughs groaned under the weight of dozens of ceramic cherubim and seraphim. Each of the little figures was personalized with the face of a celebrity who had joined the Heavenly Host: Princess Di, George Harrison, Martin Luther King, Dale Earnhardt, Pierre Trudeau, Janis Joplin, Mahatma Gandhi, Buddy Holly, John Lennon, Elvis, Marilyn Monroe, James

Dean, and an entire phalanx of Kennedys. There was a card tied to one of the branches. Angus took it down and read aloud, "I am called Angels Among Us, and I am a reminder that the great ones never die." Angus rolled his eyes. "That was the tree talking," he said. "Just in case you thought it couldn't get any worse . . ."

An hour later, we had slipped out of our wedding finery and back into our everyday lives. Taylor was in her room playing with her cats, Bruce and Benny, and I was in my room wrapping a couple of last-minute gifts and trying to get into the spirit. Except for the persistent thump of Angus's stereo, the house was quiet. When the phone rang, the fact that Jill was on the other end of the line didn't set off any bells.

"I need some clothes," she said.

"Don't we all?" I said. "But I thought you were planning to change back at the hotel."

"I need something now. There's blood all over this dress."

In a microsecond, I rocketed into full panic mode. "Are you all right?" I said.

"It's not my blood," she said. "It's his."

"Whose? Jill, what's happened?"

"There was an accident." Her voice was razor-edged with hysteria. "I've got to get this dress off, Jo. It's covered in blood."

"I'll be right there," I said. "Do you need a doctor?"

"It's too late for a doctor," she said. "I need clothes . . . Please, Jo. Just bring me some clothes."

I ran upstairs, jammed fresh clothing, socks, and shoes into a backpack, grabbed a towel and a bar of soap, and dashed down to the kitchen where Angus was making himself a grilled cheese sandwich.

"They should give you real food at a wedding," he said without looking up.

My heart felt as if it was pounding out of my chest, but I

tried to keep the mood light. "When you get married, we'll have the reception at the Between the Buns Sports Bar," I said. "Look, why don't you make a sandwich for Taylor too? I have to go out."

My son shot me a look. "In this weather?"

"It's important." I gave him a one-armed hug. "I don't know how long I'll be, but I've got the cell if you need me."

Taylor intercepted me in the front hall. "Where are you going?"

"Just to run an errand," I said. "Angus is here."

"Wait!" Taylor fell to her knees and plugged in her tree. "You've got to see this." In the blink of an eye, a hundred twinkling stars lit the celebrity cherubs, and somewhere deep in the tree's flocked heart a computer chip began to play "The Way We Were."

"You always say things work out the way they're supposed to," she said, sighing contentedly. "This is going to be the best Christmas ever."

I kissed the top of her head. "Hold that thought," I said.

Albert Street was tough sledding. Stuck behind a snow-plough, I grew white-knuckled with frustration and fear. As I crawled in the vehicle's wake, I replayed my conversation with Jill. No matter how I construed her words, they signalled trouble. There was more cause for anxiety in the outside world. Except for my Volvo and the snowplough, every vehicle headed south on Albert Street had a member of the Regina City Police in the driver's seat. When we came to the turnoff for the gallery, I tensed, hoping against hope the squad cars would continue south, towards a disaster that had nothing to do with anyone I loved. But as the caravan turned east onto the road that led to the MacKenzie, I knew that the longest night of the year had just gotten longer.

The visitors' parking lot was so choked with snow that I didn't even give it a second glance. I parked my Volvo in the first available staff space and headed towards the gallery. The lobby was blue with uniformed cops. I took a deep breath and forged ahead as if I had a right to be there. Adopting an air of entitlement was a trick I'd learned from Angus, and that night it got me through the front doors. Fate – benevolent or malevolent – intervened immediately. The first officer I ran into in the lobby was Alex Kequahtooway. He was a man with enviable control of his emotions, but I knew every inch of his body, and I recognized the throb in his temple as a sign that he was suffering.

The impulse to reach out to him was almost overwhelming, but remembering the pain of our breakup, I kept my hands jammed in my pockets. "What happened?" I said.

"Evan MacLeish is dead. His carotid artery was slit with the knife they used to cut the cake – some kind of hunting knife."

"It's called an ulu," I said.

"Well now it's called a murder weapon," Alex said dryly.

"Do you know who did it?"

I could almost hear the clang as he shut me out. "This is a police investigation, Joanne."

I slid off my backpack. "I have some clothes in here for Jill. Can I take them to her?"

"I'll check to see if the forensic guys have everything they need from her."

"Is she a suspect?"

Alex started towards the elevator. Before he touched the button, he turned back to me. "You might as well come up with me."

We stepped into the elevator together. "Is the body still up here?" I asked.

Alex's surprise was genuine. "Why would it be here? Evan MacLeish was killed in that snow fort on the east lawn."

"What was he doing out there?" I asked.

Alex shot me a withering glance. "Getting murdered," he said.

When the elevator doors opened, the sight that greeted us was eye-popping: Martha Stewart meets "COPS." The area in which Jill and Evan had cut the cake was cordoned off with yellow crime scene tape. The Rainbow Dancers were still strutting their stuff on the top tier of Kevin Hynd's brilliantly inspired confection, but the glowing cloth on which the cake-tray sat was dark with traceries of fingerprint powder. Guests who had decided to stay until the last drop of Cuvee Paradis Brut had been drunk clutched individual cake boxes and talked uneasily to note-taking cops.

My eyes darted around the room, seeking Jill. Finally, I spotted her sitting on a banquette in the shadows at the far end of the gallery. On one side of her was a female police officer, on the other was Kevin Hynd. The cop, the bride, and the pastry chef – even on a night that was adding new dimension to the term "surreal," it was a bizarre grouping.

No one stopped me as I walked towards them, but when I got close, the sweet smell of blood almost gagged me. I kept moving and when Jill held out her arms, I moved to embrace her.

"Stand back." The police officer's voice was not unkind. "There's a fair amount of blood on her dress."

I slipped off my backpack and held it out to the officer. "I've brought some fresh clothes for her. Can she go somewhere to change?"

"Don't talk about me as if I'm not here," Jill said, and the deadness in her voice chilled me.

"I'll check with the inspector," said the officer, a rosy brunette whose badge read Maria Ciarniello.

I waited until Officer Ciarniello was out of earshot, then I turned to Jill. "You need a lawyer," I said.

Kevin shrugged. "She has a lawyer. Me."

I took in his Jerry Garcia beard and white caterer's jacket. "Well, why the hell not?" I said.

Amazingly, Jill began to laugh. She laughed until the tears streamed down her face. When her laughter ended in a hic-cupping sob, she looked around. "I don't suppose either of you has a Kleenex."

"I do," I said, handing one to her.

The young police officer came back. "Inspector Kequahtooway says you can change, but I'll need to be with you so I can bag your gown for forensics."

Jill nodded wearily. "You can bring in the whole police force if you have to. Just let me get the blood off me."

Another cop came over and handed Officer Ciarniello a plastifilm bag eerily like the bag that had held Taylor's Angels Among Us tree. "Let's go," she said.

The four of us went down in the elevator together. Officer Ciarniello followed us into the bathroom; Kevin Hynd sta-tioned himself outside.

The largest of the women's restrooms at the gallery had two parts: a small area in which women could change their babies and, through another door, the usual stalls, sinks, and mirrors. Maria Ciarniello positioned herself in the doorway that separated the two rooms and slid on a pair of surgical gloves. Jill turned her back to the mirrors, unzipped her beautiful blood-stained dress, and let it fall. Like a zealous salesperson in a top-of-the-line shop, Officer Ciarniello caught the gown before it hit the floor and placed it in the evidence bag. There was a spot of blood on Jill's strapless long-line bra. When she noticed it, she began fumbling with the hooks on the back.

"I'll get it," I said. I undid her hooks and Jill ripped off the bra and handed it to Officer Ciarniello. After Jill stepped out of her panties, and Officer Ciarniello dutifully retrieved them, my friend turned to me naked. I took a washcloth from the backpack, ran a sink full of warm water, squirted soap on the cloth, and began to wipe her body. She was as still as a sick child. When I'd rinsed her body, I reached for a towel. Jill shook her head violently. "No, there might still be some blood." Obediently, I refilled the sink, soaped the washcloth, and repeated the process. It was a long while before I could persuade Jill that she was clean. When finally she was convinced that not one drop of Evan MacLeish's blood remained on her body, she picked up the towel and patted her skin dry. "You understand why I had to be sure," she said.

"I understand," I said. "Now come on, let's get you dressed. It's time to go home."

CHAPTER

5

Jill was silent as she pulled on the slacks and sweater I'd brought, but after she'd run a comb through her hair, she turned to me. "I didn't kill him," she said. "I got the blood on me when I found his body."

I indicated Officer Ciarniello with my eyes. "We don't need to talk about this now," I said.

"But I need you to know," she said.

I met her eyes. "I know."

Officer Ciarniello popped her head around the door. "Inspector Kequahtooway will be waiting."

"We can't have that." The cheekiness was vintage Jill, but the delivery was flat.

Kevin Hynd was still at his post by the door to the ladies' room. As we came out, he slid his arm through Jill's. "Don't volunteer anything," he said, then led us towards the elevator.

Alex was sitting on small couch just inside the room where the wedding and reception had been held. He was talking to a petite, curvy blonde named Pam Levine. She was an associate producer on "Canada Tonight," and when we'd run into one another Christmas shopping, she'd announced that the bodysuit she was wearing to Jill's wedding would shoot her straight to the top of Santa's list of Bad Little Girls. Nobody would have disputed Pam's claim that her lipstick-red outfit was a sizzler, but as she answered Alex's questions, she didn't look naughty, she looked terrified.

Kevin led us to a table well away from the windows that faced the maze where Evan had been killed. With his Captain Trip insouciance and grizzled masculinity, Kevin did not, at first, seem like one of nature's gentlemen, but he was courtly as he pulled out chairs for Jill, Officer Ciarniello, and me. Jill and I sank into ours, but Officer Ciarniello remained standing. When Alex came over, he dismissed her, and she left, struggling under the weight of Jill's gown in the evidence bag.

Alex sat down and Kevin took the chair opposite him. "Is there a reason that you're staying?" Alex asked.

"I'm Ms. Osiowy's lawyer," Kevin said.

Alex's eyes widened. "And you cook too," he said.

"What a long strange trip it's been," Kevin said pleasantly. He gave Alex his full name, then said, "I've instructed my client not to volunteer any information."

"Fair enough," Alex said. "I'll just ask my questions."

As he shifted in his chair to face Jill, Alex's body language and tone changed. I was hyper-alert, anxious to know how he would treat her. Alex had come to know Jill through me. He didn't trust the media. As an aboriginal cop who had come off his reserve to work in the system, Alex was wary of the institutions that govern our lives and of the people who run them, but he had grown genuinely fond of Jill.

"What happened here tonight?" he asked.

Jill chewed the nail polish on her thumbnail. "I wish I knew," she said.

"Just tell me what you can," Alex said, and his voice was soft with empathy.

Jill was a savvy journalist, and under normal circumstances, she would have seen through the warm reassurances that are standard issue for officers playing the Good Cop role. These were not normal circumstances, and when Jill exhaled and smiled gratefully at Alex, I knew she was seriously off her game. I shot a glance at Kevin Hynd.

"I'm on it," he muttered. He leaned close to his new client. "Jill, the less you say, the better."

"But I didn't do anything wrong," she replied.

"Then tell me everything you know," Alex said. There was urgency in his voice. He was pressing her because he knew the window of opportunity opened by her vulnerability could slam shut at any time. "How did you come to be out there by the snow maze, Jill?"

"I was looking for . . ." She caught herself. "I was looking for someone."

The cords in Alex's neck tensed. "Who?"

"Just a guest I hadn't spoken to. An old friend from the network. Someone told me she'd gone outside for a smoke, so I decided to join her."

Alex put down his pen and stared at Jill. "You left your own wedding reception to step outside for a smoke in the middle of a blizzard?"

Jill was cool. "I hadn't had a cigarette in three hours, and it had been a stressful day." She raised her hand to deflect a hasty interpretation. "Not because anything was wrong – just because there's stress in every wedding."

"All right, so you're out in front of the gallery, lighting up with your friend . . ."

"No," Jill cut him off. "She wasn't there. I'd missed her. I decided that since I was already outside, I'd have a cigarette."

"In the blizzard," Alex said. This time he made no attempt to disguise his scepticism.

"There's a portico out front that offers some shelter," Jill said. "Besides, by that time the wind had died down."

"And the weather had become so pleasant you decided to stroll over to the maze."

"Inspector, if you keep jerking Jill around, we're out of here." Kevin Hynd removed a rose from the centrepiece and handed it to his client with a flourish. "We're solid," he said.

It was a gallant gesture, and Jill rewarded him with a smile. "Thanks," she said. "For the flower and for the reminder that the inspector is no longer a friend."

Alex winced. He was a good officer, but he was also a man sensitive to rejection, and for a moment, I felt my heart go out to him. The feeling didn't last. If lines were being drawn, I was on Jill's side.

Jill twirled the rose between her thumb and index finger. "Here's what happened," she said. "Take it, or leave it. I was standing in the portico smoking when I heard a cry – not a cry exactly, but obviously the sound of someone in trouble. It was coming from the direction of the maze, so I went over." Jill's eyes lost their focus. She was back at the scene. I'd had my own doubts about Jill's story to this point, but suddenly her words had the ring of truth.

Alex seemed to believe her too. "You were wearing a wedding gown," he said. "Why didn't you just go inside and get somebody to call 911?"

Jill's eyes flashed. "Damn it, Alex, you *know* me. You know that if I heard someone in agony, my first thought wouldn't be what I was wearing or how I could offload the problem onto someone else. Why can't you get your head around the fact that I did what any decent human being would do?"

Alex didn't raise his eyes from his notepad. "All right," he said. "You heard a cry and you responded. What happened next?"

"When I was about halfway to the maze, the sounds stopped," Jill said. "I kept going until I came to the entrance. I went in. That's when I found Evan. The walls were blocking the light, so I couldn't see him until it was too late. He was just inside." She bit her lip. "I fell right on top of him. For a few seconds I just lay there. I was stunned. Finally, I put my hand against his throat to see if he had a pulse. That's when I touched the ulu – it was stuck here." Jill placed her fingers against her own carotid artery. "I knew enough not to take it out. That's how people bleed to death." Her eyes were vacant. It was clear she was teetering on the brink of shock, and Kevin tapped her hand with his own, bringing her back.

Jill exchanged glances with him, then she continued. "I put my ear against Evan's mouth to hear if he was breathing. He didn't seem to be. I ran back to the gallery. There was a commissionaire just inside. He phoned the police. Then I went to look for . . . ," she hesitated, and in that moment, I knew that whatever came next would be a lie. "There was a medical doctor at the reception," Jill said. "I went to see if I could find her."

"So you went back upstairs to the party," Alex said.

"Yes," Jill said. "And from that point on, there are a hundred people who can tell you what I did."

"We'll be talking to every one of them," Alex said dryly.

Jill turned to Kevin Hynd. "Can we go now?"

Kevin leaned back in his chair. "Inspector?"

Alex didn't look up. "Tell your client to stay in town. I want her available."

Jill stood up abruptly. "Thanks for the vote of confidence, Alex."

"I still need someone to identify Gabriel Leventhal's body," Alex said.

Jill's voice was icy, "And you expect me to do it."

"I'm not a monster," Alex said. "I was hoping you could suggest someone."

"Felix Schiff took over as best man when Gabe didn't show up," I said. "He's known Gabe for years."

Alex shrugged. "Point him out, and you can be on your way."

"He's not here," Jill said.

"Where is he?" Alex said.

Jill looked away. "Back at the hotel, I guess."

"You don't know? He was the best man at your wedding. I would think when he left the reception, he might say goodbye and mention where he was headed." Alex's face was dark with anger. "Jill, ever since we sat down for this interview, you and your lawyer have been dumping all over me because I'm trying to do my job. You say you're innocent. Then let me hear the truth. No more lies. No more evasions."

"I'm not lying," Jill said. "I haven't seen Felix since . . . since before I went outside to have that cigarette."

"Nobody knows; nobody tells," Alex said, seemingly to himself. "What hotel is he staying at?"

"The Saskatchewan," Jill said.

"A straight answer. Thank you very much." Alex raised his hand in dismissal. "You can leave now."

Bryn was with her aunts at the top of the staircase that curved to the main floor. The three women formed a provocative triptych. Shoulders squared, jaw set, Claudia MacLeish was stoic. Bryn, too, was composed, but tears ran down her cheeks as if somewhere inside her there was a well of sorrow that could not be stilled. Tracy's woe was unrestrained. Hands cupped over her eyes, she sobbed with such intensity that her slender body seemed to convulse. Her suffering might have touched a stranger, but we "Magictown" aficionados had caught Tracy's act before. The cupped hands and the sobs were tipoffs that, once again, the Broken Wand Fairy's powers had failed her.

If I had had magical powers, I would have made all three women disappear, but like the Broken Wand Fairy, I was mired in the real world. All I could do was watch as Jill ran to Bryn, clasped the girl's bare shoulders, and assessed her anxiously. "Are you all right?"

"I'm fine," Bryn said. The tears were still flowing, but her words did not suggest deep and abiding grief. "I'm glad he's dead," she said.

Jill drew the girl to her. "Shh . . . ," she murmured. "You mustn't say that."

Bryn broke away. "Why not? It's true. It's not like I haven't told you a million times that I hated him." She whirled to face her aunts. "I told you too. He deformed my life, and nobody did anything about it. Now somebody has. Just don't expect me to be a hypocrite like everybody else."

It was a situation that demanded quick and deft handling, and Kevin Hynd supplied it. "We haven't met," he said, extending his hand to Bryn. "I'm Jill's lawyer. Since you're her stepdaughter now, I'm going to give you some legal advice."

Bryn took his hand warily. "What's the advice?"

"Put a sock in it," Kevin said equitably. "There are cops hanging off the rafters here. If you want to rant, wait for a change of venue."

"I'm not leaving Jill," Bryn said quickly.

"You don't have to," Jill said. "We'll figure something out."

"Stay with us," I said and immediately regretted the invitation. I would have shared a pup-tent with Jill, but the idea of having Bryn at close quarters was not appealing. I didn't like her, and Angus's readiness to leave the reception suggested I wasn't the only one who suspected his goddess had feet of clay.

"Finally, a decision." Claudia shifted into full take-charge mode. "Let's move," she said. "The only thing that calms Tracy down when she's this hysterical is one of her pills and a massage, and these healing hands of mine won't be able to do their job unless they've spent some time wrapped around a big glass of Johnny Walker. Bryn can pick up her stuff when you drop us off at the hotel."

Bryn's eyes widened. "No," she said. "I'm not going back there. Just pack up my things and send them to Joanne's in a taxi."

Claudia frowned. "If that's what you want . . ."

"It is," Bryn said.

"And that's it?" Tracy's voice was jagged. "After seventeen years, you just walk out of my life?"

"Oh *please*," Bryn said. "Like you care about anybody but you."

Jill turned to Claudia and Tracy. "She's had a lot to deal with today."

Claudia made no attempt to hide her exasperation. "Bryn, I may not have done enough, but I did the best I could." She gestured towards Tracy. "So did she."

"Bite me!" Bryn snapped, then flew down the spiral staircase. I watched her, surprised and oddly heartened. For the first time since I'd met Bryn, I knew I had heard her true voice. It wasn't pretty, but it was authentic. As she disappeared into the lobby, I found myself hoping that despite everything that had been done to her, the bouncy egotism of the seventeen-year-old would get Bryn through.

When we came in, Taylor was lying on the hall floor with her head on Willie's side, gazing at the angels suspended from the flocked tips of her tree. The invisible music box was still playing "The Way We Were." As I listened to its endless, tinny repetitions, I knew I had discovered a fresh circle of hell.

The blast of cold air from the open door roused Taylor from her reverie. "Is the party over?" she asked, looking up at us.

"Yes," Jill said. "It's over – big time."

Kevin had gravitated towards Angels Among Us. "Serious foliage," he said.

Taylor bobbed her head in agreement. "Do you know who all the angels are?"

Kevin perused the tree carefully and nodded. "Every last one."

"They're all dead," Taylor said. "But look at the card."

Kevin put on his wire-rimmed glasses and read. "It's true," he said. "The great ones never really die."

Angus loped down the stairs and took in the scene. "What's going on?" he asked.

"Let's go up to your room," Bryn said. "I don't feel like talking about this in front of everybody else."

"If you want privacy, you can use the family room," I said. "Nobody's in there."

Bryn glared at me, but my son shot me a look of relief. "Good plan. My room's pretty much of a slag heap."

After Angus and Bryn left, I turned to Jill and Kevin. "Slag heap or living room?"

"Normally I'm a slag heap man," Kevin said. "But this is a professional visit."

I didn't remember a chapter in Ms. Manners' book of etiquette that covered entertaining a friend who was a murder suspect and her lawyer, but I did my best. As we walked into the living room, I turned on lights, flicked on the gas fireplace, and made the hostess's offer. "What can I get you?" I asked. "Coffee? A drink? It's the holiday season, so I'm well stocked."

"Actually," Jill said. "What I'd like is a joint."

"Can't help you there," I said.

"I can," Kevin said. "As long as Joanne doesn't mind."

"Joanne doesn't mind." I said. "It's for medicinal purposes."

Kevin pulled a baggie out of his pocket, rolled an expert joint, and handed it to Jill. He rolled a second one and offered it to me.

I shook my head. Kevin shrugged, touched the tip of the joint with a lit match, and sucked deeply. Beaming like a benevolent Buddha, he leaned back in his chair. "Truth-telling time," he said. "And, Joanne, I know how this sounds, but I think it would be better if you left."

Jill started to protest, but I cut her off. "Kevin's right," I said. "What you tell him is covered by lawyer-client privilege, but what you tell me is fair game. Besides, Taylor and I are at a critical juncture in *Little Women*. Beth is just about to leave this vale of sorrow, suffering, and tears."

Jill inhaled and gave me a half-smile. "I love that part. Beth always made my fillings ache."

Apparently Taylor shared Jill's opinion of the saintliest March sister. When Beth breathed her last, Taylor rolled over with a satisfied sigh and fell into a sound sleep. I turned off the light thinking Claudia's idea of a super-sized Johnny Walker had much to recommend it. Willie had other plans. He was waiting on the threshold of Taylor's room, and he leapt to attention as soon as he saw me. It was well past time for his after-dinner walk, and as I followed him down the stairs, his tail stump wagged with anticipation. Once again, the universe was unfolding as it should. I hadn't made it much past the landing when Angus caught up with me. "I can take Willie," he said.

"Thanks," I said. "But if you want to stay with Bryn . . ."

Angus lowered his voice, "Actually, Mum, I'd kind of like to get out of here for a while."

"Situation getting a little intense?" I said.

He shook his head in bemusement. "It's not intense at all."

"Bryn did tell you about what happened to her father?"

"Yeah. He's been dead – what? Four hours? Bryn's already got the whole situation wrapped up and put away. When Dad died, I was a fucking zombie for months."

"People handle things differently," I said.

"I guess," Angus said. "But all Bryn seems to care about is whether she's still going to go to New York for New Year's Eve. Don't get me wrong. I feel sorry for her, but she weirds me out."

"Then stay away from her," I said. "Take Willie for his walk, and I'll help Bryn get settled."

"I don't think she needs any help," Angus said. "She's watching *Miracle on 34th Street*. She said that when she gets tired, she'll go to bed."

"I'll get her some towels," I said. "I'll even put that lavender aromatherapy candle you gave me in her room. It might help her relax."

Angus sniffed the air. "If she wants to relax, she should just stand here for a while. Somebody's got themselves some pretty sweet ganja."

"Jill and her lawyer needed to unwind," I said.

"So the next time I'm tense, I can roll a spliff?"

"Is that what they call it now?"

"Yeah. Spliff, doob, dart. Joint is still perfectly acceptable though."

"You're quite the font of information," I said.

"Well you know how it is, Mum. Every so often I just check out *High Times* on the Internet." He read my look. "Time for me to hit the trail before I dig myself in any deeper?"

"You're a clever lad," I said.

Watching Willie pull Angus through the snowdrifts was a

powerful antidote for a lousy day. The combination of a boy, a dog, and a contact high had made me feel almost human again when a silver Audi I knew only too well pulled up in front of my house.

There had been times when Alex Kequahtooway and I had been so eager to touch one another that we had come together like teenagers, but those times were long past. Tonight, Alex came up the walk slowly, and I watched him approach with my arms folded across my chest. Under the harsh porch light, his face looked grey and tired, but mindful of Jill and Kevin in the living room, I didn't invite him in.

"I know I'm *persona non grata* around here," he said. "But I'm going to have to insist that someone in Jill's little wedding party comes down to make a formal identification of Gabriel Leventhal's body. We haven't been able to locate Felix Schiff, and we need to move before the trail gets any colder."

"What trail? Gabe died of a heart attack."

"Maybe not," Alex said. "Apparently the medical examiner found something that raised a red flag for him. He says we should treat this death as a potential homicide."

"Gabe was murdered?" I said, and as soon as I'd formed the words, I knew the possibility had been in the back of my mind all along. Perhaps that's why instead of reacting with tears or disbelief, I was suddenly furious. Gabriel Leventhal was one of the good guys, the kind the rest of us hope will stick around. "This is all so wrong," I said.

"Then do what you can to make it right," Alex said. "Come down to the morgue, so we can get moving on the investigation."

"I'll get my jacket," I said. As I passed by the living room, I opened the door a crack. Jill and Kevin were together on the couch, talking quietly. "Alex is here," I said. "They can't find Felix, so it looks like I have to make the identification."

Jill started towards me. "Jo, you don't have to do this. Gabe didn't have any family. There's no rush."

"I'll fill you in later," I said.

I pulled the door closed and went back to Alex. "I'll be ready in two minutes," I said.

He stared studiously out the window as I put on my boots and coat. "Ready," I said finally, and that was the only word that passed between us until we walked into Pasqua Hospital, a health centre that contains a first-class cancer facility, medical offices where specialists treat the myriad weaknesses to which our flesh is heir, and a wing devoted to discovering how the dead came to be dead. That night, Pasqua's lobby was festive. Alex gazed with distaste at the lights that framed the entrances to the coffee and gift shops, the shook-foil garlands that hung from the ceiling, and the tree decorated with homemade paper angels. "I hate hospitals at Christmas," he said. "Bad enough to be sick and scared without having to look at decorations that remind you of a time when you were happy."

Unless your personal happy times involved the scent of body parts floating in formaldehyde, there was nothing in the Pasqua morgue to trigger a madeleine moment. The medical examiner on duty was a Charles Addams cartoon of a man: tall, pale, and sepulchral. When we came in, he was hard at work, and as luck would have it, the cadaver he was working on was Gabe Leventhal's. Battered, bloody, bruised, and broken, it seemed impossible that any new indignity could be visited upon the body of this decent man, yet the Y-shaped incision that bisected Gabe's torso looked fresh.

My head swam. Out of nowhere, a memory: Alex at my kitchen table telling me there was a rule about rookies and autopsies – the bigger the rookie, the faster he fell. "It takes them a while to learn to disassociate," he had explained. I closed my eyes, trying to distance myself. Behind me, the medical examiner's voice resonated with the confidence of a bass in a church choir. "Breathe deeply, then just look at the face, and say the name."

I followed instructions. "It's him," I said. "It's Gabriel Leventhal."

"Thank you," the medical examiner said. "The woman at the desk outside will give you the appropriate papers to sign."

I'd been dismissed, but I didn't head for the door. A window ran the length of the lab, and I gravitated towards it. As I stared at the snow-stilled city, Alex and the M.E., oblivious to my presence, talked shop.

"So what have you got?" Alex asked.

"For starters, a real pharmaceutical stew in the bloodstream – I can't be more specific until we get the rest of the lab results, but for the nonce, let's just say the preliminary screens are puzzling. And there's the bruising."

"Two tons of truck backed over him," Alex said.

"Acknowledged," the M.E. said. "As is the fact that he apparently spent the night in a snowbank. All the same, some of those bruises look old to me – and here's the capper: there are traces of skin and blood under his fingernails."

"He was in a fight," Alex said.

"Or defending himself against an assault," the M.E. said. "Whatever the case, someone's given you a Christmas present, Alex. All you have to do is find a match for the DNA under Leventhal's fingernails."

"Start with a sample from Evan MacLeish," I said.

The two men turned towards me. From their expressions, it was clear they had forgotten I was in the room. The medical examiner pointed to the door. "The exit's that way," he said.

"Let her stay," Alex said. "She may be able to shed some light on this."

The M.E. shrugged. "Your call, Alex." Then he turned to me. "So start shedding light."

"This morning I noticed Evan was wearing concealer," I said. When the two men looked blank, I explained. "It's heavy-duty makeup – the kind you use to cover a blemish. Evan said he'd cut himself shaving, but his jaw was swollen."

The M.E. beamed "Your lucky day, Alex. Not only are you getting an early Christmas present, it's tied up with a pretty bow."

Alex shook his head. "This present's more shit than pony," he said. "Have you had any deliveries in the last hour or so?"

"I don't know," the M.E. said. "I've been stuck in here. This is our busy season. We've got a woman from pathology helping out. She'll be able to tell you if we have any new arrivals."

"No need to trouble her," Alex said. "Evan MacLeish was murdered this afternoon."

The medical examiner's expression grew even more lugubrious. "Well hell," he said. "Just when I was starting to believe there really was a Santa Claus."

When Alex dropped me at our house, Angus was outside, shovelling snow.

"Being kind to your old mum?" I said.

"I just didn't want to hang around inside."

"What's going on," I said.

"Nothing," he said. "Just Bryn."

"She wanted to get up-close-and-personal?" I said.

"I don't know what she wants," he said. "After you left, Jill and her lawyer took off."

"Where did they go?"

"To his store. He said they needed to be sure nobody walked in on them, which didn't make any sense – I mean, who's going to walk in on them in our house? Anyway, Jill asked me to keep an eye on Bryn, so I went in to watch the movie with her." My son looked down at his boots. "Mum, I was there about three minutes when she started coming onto me."

"And that was a problem?"

"Yeah," he said. "It was a problem because it was totally BS. Bryn is really hot, Mum. What's she doing faking this big passion for a guy like me?"

"I don't know," I said. "I don't know anything – except that all of a sudden, I'm not crazy about the idea of going inside either."

"Want me to get you a shovel?" Angus asked.

"Good idea," I said. "Let's move a little snow around – shovel the day away."

It took us half an hour to clear the walk and the driveway. The snow from the blizzard was crisp, even, and very, very, deep. By the time we were finished, my lungs were aching, and my muscles were crying foul, but as I looked at the path we had cleared, I felt a twinge of hope. Evan MacLeish was dead; Jill was safe; we didn't have to let the misery bury us. Tomorrow the sun would rise earlier and stronger. The northern hemisphere was beginning its movement towards the time of budding life and fresh beginnings. Buoyed by possibilities, we headed for our front door. We'd almost made it when Angus stopped and pointed upwards.

Behind the filmy curtains of the bedroom, Bryn's silhouette was ghostly. As soon as she realized we'd spotted her, she opened the window and called down. "It was fun watching you," she said. "Especially since you didn't know I was here." She waved, then closed the window.

Angus ripped off his toque. "See what I mean, Mum," he whispered. "She's totally psycho."

"Let's hope you're wrong," I said, but my voice lacked conviction. I knew that in celebrating the end of the time of cold and darkness, I'd been woefully premature.

CHAPTER

6

The next morning I was jolted from a sound sleep by the shrill of the phone on my nightstand. I opened one eye to read the numbers on the alarm clock: 6:00 a.m. – half an hour past my usual wake-up time, but too early for anyone to be calling with good news. The voice on the other end of the line was apologetic but not overly so. "It's Claudia MacLeish. I know it's early, but I need the name of your doctor."

"What's happened now?" I asked, but even as I formed the words, I knew I didn't want to hear the answer.

Claudia sounded as exhausted as I felt. "Nothing that someone prepared to write a scrip for a beta blocker can't cure. You've probably noticed that Tracy's been high-wiring since we got here. As long as she has her medication, she can function. We travel with our own little pharmacy, but this morning one of her essentials is missing. I've torn apart the hotel room looking for her beta blockers, but they are nowhere to be found, and she has to take them every day."

"Can't her doctor in Toronto just fax out a prescription renewal?"

"He's away for the holidays. I suggested going to a medi-centre or an emergency room, but Tracy doesn't want her public to see the Broken Wand Fairy twitching."

"The Broken Wand Fairy may have more serious problems than bad PR," I said. "The medical examiner is concerned enough about what he termed 'the chemical stew' in Gabe Leventhal's bloodstream to ask the police to treat Gabe Leventhal's death as a homicide."

Claudia clucked dismissively. "You're not suggesting that Tracy . . ."

"I'm not suggesting anything," I said. "Let's just hope they don't find beta blockers in Gabe Leventhal's blood samples. Otherwise, the police are going to be knocking on your door."

"They can knock, but they can also cross Tracy off their list."

"Gabe told me he had a history with her."

"And it was nasty, brutish, and short. It was also a long time ago. Tracy wouldn't have emptied out her pill bottle for him – she needs that medication. Give your doctor a call – please."

"There's a psychiatrist I can call," I said, "but I can tell you right now, Dan Kasperski will have to see Tracy before he writes a scrip for anything."

"Whatever it takes," Claudia said.

When I hung up, Jill was standing in the doorway. "Phone wake you up?" I asked.

"I wasn't sleeping," she said. "Just lying there, mulling over the options."

"Something new has been added to the mix, and I'm afraid it isn't good." I patted the bed. "Come and sit down."

The night before, Alex had accused Jill of offering him nothing but lies, half-truths, and evasions. I'd chafed at the attack, but in my heart, I knew there was truth in what he said.

Jill *was* holding back, and as I filled her in on the latest developments, I watched her carefully – trying to read the signs.

She was rapt but silent until I mentioned Claudia's phone call about the missing beta blockers. Suddenly, she was shaping the story. "No big mystery there – Tracy misplaced them. She's a flake. She loses stuff all the time."

"If she's as dependent on her medication as Claudia says, I think it's the one thing she might be careful about."

Jill turned on me. "Damn it, Jo, the last thing I need is you hovering around playing Hercule Poirot. I've got enough problems."

I stood up. "Okay," I said. "I'll stay out of it. I'll take Willie for his walk, and when I come back, you tell me how I can help."

Jill punched the air in frustration. "I'm sorry. I'm being a total asshole. It just makes me sick knowing that the police are out there digging around in our lives, and there's nothing I can do."

"Come off it," I said. "You're not exactly without resources. You're a journalist. You know the most potent weapon anybody has in a tight spot is information."

"'And the Truth shall set you free,'" Jill said. She raked her hands through her hair. "That *is* the way it's supposed to work, isn't it?"

When Willie and I got back from our walk, the coffee was made, and the table was set. As I passed down the hall to the shower, Jill came out of her room.

"Is it okay if I borrow something of yours to wear? Everything I've got with me was supposed to make a statement in the Big Apple."

"Help yourself," I said. "I don't own a single item of clothing that even whispers."

I'd stripped and was ready for the shower when the phone rang. I picked it up. So did somebody else. "I've got it," I said and waited for the click that would indicate the other phone had been hung up. The click never came.

"Could I speak to Joanne Kilbourn, please?" The man's voice was familiar, but I couldn't place it.

"This is Joanne," I said.

"Kevin Hynd. How's it going?"

"We're hanging in," I said. "Jill's getting dressed. I'll call her."

"You're the one I want to talk to."

I was certain I could hear the faint sound of our kitchen radio in the background. There *was* someone on the other end of the line. "This isn't a good time," I said. "Can I call you back?"

"Actually, I was hoping we could get together this morning."

"If it will help Jill, of course," I said.

"Would it be possible for you to come down here?" Kevin asked. "I'm working on something."

"Another case?"

He laughed. "Pigs," he said. "Six dozen marzipan pigs."

"I've always wanted to learn how to make those."

"Today's your lucky day. The marzipan's wrapped and ready. I was planning to start cranking out porkers mid-morning."

"I'll be there around ten," I said. Kevin hung up, but I stayed on the line until I heard a second click. I wasn't imagining things. Someone had indeed been listening in.

Taylor was at the kitchen table in her pyjamas when I came down. She had a fork in one hand, a knife in the other. "Pancake day," she said happily.

"So it is," I said. "I'd better get cracking."

I made the batter, then Taylor came over and, with great

precision, poured her initials onto the griddle. She was doing the final stroke on the *K* when Angus swooped in. "Make way for a hungry man," he said. "I skied along the entire creek, and now I'm up for some quality time with my new drum kit. But first, I need F-O-O-D!"

Angus was pouring syrup on his stack of pancakes when Bryn and Jill came downstairs. Bryn immediately drifted towards my son. With her alabaster skin, her dark hair falling loose to her shoulders, and her chocolate-brown leather pants and matching turtleneck, she had the casual chic of a model in a Ralph Lauren ad. She glanced at my son's plate. "Do you do this all the time?" she asked.

"Every Saturday," Angus said.

"Lucky," she said. Her tone was wistful, not mocking, and the pang I felt was as sharp as the one that I'd felt when Evan had confided that his mother called him "the snowman" because he was unable to love.

After breakfast I called the home number of Dan Kasperski, the best and only psychiatrist I knew. If I'd needed further proof of his excellence, the fact that he didn't make me grovel before he agreed to see Tracy that morning at 9:30 would have been plenty. I hung up and poured myself a second cup of coffee. I was going to need the extra caffeine; it was only eight o'clock, but my dance card was filling fast.

Angus volunteered to take Taylor to her art class, but when Bryn suggested she go with him, Jill cut in. "Why don't you come with me, Bryn?" she said. "I'm going over to NationTV and I want to show you off." When Bryn left to pick up her jacket, Jill and my son exchanged glances that said more potently than words that she understood exactly how he felt about her stepdaughter. Despite her own troubles, Jill had extricated Angus from a tight spot. She was a good human being, and as I left to pick up Claudia and Tracy,

I was determined that, this time out, virtue would not have to be its own reward.

Given the proliferation of trees in our house, it seemed impossible that I could have forgotten it was Christmas, but when I walked into the lobby of the Hotel Saskatchewan that morning, the combination of muted carols and pungent evergreen was a jolt. The Big Day was only two sleeps away. I'd come early, hoping to talk to Felix Schiff before I hooked up with the weird sisters-in-law. I was standing at the reception desk asking the clerk to ring Felix's room, when the man himself walked in the front door. He was dressed trendily with an expensive backpack and an outfit that conjured up images of sunshine, oxygen, and a day on the slopes, but Felix's pallor and bloodshot eyes suggested that even navigating his way to the coffee shop was going to be a stretch. Not to put too fine a point on it, he looked like hell. When he spotted me and came over to shake my hand, I could see the sheen of sweat on his forehead.

"Are you okay?" I said. "Everyone's been looking for you."

"I've been checking out your city's club scene," he said. "Not cutting edge but, given my impaired memory of it, not without appeal."

"You found the possibilities of Regina after dark so seductive that you couldn't wait until the reception was over?"

He shook his head. "It wasn't that."

"Watching Jill marry Evan wasn't easy for me either," I said.

"You had your family. I needed to be with someone too."

"But with strangers? Felix, that was . . ."

"I know. It was stupid and self-indulgent." He ran his hand through his hair, mussing it appealingly. "If it's any consolation, I'm suffering. Can you forgive me?"

His expression was painfully earnest, and I felt myself warm to him. "Hey, I have to forgive you," I said. "Reliable 'go-to' guys are in short supply."

Felix's mouth curled in the smallest of smiles. "That is my role, isn't it? The dependable one – the one everyone counts on."

"There are worse roles," I said.

"And better ones," he replied, "but like the knights in medieval romances, we must take the adventures God sends us." He straightened his shoulders. "Speaking of, it's time for me to behave in a courtly manner and wish Jill and Evan well before they go on their honeymoon."

I looked at him hard. "You haven't heard?"

"Heard what?"

I put my hand under Felix's elbow and guided him across the lobby to the gift shop. There were stacks of newspapers just inside the door. I picked one up. The photo of Evan that dominated the front page was a good one. He was leaning toward the photographer, his face animated, one hand raised as if he were explaining something. The type announcing his murder was seventy-six point, the size reserved for the tragedies of princes, prime ministers, and pubescent heartthrobs. Felix's hands were shaking so violently, he could barely hold the paper, but he read the story through to the end.

"I have to make a phone call," he said.

"To Jill? She's staying with me, but she was planning to go over to NationTV to see whether they're sitting on any information that hasn't been made public."

For a beat he stared at me without comprehension. When he emerged from the thicket of confusion, he was stunned but functioning. "I can help at NationTV," he said. "I still have connections there."

"Good, because Jill's going to need all the help she can get."

Felix zipped his jacket and pulled on his winter gloves. When he touched his hand to his forehead in a little salute, I felt a welcome rush of reassurance.

They say that timing is everything. That morning the timing of Evan MacLeish's small coterie of mourners was abysmal. Thirty seconds more and Jill's knight errant would have been out of the building. As it was, Felix was crossing the lobby just as Claudia and Tracy stepped out of the elevator. Given her temperament, I would have put my money on Tracy as the one to strike, but Claudia was the viper.

When she spotted Felix, she strode over and stepped in front of him. "Satisfied?" she said. "The path's clear now. You'd better stock up on vitamins, lederhosen-boy. You're going to be busy."

Felix reacted quickly. "Keep your mouth shut." He grabbed her shoulders and pushed with such force that she lost her footing. Circled by bystanders whose faces registered both shock and delight, Claudia went down like the proverbial bag of hammers. Felix didn't hang around to witness her humiliation. He was already at the front doors. The young man in livery didn't miss a beat. He held the door for Felix and touched his hat. "Have a good day, sir," he said, but he didn't wait for a tip.

I helped Claudia to her feet. "What was that all about?" I asked.

"Family honour," she said. Her tone was sardonic, but she was pale, and she seemed a bit dazed.

"Why don't I drive you to Dan's office," I said.

Claudia laughed shortly. "Tracy and I don't seem to be managing very well on our own," she said.

I led the two women down a short flight of stairs to a side door. It meant walking an extra block to the car, but I didn't want to risk a rematch between Felix and Claudia. Before we hit the street, Tracy donned a pair of Jackie O sunglasses.

"I don't know why you bother with those," Claudia said peevishly. "Nobody recognizes you without your tutu and your orange sneakers."

Dan Kasperski's office was in a converted garage at the back of his house in central Regina. A large proportion of his clients were adolescents, and his office was fitted out with posters of cool-for-the-moment bands and magazines that covered the range of adolescent dreams from *Seventeen* to *Modern Drummer*. When I'd needed advice about a drum kit for Angus, I'd known exactly where to turn. Dan knew everything there was to know about drummers and their art. The space next to his waiting room housed his personal passion: a Red Yamaha Stage Customs drum kit and a dazzling array of Sabian and Zildjian cymbals. He had sound-proofed his garage himself.

He had also replaced the hard-packed cinder of the yard with good soil in which he planted wildflowers and indigenous grasses that murmured in the wind. In warm weather, Dan's young patients sat beside him on a bench, listening to the grasses, smelling the wildflowers, and watching koi swimming placidly in a pool hand-dug in an area that had once between a cemetery for abandoned car parts. The metaphor was ready-made, and Dan used it when he talked to kids who said they could never turn their lives around.

As Tracy rushed towards the garage office that chilly day, she didn't spare a glance for the half-dozen bird feeders placed with such care around the garden, nor did she notice the pains Dan had taken to ensure that each stone in the garden wall complemented its neighbours. She was a woman on a simple and well-defined mission. She wanted to get a

prescription and she wanted to get the hell out. Venturing
into this weird place was simply the price she had to pay.

We heard Dan before we saw him. He had been drumming, and when he opened the door of the converted garage,
he was glistening with perspiration and life. It was twenty-
five below zero, but he was wearing cut-offs and a sweatshirt. I made the introductions. He shook hands with Tracy
and Claudia, and drew Tracy inside. "Come talk awhile," he
said. He looked at me. "Kitchen's unlocked," he said. "You
know where the tea is."

"All I want is to get out of the cold," Claudia said. She was
warmly dressed, but she was hugging herself and her teeth
were chattering. "It's bitter out here."

We sat down at Dan's kitchen table, slid off our coats, and
stared silently at the snowy garden. Finally, I said, "So do we
talk about the elephant in the living room or not?"

"I don't want to talk about anything," she said. "In the last
twenty-four hours, my brother was murdered; a man I liked
died under questionable circumstances; a man I don't like
humiliated me in public; and the child I cared for from the
day she came home from the hospital told me to bite her."

"I'm sorry," I said. "I guess I hadn't added up all you've
had to deal with." I leaned forward. "Claudia, I never knew
you'd taken care of Bryn."

"Who else would have?" she said.

"I just assumed her parents . . ."

"They were building their careers. Focused. I was twenty-
three years old with a shiny new diploma and no idea at all
about what I was going to do with the rest of my life."

"And you took over the care of an infant. That's a pretty
selfless decision for a twenty-three-year-old."

"Not for a twenty-three-year-old who'd had the kind of
parenting I'd had."

"That bad?" I asked.

Claudia's mouth curved in an ironic smile. "No point talking about it," she said. "It was no worse than what happened to Evan – no worse than what happened to the other kids we knew. The unwanted children of the rich live in their own particular hell. It's just so difficult to spot under their picture-perfect lives of private schools, ski holidays, and idyllic camps in the Muskokas."

"Where were your parents?"

Claudia tented her fingertips and regarded them thoughtfully. "Well, my father had the good sense to be dead by that point. That left Caroline, and the only reason she had children was because contraception was an imperfect science, and my father had scruples about abortion."

"Your mother told you that?"

"No, our housekeeper. Mrs. Carruthers made that particular contribution to our education. Caroline pressed her into service to care for Evan and me until we were old enough to be packed off to school. When Bryn was born, I saw that history was about to repeat itself, so I stepped in."

"And Annie didn't mind?"

"She never noticed. Annie and Tracy were living the high life. They'd ignore Bryn for days, then they'd wake her up in the middle of the night so Evan could film them playing with her. I don't have a maternal bone in my body, but I knew that was wrong."

"And you came to love Bryn," I said.

Claudia shook her head. "She wasn't an easy child to love, but I did come to feel responsible for her – for both of them. After Annie died, I was all Bryn and Tracy had."

"Caroline was there," I said.

"In body if not in spirit," Claudia said. "And to give Caroline her due she has allowed us to share her beautiful home on Walmer Road for lo these many years. Our family may be dysfunctional, but we have nice digs."

Tracy didn't bother coming inside when she and Dan emerged from his office. She spotted us through the window, waved the prescription in her hand, and gestured for us to join her. Neither Claudia nor I had to be asked twice. When the two women headed for my car, I turned to thank Dan. He was a man with a ready smile, but in that moment he looked deeply troubled. "Keep an eye on her, Jo. I'm faxing her psychiatrist's office. I know he's out of the country, but someone must be covering for him. I'd rest easier if I knew someone familiar with her case was handling Tracy Lowell. Until then . . ." Dan waved his hands in apology. "I've said too much already."

"Not too much," I said. "Dan, I put you in a tight spot. I shouldn't have presumed on our friendship."

Dan shook his head. "You saw someone who needed help, and you got help. That's not presuming on friendship; that's being a responsible human being."

"One more question, and this is hypothetical. Could an overdose of beta blockers be fatal?"

"Jo – an overdose of Aspirin can be fatal. But if I can read your subtext here, Tracy's prescription is short term."

"But if someone – not Tracy – we're still talking hypothetical here – were to be given a larger dose?"

"It would depend on the dose and on the person. It always does. You know how beta blockers work. They slow the heart rate and reduce the force of heart muscle contractions. An overdose could cause hypotension and bradycardia."

"In lay terms?"

"Severe low blood pressure. Severe low heart rate. Heart failure."

"Death."

"It could happen."

Claudia insisted that she and Tracy take a cab back to the hotel. She said I had already done enough, and I didn't argue the point. I *had* done enough. That didn't change the fact that there was still more to do, and I welcomed the chance to be alone to ponder Dan's information before I made the next stop on my rounds. Kevin Hynd's Day-Glo painted patisserie, Further, was in the Cathedral Area, so-called because its citizens lived their lives beneath the shadows cast by the twin spires of Holy Rosary. As I drove past newly gentrified houses and specialty shops, the dark possibilities of pharmacological dirty work seemed a world away.

Kevin's business on 13th Avenue was flanked by shops called The Little Red Meat Wagon and Pinky's Nail Salon – steak, cake, and fake – one-stop shopping for the unreconstructed hedonist. If we can judge a human being by the kitchen he keeps, Kevin Hynd was stellar. The walls of his shop were painted the rosy gold of peach butter. Like me he had a pegboard wall, hung with pots, pans, sieves, and strainers. Unlike me, his kitchen had gleaming industrial-sized ovens, three Kitchen Aid mixers, a stainless-steel Sub-Zero refrigerator, and a wooden worktable smoothed by use and so beautiful that I would have traded my signed copy of *Mastering the Art of French Cooking* for it. Julia Child would have approved, and she would have approved of Kevin, a chef who might have been a dead ringer for Jerry Garcia but who was approaching the mound of pink-tinted marzipan in front of him with the reverence of the serious cook.

"Greetings," he said. "Wash your hands, put on some gloves, and be bold. We're all novices."

"Okay," I said, "but we need to talk first. The preliminary findings of the autopsy on Gabe Leventhal suggest he didn't die of natural causes."

"Whoa!" Kevin flopped the marzipan onto a marble pastry slab. "So what happened?"

"His blood sample was suspicious; he had bruises that didn't come from the truck driving over him; and there were scrapings of tissue and blood under his fingernails."

"Evidence that he was defending himself against somebody," Kevin said.

"Right," I said. "And my guess is the pathologist will discover that the mystery assailant was Evan MacLeish."

"Is that just a gut feeling?"

"No, but everything I'm going on *is* circumstantial. Evan was wearing makeup the day of the wedding, but I could tell he'd been in a fight, and when Gabe disappeared, Evan moved in a little too quickly with his explanation that Gabe was a hypochondriac who refused to deal with any doctor except his own in New York."

"Certainly an avenue worth exploring." Kevin broke off a chunk of marzipan the size of a baby's fist for each of us.

"So where do we start?" I asked.

"First you have to Think Pig."

"To catch the tiger, you must imagine the tiger."

Kevin raised an eyebrow. "Excellent. Now working with marzipan is like working with Plasticine. Pinch off what you think you'll need, roll it between your hands into sausage shapes, and give each little sausage a nip, a bend, or a flatten until it looks the way you want it to look." Kevin made two balls, stuck the smaller one onto the larger, and smoothed it effortlessly into a snout. He made indentations for the eyes and then made and flattened two balls into ears. I started working with my own marzipan, copying what Kevin had done. He watched until he seemed to decide I could continue on my own. Then he broke off a larger piece of marzipan and worked it into a body.

"So we have ourselves a puzzle," Kevin said. "If Evan killed Gabe, who killed Evan?" he said.

"I don't know," I said.

"Then it's a time for caution," he said. "At this point, we don't know much about anything or anyone." Kevin shaped a solid little leg with his thumbs. "I had a battle with myself this morning," he said. "Jill is my client, and in calling you I'm going behind her back and probably against her wishes. But you don't have to be Eddie Greenspan to know that Jill's the star suspect in this case, and she refuses to help herself."

"She didn't open up to you?"

"Not a crack. You could drive a tour bus through the holes in that story of hers about what happened last night. You know it. I know it, and, most significantly, the cops know it. I tried to make her aware of the importance of full disclosure to her lawyer, but no dice." He transformed a ball of marzipan into a jaunty little bowler hat, placed it on his pig's head, and filled the tiny eye indentations with white royal icing. "Jill's protecting somebody," he said.

"Not just somebody," I said. "Her stepdaughter, Bryn. At least that's my guess. I think when she went outside the night Evan was killed, she was looking for Bryn, and I think when she ran back inside, she was still looking for her."

"Maybe I should talk to Bryn," he said. "If she's as crazy about Jill as Jill is about her, she won't want to leave her new stepmother out to dry."

"You'd be wasting your time," I said. "From what I've seen the only person Bryn is crazy about is Bryn."

"My grandmother always said every cookie has two sides," he said. "Maybe Jill sees a side of her you haven't."

"As a rule, I'm with your grandmother, but so far what I've seen of Bryn is not appealing. I'm certain that when you called today she was listening in on another phone. And last night when Angus and I were out shovelling snow, we looked up and she was at the window. She taunted us about how she'd been watching us all the time, and we didn't know it."

"She's a voyeur?"

"If she is, the pathology is understandable. Kevin, Bryn has not had an easy life. Gabe Leventhal told me that her father has been filming her from the day she was born – the movie of Bryn's life was going to cap his career."

"My God, no wonder she hated him." For a beat Kevin was silent, then he peered at me thoughtfully through his wire-rimmed glasses. "And Jill's hedging about what really happened the night Evan died because she's afraid Bryn hated her father enough to kill him."

I nodded. "So where do we go from here?"

"For starters, let's get our hands on that footage before the police do. That'll at least buy us some time to come up with a strategy for defending Bryn if we need one. Were Jill and Evan living together before they were married?"

"Does it matter?"

"It would if Evan kept projects he was working on at home. If he and Jill were cohabiting, as they say, she could just send a friend in to scoop up what we need."

"But even if they didn't live together before, Jill and Evan *were* married when he died," I said. "She must have some rights."

"Sure, but the scope of those rights could be limited if there was a pre-nup." Kevin gazed sadly at the half-formed lumps of marzipan in front of me. "You're not exactly wailing there, are you?"

"No," I said.

"Your vision is clouded by anxiety," he said kindly. He dotted his pig's eyes with chocolate, dipped the bowler and base into chocolate, and handed the dapper little porker to me. "Take this one home to contemplate," he said.

"Thanks," I said. "So when do you want to talk to Jill?"

"This time out, it's better if you do the talking. Friends can suggest things lawyers can't."

"For example, a friend could – hypothetically – recommend that if there was anything damaging in the footage of Bryn, Jill might want to get it out of harm's way," I said.

"No flies on you," Kevin said approvingly.

"Thanks," I said, "for the compliment and for the marzipan lesson. I'll do better next time." I wrapped my pig carefully and dropped it in my purse. "Who wants all these pigs anyway?"

Kevin checked the order on the bulletin board over his counter. "Dumped Dames," he read. "Seemingly, an organization of ladies who do not go gently."

Jill was standing on the front steps smoking when I got home. "How was your morning?" I asked.

"Shitty," she said. "And yours?"

"Instructive," I said. "I learned that Felix has the hots for you; that Tracy Lowell shares a home with the MacLeish family; that beta blockers can kill; and that I have no talent for making marzipan pigs."

Jill doused her cigarette in a snowbank. "Tell me something I don't know."

"Okay," I said. "How about this? Your next move is to pick up the phone and arrange to get everything about the projects Evan was working on at the time of his death out here."

"You think Evan's work might point to who killed him?"

"His movies cut close to the bone, Jill. Evan might have captured something on film that someone didn't want revealed."

Jill pulled her cigarette pack out of her jacket pocket. On the front was a vivid photo of a diseased lung. She glanced at it briefly and removed a cigarette. "Do you think there'll be footage of Bryn?" she asked.

"I don't know," I said. "Probably."

Jill lit her cigarette. "Can you believe that I didn't even know Evan was shooting that movie until the night of the rehearsal dinner?"

"How could you not know?" I asked.

"As it turns out, there's a lot I didn't know," she said. "What's that old saw? 'Marry in haste; repent at leisure.' My opportunities for penance seem to be coming at warp speed. I might as well tell you this because you'll find out soon enough. Evan and I had a pretty heated argument after the rehearsal. When we got back to the hotel, I suggested we have a drink and hash out the question of the morality of what he was doing to Bryn. I thought the footage should be destroyed; Evan had other ideas. We went into the hotel bar, and I guess we forgot to keep the decibels down. The one shining nugget Felix and I uncovered at NationTV today was the fact that at least half a dozen people remember overhearing Evan and me fighting."

"So it shouldn't come as a surprise that the police are expressing a more than casual interest in you."

"No, it doesn't." Jill drew on her cigarette and blew two perfect rings, the second inside the first. "Remember when doing this was an accomplishment?" she said.

"I remember," I said.

"Life gets harder," she said. "All the more reason to keep one step ahead of the other guy." She stood up. "Evan has a binder he carries with him everywhere. He calls it 'his Bible' – it's an update on the status of his works-in-progress. I'll dig that up. And I'll call our office manager, Larissa, in Toronto and get her to courier everything connected to Evan's work out here. Now the question is where should she send it?"

"I have an idea," I said.

As soon as the arrangements were made, I called Kevin Hynd. "We're rolling," I said.

"Is the stuff coming to your place?" Kevin asked.

"Do you really want to know?"

"Nope. As long as I can go through everything as soon as it gets there."

"Not the most festive way to spend December 24."

"Helping somebody else? Hey, it's Christmas, Joanne. As the man says, loving well is one way of participating in the mystery."

CHAPTER

7

When you live close to the 50th parallel, darkness comes early in deep winter. Sometimes as people gather on these long evenings, the awareness that we are separated from the cold and dark by a glass-thin membrane can create a sense of community that is almost mystical. On the evening of December 23, there was no transcendence at my dinner table, but there was civility, and that was miracle enough for me. Late that afternoon, Claudia and Tracy had stopped by with a new robe and pyjamas for Bryn. While the golden child was checking out her gifts, Claudia had leaned towards me. "I hate shopping," she whispered, "but even a trip to the mall beats sitting around a hotel room watching reruns of 'Magictown' with Tracy."

The women in Jill's new family had brought me no joy. More than once I had made some rough calculations about when they might cease to be part of my life. But it *was* Christmas, and Kevin Hynd was right. Loving well was one way of participating in the mystery.

I turned to Claudia. "Why don't you two come for dinner," I said.

And the die was cast. An hour and a half later, Claudia and I had put a meal together, Jill and Bryn were wrapping Christmas gifts in their room, and Tracy, Taylor, and Taylor's cats were in the front hall marvelling at the new tree and listening to "The Way We Were."

Claudia and I had agreed to do our bodies a favour and order takeout from my family's favourite vegan restaurant, Heliotrope. But when we stopped by the liquor store, Claudia threw a bottle of Jack Daniel's into the basket. "Perfect antidote to virtuous eating," she said. And it was.

Standing side by side, sipping bourbon and ladling out Moroccan stew, Claudia and I achieved harmony. "Great menu," I said, handing her a piece of desem pita.

"Great company," Claudia said. "Being in an enclosed space with Tracy is like ancient water torture – drip, drip, drip till the victim goes insane."

"How have you managed to share living space all these years?"

Claudia shrugged. "It's a big house," she said. "Lots of room to hide. And that's what we do – lead separate lives."

"But your lives must intersect," I said. "And you must have spent a lot of time with Bryn."

Claudia's face grew soft. "As much as she'd let me."

"Are you worried about her?" I asked.

Suddenly, Claudia was wary. "Worried in general or worried because of what happened to Evan?"

"Both, I guess. I know there were tensions between Bryn and her father, but he *was* her father. Even Angus, who's not exactly Mr. Touchy-Feely, thinks that Bryn may not be dealing with Evan's death in the healthiest way."

Claudia's mouth tightened. "Who decides what's healthy? People do what they do. Look at me. I loved my brother, but I'm not going to let you or anyone else see me wailing and rending my clothing. When I woke up this morning, I made a mental list of what I needed to do. Take care of Tracy. Take care of Bryn. Endure. Three items, and I'm handling them all. I don't need anyone second-guessing me."

"I didn't mean to sound judgmental," I said.

Claudia's shoulders slumped. "I know, and I know Angus is right to be concerned about Bryn. I am too. But Joanne, Bryn isn't like Angus – she's not like anyone I've ever known. I've tried to make her more . . . *aware* of other people. But the truth is she's just not hard-wired for empathy, no more than Evan was." Claudia began placing the filled bowls on a tray. "There's only so much you can do. You know that. You have kids."

"Nature versus nurture?"

"And nature wins every time," Claudia said. "All we can do is look at our kids honestly, and do the best with what we have."

I touched her hand. "You're right," I said. "That is all we can do."

We both had tears in our eyes. "Oh for God's sake," Claudia said. "Enough already. Soup's on. Let's declare this house a grief-free zone and spend the evening getting to know each other."

And so we did. During dinner, the seven of us took part in a no-holds-barred, rapid-fire, round-robin exchange of personal trivia. We identified our favourite colours, Christmas movies, actors, brands of toothpaste, poets, kids' books, and breakfast foods. By the time we were onto the peach cobbler, we were relaxed and easy, and Bryn had confided that she never really got the point of *Charlotte's Web* and that, in her opinion, taupe was seriously underrated.

Buoyed by our new camaraderie, we sailed through the after-dinner cleanup and when Bryn stood in the shining kitchen and slid her hand into my son's, he did not look uncomfortable. "This has been the best evening," she said.

"Why don't we all take Willie for his walk? Like a real family."

It was a poignant statement of longing by a young woman who didn't often reveal herself, and the people who loved her were quick to respond.

"We *are* a real family," Jill said.

"*All* of us," Tracy said. "Nothing can ever change that."

"I wonder how Evan would have felt if he'd seen us like this," Jill said.

"Who knows," Claudia said. "I never knew how my brother felt about anything. Maybe if I had understood him more, I could have helped."

"I've been thinking about that too," Jill said, and it seemed she was speaking more to herself than to us. "I never really got to know Evan. That sounds crazy, doesn't it? But it's the truth. I never knew my husband. I wonder now if anyone did."

Jill's voice was wistful. It was the first time I'd heard her speak of Evan with emotion, and I wondered if the moment for grief had come. "The night I met Evan we talked about that illumination I gave you," I said.

Jill smiled. "Not many people can claim that Philo of Alexandria brought them together, but that's what happened with Evan and me. Felix introduced us, but it wasn't until Evan saw that illumination hanging in my living room that our relationship moved from the professional to the personal." Jill's voice was filled with pain. "Evan never talked about his feelings, but those words seemed to resonate for him. I guess he wanted me to ask about the great battles he was fighting, but I never did."

Had we been alone, Jill's remembrance of things past might have opened the door for an intimate discussion. But we weren't alone.

Tracy had listened to Jill's words without interest, drumming her fingers on the kitchen counter to indicate her impatience. Finally, she offered an opinion that was as astringent as a bucket of cold water in the face. "It's too late to talk about what Evan wanted," she said. "He's dead. But we're not, so we might as well go for that walk Bryn's so keen on."

We stepped out into a star-bright night. The cold air was wisped with smoke from wood-burning fireplaces, and across the creek, kids screamed with delight as their toboggans ripped down the bank onto ice made thick by six straight weeks of temperatures stuck at twenty below. It was good to be alive on such a night, and from a distance we really could have passed for an extended family that had special cause for gratitude. The house we had come from, like all the houses that backed onto Wascana Creek, was substantial and handsome. We were well fed and expensively clothed. We moved easily, laughed often, and seemed content in one another's company. Enviable people leading enviable lives, but there were fault lines in the image we presented, and we knew it. And so, as we walked along the levee, we kept it light: reminiscing about other winters; vying with one another to see who could arc a snowball over the shining ice to the bank across the creek; running with Willie as he swam through the snow.

Carefree times, but as we started for home, Willie ceased to be a diversion and became a problem. When he failed puppy socialization class, I had been too humiliated to re-enrol him, and he was making me pay for my cowardice. Inside the house, Willie was the best of dogs: sweet, compliant, and loyal; outside he was a brute and a brat who demanded his own way. That night as he recognized the landmarks that meant his walk was winding down, he balked: dragging me towards every garbage bin in the alley to check out what Taylor called the dog mail; barking when I called him to heel. Finally, when he grabbed at the leash and began a game of tug-of-war with me, Claudia intervened.

"Why don't you let me take him?" she said.

It was an offer I couldn't refuse. I handed her the leash. "He's all yours," I said.

She grabbed Willie's collar. "Time to learn some manners," she said. With two quick manoeuvres, she flipped him into the snow and pinned him on his back, then she began talking to him. At first he flailed, but as he calmed, her words became endearments. Finally, she put her mouth beside his ear and cooed, "Ready to try again, big boy?" When Claudia brushed herself off and started down the alley, Willie trotted beside her like a show dog.

I opened the back gate for them. "That was nothing short of amazing," I said.

"It was just a first step. There's no quick fix. You're going to have to do this every day, and you're going to have to enrol him in obedience school. Willie is never going to earn a Ph.D., but he might surprise you." Suddenly, Claudia laughed her wonderful wry, throaty laugh. "What a life I have – Bouviers and Broken Wand Fairies."

I was basking in the self-generated glow of the doer of good deeds when Jill and I drove Claudia and Tracy back to their hotel. The evening was nearing an end and, given the players and the circumstances, it had been a triumph. The first time we stopped for a light, Jill gave me a surreptitious thumbs-up. The second time we stopped for a light, Tracy unsnapped her seat belt, leaned into the front seat, and, without pre-amble, dropped her bombshell. "Claudia and I have decided Bryn should come back to Toronto with us."

"Nice build up there, kiddo," Claudia said furiously. "At least you could have waited until the car stopped."

"I'm not taking the flak for this one," Tracy snapped. "It was your idea."

Jill turned in her seat so she could see Claudia's face. "Why didn't you bring this up back at Joanne's?"

"Because I knew you wouldn't exactly leap at our suggestions, and I didn't want Bryn to hear us fighting," Claudia said. "She has enough to deal with as it is."

Jill's hands were clenched, but she kept her temper in check. "Bryn does have enough to deal with," she said levelly. "That's why she doesn't need the three of us tearing at her as if she were a doll. There's nothing to discuss here. The moment I took those marriage vows, Bryn became my daughter. I want her with me. She wants to be with me. Before we left Toronto, Evan and I talked to a lawyer about arranging for an adoption. We wanted to make certain my relationship with Bryn was protected."

"You can't do that," Tracy said.

"Don't say anything stupid," Claudia said, and her tone was the same one she had used on Willie in the back alley.

"Evan was the one being stupid if he thought he could get away with this," Tracy said furiously.

Claudia was conciliatory. "Why don't we just drop this for now? Jill, if things get complicated, the offer is always open."

"That's right," Tracy said. "Something could happen to make you change your mind." She laughed her trilling Broken Wand Fairy laugh. "You never know, do you?"

We watched in silence as the two women walked into the hotel. "Felix was right," Jill said.

"About what?"

"About Evan's family. After we went to NationTV this morning, he came back to the house to talk. He told me not to trust anyone in Evan's family. He said they're the kind of people who don't stop until they get what they want."

"How well does he know them?" I said.

Jill shrugged. "Obviously better than I do," she said.

We came home to more surprises. Bryn and Angus were cuddled on the couch watching *A Christmas Story* and Taylor, the archetypal younger sibling, was sitting on the floor blocking their view.

As soon as she spotted us, Bryn was on her feet. "Come sit down with us," she said, and her smile was winning. "This is exactly the kind of movie we should be watching together. It's about this boy named Ralphie. All he wants for Christmas is a Red Ryder air rifle, but everybody keeps telling him he'll get his eye shot out. It is so sweet."

"Thanks for asking," Jill said, embracing her stepdaughter. "But Jo and I have some things to discuss."

Bryn's eyes narrowed, and the cheerleader glow left her translucent ivory skin. "You're not changing your mind about me moving to New York?"

"Of course not," Jill said. "I don't want you to worry about that or about anything else. Now, get back to your movie. Jo and I are going to grab a beer and find a quiet place to talk."

We took our bottles of Great Western into the living room where the traditional Kilbourn tree still held sway. I plugged in the lights. "Beautiful," Jill said. "It looks exactly the same every year."

"That's why Taylor hates it," I said.

"She'll appreciate it some day. Bryn already does. She told me she thought it would be wonderful to have a tree with homemade decorations." Jill sipped her beer. "It's been good for her to be here, Jo. I think she's starting to connect more with other people."

When I didn't jump in to agree, Jill pressed me. "You'll have to admit it was thoughtful of her to ask us to watch the movie with them."

"It was thoughtful," I said.

"But you still don't like her," Jill said.

"I don't know her," I said, "and I'm not sure you do either. Claudia and I were talking about this today. She told me she thinks Bryn just isn't hard-wired for empathy."

Jill tensed. "And when did Claudia become an expert on genetics?"

"She may not be an expert," I said, "but she *has* cared for Bryn since she came home from the hospital. That has to count for something."

The Christmas lights played out the spectrum of colours across Jill's face, but she looked wan and abstracted. "Nobody told me," she said. "No wonder she wants to hang on to Bryn."

"Jill, how long did you and Evan know each other before you got married."

"Seven weeks." Jill chewed her lip savagely. "What the hell was I thinking of? Why wasn't I asking questions? Why wasn't I paying attention?"

"Love makes us do strange things."

"I never loved Evan."

"You love Bryn," I said.

Jill placed her palms together and lowered her head. "I do," she said. "And she needed to be rescued."

"From what?"

"From that house she lived in. It's a museum – exquisite, but not a place where people live. Evan's grandfather was a diplomat in the days when treasures went cheap. Everything you sit on or look at or drink from is priceless: shoji screens, lacquers, Japanese wood-block prints, the most incredible red sandstone Buddha."

"Not an easy place for a child to grow up."

"No, and the people in that house weren't easy people to grow up with. Bryn's mother was a real piece of work. And you've seen Tracy . . ."

"Annie's been dead for almost fifteen years. Why does Tracy still live there?"

Jill raised her hands in the universal gesture of the confounded. "Who knows? My guess is that when Tracy discovered that the spotlight would always shine on her sister not her, she just followed the path of least resistance."

"A role in a children's show and living at home – someone else's home at that. Not exactly a sparkling destiny," I said.

"No one in that house has a sparkling destiny – it's a house of half-lived lives."

"Claudia seems to fill her days."

"A pair of Rottweilers, a niece who can't wait to leave, a sister-in-law who's a basket case, and a mother who hasn't been out of the house in forty years – not my idea of a fully realized life."

"Caroline hasn't been out of the house in forty years?"

Jill nodded. "Apparently after Claudia was born, her mother suffered a postpartum 'incident.' That's when the agoraphobia began."

"Claudia told me today that her mother never wanted children," I said. "Was the incident caused by guilt?"

Jill shrugged. "Who knows? That family is full of secrets."

"Still, someone must have tried to get treatment for Caroline."

"Of course, they did," Jill said. "Her husband was a professor at U of T. He tapped every colleague and acquaintance he had at the School of Medicine. They offered to psychoanalyze her, medicate her, and modify her behaviour. Caroline turned them all down flat."

"Why?"

"According to Evan, his mother saw herself as a woman like Virginia Woolf – a person with an exceptional mind and exceptional problems. Apparently, she simply refused to

allow people she considered to be her intellectual inferiors
to roam around in her brain."

"And her family accepted that?"

"They had no choice." Jill ran a thumbnail down the label
of her Great Western. "For all her problems, Caroline is a
force to be reckoned with. She has a lot of money and she
really is brilliant. She has one of those quicksilver minds
that shimmers from one idea to the next."

"Her illness must have put a pretty serious dent in her
shimmering."

Jill nodded. "It's been devastating for her. She should have
been setting the world of ideas on fire. Instead, she has
nothing more to do than muse over her tchotchkes, supervise
her garden, and read everything ever written about agoropho-
bia. She's an expert there – in every way. She's so knowledge-
able, she's written articles that have appeared in medical
journals. She just can't break out. She says it's as if she's in a
fairy tale and some evil witch cast a spell on her, so that every
time she tries to step out of the house, the demons attack."

"Is she bitter?" I asked.

"People make accommodations . . ." Jill gazed at her
bottle. "Empty," she said.

"Are you up for another round?"

"Nope," she said. "I think I've had enough fun today. I'm
going to hit the sack."

After Jill went up to bed, I checked on the kids. Angus and
Bryn were engrossed in the movie credits, but the question
of whether Ralphie would ever get his Red Ryder so he could
shoot his eye out would remain unanswered for Taylor. She
was sound asleep.

I tapped my son's shoulder. "Santa's still doing his evalu-
ations," I said. "Are you up for a good deed?"

"You want me to carry Taylor upstairs?"

"I do," I said. "It's the end of the day, and your sister is no longer a featherweight."

We climbed the stairs together and tucked Taylor in. "Dismissed with thanks," I said.

Angus didn't leave. "Mum, have you got a minute?"

"Of course."

He followed me down to my room, closed the door, and stared at his shoes.

"Let me help," I said. "Is this about the fact that Bryn is back on the A list."

Angus coloured. "We had a long talk. She told me that sometimes she doesn't know how to behave. Like with her dad dying – she says she must have been in a state of shock or something."

"She seemed pretty focused to me," I said. "She wants to move to New York and she isn't about to let anything interfere with her plans."

"I know that's how it looks," Angus said. "But she's trying. You saw how nice she was tonight."

"Yes," I said, "I did."

Angus looked at me hard. "You don't think she's sincere."

"Just take it slow," I said.

"Because?"

"Because the fact that a young woman believes taupe is an underrated colour isn't enough to build a relationship on."

As if on cue, the taupe-lover herself burst through the door. This time there was no mistaking Bryn's sincerity. She was so agitated her words tumbled over one another. "There's something going on in the back alley. A lot of lights, and I think police cars. Should I get Jill?"

"No," I said. "Let her sleep till we find out what's happening."

As we followed her, Bryn filled us in. "The dog was making this weird noise, so I let him out. The minute he got in the backyard, he started to bark. I went out to the deck to see what was going on. That's when I saw . . . ," she shrugged, "whatever I saw."

We all put on coats and boots; I called Willie, snapped on his leash, then the four of us went to investigate. As soon as I unlatched the gate that opened onto the alley, Willie made a sound I'd never heard him make before: a low, guttural warning growl. I knew how he felt. The quiet alley along which we'd walked an hour before was floodlit, and khaki tarpaulins had been thrown over the snow. Half a dozen police officers were tipping garbage bags from the bins onto the tarps, then searching through their findings. It was not a pretty sight.

"What's going on?" I said.

"Police business," a cop who didn't look much older than Angus said.

"That's my garbage you're going through," I said. "So it's my business too. What are you looking for?"

The young cop took a step towards me, and Willie strained at the leash, growling at him with bared teeth.

"Hold that dog back," the young officer said.

"He doesn't do anything without a command," I said.

"I'll get the inspector."

Alex Kequahtooway came back with the young cop and, in an instant, Willie morphed from killer to buddy. Tail wagging, he leapt up and began licking Alex's face. The corners of the young cop's mouth turned up as he looked at me. "Looks like your dog needs a command," he said.

"Heel, Willie," I said in my new Claudia-inspired voice, and amazingly, Willie came and sat at my feet.

I glanced at the tarpaulin – and recognized some treasures from our garbage: takeout containers from Heliotrope, some wizened tangerines that had been hiding in the back of the crisper, an empty bacon package. A young cop was going through the detritus with the fervour of a man panning for gold. "So, Alex," I said, "what exactly is it that you're looking for?"

Alex's left eye twitched, a sure sign of tension. "I can't answer that," he said. "This is a police investigation. I think you should leave."

"It's a pleasant night," I said. "And this *is* public space."

"Suit yourself," Alex said.

After five minutes, my bravado had dissipated and my feet were cold, but at least I wasn't alone. Angus had stayed with me, so – surprisingly – had Bryn. Both were uncomplaining, but I was just thirty seconds from calling it quits when the young officer closest to us held up an empty prescription pill bottle. "Bingo," he said.

Alex gave the discovery the briefest of glances and said, "Good work. Bag it for forensics."

I stepped towards the tarpaulin. "All that effort for a pill bottle," I said.

Alex hesitated before responding; when he did, it was clear he had decided to push my buttons. "It's evidence," he said. "A conscientious citizen told us we might find something helpful to our case here, and sure enough we did." He looked hard at me. "What's the matter, Jo? You seem a little shaken."

"Just concerned about my neighbourhood. I hope your people are planning to clean up this alley – kids play out here."

"Unlike civilians, we don't leave messes we're not prepared to clean up," Alex said. Then he turned to Angus, and his voice grew gentle. "Could I have a minute with you?" he asked.

"Sure," Angus said.

"Bryn and I will go back to the house," I said. "You can catch up with us."

We were barely out of earshot when Bryn pulled me close. "Was that my aunt's pill bottle they found?"

"We can talk about it inside," I said.

Bryn was relentless. As soon as we stepped through the kitchen door, she turned to me. "So was it hers?"

"I don't know," I said. "I'm guessing it was."

"Then she killed Mr. Leventhal?"

"Bryn, what do you know about the way Mr. Leventhal died?"

"Enough," she said. "There's not a lot that happens I don't know." Her eyes were glittering and her cheeks were pink. She seemed almost feverish with anticipation. "So do you think the police will arrest her?"

"If it's Tracy's prescription bottle, they'll certainly want to talk to her."

Bryn seemed oddly gratified. "Then they'll stop thinking it was Jill," she said and added, as if to herself, "It was a lucky thing the police were out there."

"Lucky for who?" I said.

She looked incredulous. "For Jill and me." She stifled a yawn. "I'm really tired. Angus and I are going shopping tomorrow morning, so I'd better get some sleep." Suddenly, she remembered her manners. "Thank you very much for the nice evening," she said.

I was still reeling when Angus came in.

"Everything okay here?" he asked.

"Couldn't be better," I said. "Bryn had a nice evening and she's gone to bed."

"She wants to go shopping tomorrow," he said.

"She mentioned that," I said. "What did Alex want?"

Angus unzipped his jacket and turned away. "He just wanted to say Merry Christmas. He's still a great guy, Mum. He taught me how to drive. He taught me a lot of stuff. I always kind of thought you two would end up together."

"For a while, we kind of thought the same thing," I said. "But it's not going to happen, Angus. It's over."

My son gave me a bear hug. "Well, it was fun while it lasted," he said.

"You're right," I said. "It was fun."

Suddenly alone, I moved to the glass doors that over-looked the alley where Alex was supervising the search for evidence. Despite everything that had gone wrong between us, I still felt connected to him, and I longed to tell him it was time he came in from the cold. If, as Nadine Gordimer says, human contact is as random and fleeting as the flash of fireflies in the darkness, Alex and I had made the most of our moments. Hands joined as we sat at the symphony listening to Mozart; heads bent towards one another as we played killer Scrabble in front of the fireplace; bodies touching as we lay on the sand at the lake, our books forgotten, listening to the pounding of the waves and thinking ahead to the possibilities of the old couch on the screened porch, we had always been smart enough to know we were happy. But at some level beyond the reach of reason, we had both known that our firefly moments were numbered.

My encounter with Alex might have provided conclusive proof that our relationship was over, but it had also raised some unsettling questions that had nothing to do with our personal relationship. I would have bet the farm that the prescription bottle in the dumpster had belonged to Tracy Lowell, but how it had made its way from her room at the Hotel Saskatchewan to my back alley was a mystery. The identity of the helpful citizen who had called the police tip-line was less enigmatic. Bryn was both fastidious and self-involved; yet she had stood in the cold with me watching a police officer paw through garbage until he came up with exhibit A.

A cynic might conclude that she had known all along that he would find what he was looking for.

CHAPTER

8

On a normal day, few things gave me as much pleasure as dialling my daughter's number and waiting to hear her voice. On the morning of December 24, I dreaded making the call. Since Thanksgiving, we had been making plans to spend the holiday together in Saskatoon. After the birth of my granddaughter, Madeleine, we had made the trip to Saskatoon at least one weekend a month, and Mieka and Greg had put more than a few kilometres on their Volvo wagon coming to see us. We were a family that enjoyed one another's company, and we had all been counting the days till Christmas. I'd been ready for two weeks: presents wrapped, stocking stuffers bagged, casseroles frozen, but once again Robbie Burns was right on the money, and the best laid plans of mice and men had "gang agley." Given the fact that the police had told Jill, Tracy, Claudia, and Bryn to stay in Regina until further notice, there was no way I could leave Jill alone at Christmas.

When I broke the news, Mieka erupted in tears, but, as she pointed out between sobs, she was eight and a half months' pregnant with her second child, hormonally driven, and not her best self. She was, however, cheerful and pragmatic by nature and that morning we rejigged and rescheduled most of our plans within five minutes. By the time Jill walked into the kitchen, Mieka and I were reassuring one another that, whenever we got around to celebrating it, this would be the best Christmas ever.

Jill was frowning when I hung up. "Sounds like you were bailing on Mieka," she said.

"Not bailing, just shifting things around a little."

"Because of me," Jill said.

"Yes," I said. "But the decision has been made, so live with it. 'All will be well,' as my yoga teacher says. Speaking of transcendence, you're looking more like your old self this morning."

"Actually," Jill said. "I'm feeling not bad. I had a good night's sleep, and when I stepped on your scales, I discovered I'd lost three pounds."

"Every cloud has a rainbow," I said.

Jill smiled. "Are you sure you're okay about not being with your incomparable granddaughter and her parents tomorrow?"

"I'm sure," I said. "We'll have two Christmases: Taylor and Madeleine will be surfing the bliss wave. My only problem now is poultry. I'm trying to think of a butcher who would still have a fresh turkey big enough for all of us."

"Problem solved," Jill said. "I'll take care of dinner. We'll eat at the Saskatchewan. These old railway hotels really know how to do holidays. I brought this not so merry band into your life, the least I can do is feed everybody."

"The hotel will cost you," I said.

Jill sliced a bagel and popped it in the toaster. "At 5:00 p.m. last night, I became a woman who will never have to worry about money again."

"Evan made that much from his movies?"

"Nobody gets rich making movies," Jill said. "Evan inherited money, and he played the market. Luckily for me, unlike his sister, my husband knew when to hold them and when to fold them."

"Claudia *is* a woman with money worries?"

"Big-time, but she's not paying for dinner."

"In that case, the Kilbourns accept your invitation with pleasure. Taylor will be thrilled that she gets to wear her swooshy dress again."

"Good." Jill smeared peanut butter on her bagel. "So what's going on around here?"

"Eat first, then we'll talk."

"Let's talk now," Jill said.

As I told her about the police garbage-seining operation, she slumped. "Why is it that lately all the news has been bad news?"

As if on cue, the phone rang. Jill and I exchanged glances. "Don't answer it," she said.

"It could be deliverance," I said.

"Fat chance," Jill bit into her bagel morosely.

When I heard the voice on the other end, I mouthed the name "Claudia," and Jill rolled her eyes.

Claudia got straight to the point. "We had a visit from the police last night. Tracy needs a lawyer," she said. "Can you suggest someone? A woman would be best. Tracy tends to be manipulative with men."

"Let me think," I said. "There's a lawyer named Lauren Ayala in my yoga class. She has a sound reputation, and when she says *namaste* at the end of class, her face is incandescent."

"Perfect," Claudia said. "Competent and centred enough to deal with Tracy. Have you got her number?"

"I'll look it up." I cradled the phone between my ear and my shoulder and flipped through the book till I found an ad for Lauren Ayala's office. Her area of special expertise was criminal law. I gave Claudia the information, hung up, and turned back to Jill. "You heard everything?"

"I did," Jill said. She touched her napkin to her lips. "Do you think the kids would be all right if we went out for a while?"

"Sure," I said. "I have to drop Taylor off at a friend's, and Bryn and Angus are driving around doing what Angus calls his kamikaze Christmas shopping. What did you have in mind?"

Jill stood up and stretched. "Might be useful to hear Tracy's story before your lawyer friend helps her get her chakras realigned."

I grinned at her. "You're not nearly as dumb as you look," I said.

After Taylor waved us off from her friend Jess's house, Jill and I drove downtown. Claudia struck me as someone who didn't like surprises, but when she opened her door to us, she was cordial. "You should have told me you were coming," she said. "I would have ordered fresh coffee." She stood aside to let us pass. "As you can see, I've finished, but Tracy hasn't even poured her tea."

A room service breakfast was laid out on the table. Only a yolk smear remained on Claudia's plate, but Tracy's fruit and yoghurt were untouched. Tracy herself was crumpled in an oversized armchair by the window. She was wearing a peony-strewn kimono, and in one of those sudden eruptions of memory that are all the more devastating because they're unexpected, I remembered Gabe's characterization of Tracy as a dewy bloom in the hero's lapel. That morning as the unforgiving winter light revealed every blemish and sag, it was clear that the once-dewy bloom had become a slightly past-it posy.

At first, she didn't seem to realize we were in the room, but when she did, the effect was galvanizing. Suddenly, she was an actress with an audience. She drew herself up and ran a hand tenderly down the side of the long and graceful neck that was her best feature. In a breathless theatrical voice, she told her story. "The police came last night. They found my prescription in the alley outside your house, Joanne, but the bottle was empty."

Jill eased into the chair opposite Tracy's. "I was asleep," she said, "but Jo saw the lights and went out and watched the police dig through the garbage."

Tracy showed no interest in the fact that there was an eye-witness in the room. Unpleasant as this drama was, she was its star and she wasn't about to share centre stage.

"Those pills were stolen from my bag," she said. "Some-one is trying to set me up."

Claudia was standing behind Tracy; she dropped her hand to Tracy's shoulder and began to rub it. "Eat your yoghurt and button your lip," she said. "This is no time to be a loose cannon. Someone could get hurt."

Tracy jerked her shoulder away from Claudia. "*I'm* being hurt right now," she said. "I'm the one the police harassed."

"No one harassed you," Claudia said. "Given the circum-stances, the questions Inspector Kequahtooway asked were perfectly logical."

Tracy drew her peony kimono tight. "The questions may have been logical," she said, "but that doesn't change the fact that someone is trying to implicate me."

"You're right," Jill said. "Maybe it's time you started thinking about the evil twins: motive and opportunity. Tracy, who had access to your bag the night of the rehearsal?"

"Everybody," Tracy said. "We were all in and out of each other's rooms that night. Even Gabe came down to talk to me."

"What did Gabe want to talk about?" Jill asked.

Claudia clamped a hand on Tracy's thin shoulder. "Per-sonal matters," she said. "Tracy is going to have to go through all this with the lawyer. I think once will be enough for her."

For a beat there was silence. I could feel Jill deliberating about where to go next. She decided on conciliation. "You're probably right," she said. "This isn't an easy time for anybody. We should be kind to one another. Speaking of . . . I take it you two will be in town for Christmas."

"Inspector Kequahtooway was pretty clear about the fact that we shouldn't expect to leave," Claudia said.

"Jo and I thought it might be fun to have dinner here at the hotel," Jill said. "All of us."

Claudia and Tracy exchanged the briefest of glances. "It would be nice to have another Christmas with Bryn," Claudia said.

"It's settled then," Jill said, pushing back her chair and standing.

Claudia walked us to the door. "I'll give you a call about the time," Jill said.

"We mustn't forget Felix," I said.

"Of course," Jill said. "We can't leave out the go-to guy."

I looked hard at Claudia. "Will it be a problem for you having Felix there?"

Claudia met my gaze. "Beggars can't be choosers," she said. "I'll behave myself if he will."

When the elevator doors closed, Jill turned to me. "Some weird dynamics during that little encounter. Was Claudia trying to protect Tracy against herself or just shut her up?"

"Beats me," I said. "But Christmas dinner should be interesting."

"Speaking of," Jill said. "What was behind that exchange about Felix?"

Jill seemed genuinely baffled when I told her about the ugliness between Felix and Claudia. "I don't get that at all," she said. "Felix and Evan's family go way back."

"Could Claudia be jealous of Felix's relationship with you?"

"No," she said. "There is someone in Felix's life, but it isn't me."

"Who is it?"

"Your guess is as good as mine." Jill wrapped her scarf around her neck. "Felix and I are just business partners and friends – or at least we used to be friends."

We were silent as we walked across the crowded lobby, but when we hit the street, I turned to Jill. "So what happened to your friendship?"

The light turned green and we started across. "You know that Felix and I have always worked well together," Jill said. "But after the wunderkind incident, we really got tight. When Felix was pitching the show in New York, we were like kids. We'd parse every sentence the network and cable guys came up with – trying to read the signs. We went nuts when we finally got a buyer."

"What went wrong?"

Jill shrugged. "At first, it seemed as if the Bluebird of Happiness was flying low, showering us with lucky breaks. The day after we sold the show, we had a call from one of the networks. They said that 'Comforts' wasn't for them, but they liked our approach and they had a counter-proposal. They'd noticed their audiences were intrigued with seeing ordinary people confronting situations that could easily destroy them and they wanted us to develop a program around that concept."

"Sounds like a natural for you," I said. "The dark side of 'Comforts of the Sun.'"

"Exactly," Jill said. "The problem was we had to move quickly, and Felix and I were both crazy busy trying to put an American face on 'Comforts.' So Felix brought Evan MacLeish into the project. That was two months ago. The rest, as they say is history."

"Not great history for Felix," I said.

"Not great history for any of us." Jill looked down the street. "Son of a bitch," she said and broke into a sprint. Half a block away a commissionaire was standing beside my Volvo writing up a ticket. Jill caught up with him, took something from her purse, and handed it to him. He glanced at it, then ripped up the ticket.

"Did you give him money?" I asked when I caught up with her.

Jill raised her hands in mock horror. "Of course not," she said. "That would be bribery. I gave him my business card. You have no idea how many people have a special Sunday-morning experience they want to share with Canada."

The unadorned plantation pine wreath on the door of Kevin Hynd's shop was so serene in its perfection that it soothed me to look at it. The scene inside Kevin's shop was tranquil too. He was sitting at his work table holding a fine-pointed bamboo brush and meditating on a square pastel-iced cake. When he heard us come in, he peered at us over his wire-rimmed glasses.

"Greetings," he said. He dipped the point of his brush into a tiny porcelain dish of linden green colouring and painted what appeared to be a stylized leaf on the cake's centre. "I've been thinking about this design for an hour," he said. "I had to execute it while the idea was still fresh. Take off your jackets and come over here and tell me what you think."

"It's exquisite," I said. "You've come a long way from Dumped Dames."

Kevin gave me a beatific smile. "Not far at all," he said. "What do you think this drawing signifies?"

"I have no idea," I said.

"It's a wet leaf," Kevin said. "The kind that sticks to your foot and won't shake off. It's the Japanese character for what my client tells me is called 'a retirement divorce' – the kind that happens when a man leaves the workforce and finds himself trailing his wife around the house all day. My client's language is more piquant than mine."

"You seem to have cornered the Angry Woman market," I said.

"Everybody deserves a cake," Kevin said equitably. "And I do my best to give them what they want."

"That cake you made for me was a work of art," Jill said. "Too bad it was wasted on a disaster."

"But there was a moment when it brought you plea-sure," Kevin said. "That's all we can ask for in this change-able world." He dipped his paintbrush into the porcelain dish and drew a smaller wet leaf on the side of the cake. "So what's new?"

Kevin continued to paint his pattern as Jill brought him up to speed. When she'd finished, he sat back on his stool. "Curiouser and curiouser," he said. "Short-term, the pre-scription bottle is good news for you. The police will have to divert some of their energy into finding out what was up with that. But long-term, the picture is still murky."

"I know I'm still front and centre," Jill said.

"Do I have your permission to talk about your financial situation with Joanne present?"

"Of course,"

"Good," Kevin said. "Let's start with the fact that, for you, becoming a wealthy woman overnight is both a curse and a blessing."

Jill gave him a sidelong glance. "Where's the blessing?"

"Money's always useful," Kevin said. "Chances are that the person who dropped that prescription bottle in the garbage bin is someone you know. Who's your candidate?"

"I don't have one," Jill said quickly.

"Because you lack knowledge about the possibilities," Kevin said. "Money can buy you that knowledge."

Jill set her jaw. "I won't do that. I won't hire some sleaze-ball to ferret out secrets about Evan's family."

"Your choice," Kevin said. "But unless you do something to help yourself, you're in for serious grief. The police are thorough, and you've worked in media. You know this will be a bonanza for the press. A lot of things about your private life are going to come out."

"I haven't done anything I'm ashamed of," Jill said.

Kevin gave her a half-smile. "Neither have I," he said. "But if I had a seventeen-year-old, there are a few things I'd rather explain to her myself. Face it, Jill, paying a little money to arm ourselves with information is the lesser of two evils."

Jill ran a hand through her hair. "Jerry Garcia always said that the lesser of two evils is still evil."

"You're not going to shame me out of giving you the best advice I can."

"All right," Jill said. "Do it, but I don't want anyone going around asking Bryn's friends and classmates about her. She's off limits."

Kevin and I made eye contact, but neither of us said a word.

Jill's voice was steely. "That's the condition," she said. "Keep Bryn out of it."

"So where does that put us with examining Evan's current projects?" Kevin asked. "If Bryn appears in a frame of film, do I hit the *off* switch?"

Jill shook her head. "I'll need to know everything about Bryn, but it can't go any further."

Kevin turned to me. "I wrote down the address you gave me. Who are we dealing with?"

"A psychiatrist named Dan Kasperski," I said. "He's a good choice. He's absolutely trustworthy, and his speciality is troubled adolescents. Bryn has been through a traumatic experience. The police will believe it's logical for Jill to be visiting his office."

"And while Jill's visiting the good doctor, she can examine her late husband's stuff," Kevin said. "Very handy."

"In more ways than one," I said. "You heard Bryn say she hated her father."

Kevin nodded. "On the night he was killed. It's occurred to me since that she must have some complicated feelings to sort through."

"She does," Jill said. "But there's no way Dan Kasperski can help her if she refuses to see him. I've asked her if she wanted to talk to someone about her father, but she says what he did to her gives her every right to hate him."

Kevin leaned forward. "What did he do to her?"

Jill's voice was bleak. "He's used her for material. Starting on the day she was born, he began filming her life. He never stopped. The night he died, Bryn said she couldn't remember a time when he wasn't stalking her. She begged him to leave her alone. He just kept on shooting."

"Why wouldn't he stop?" Kevin's voice was barely audible.

"Because the film about Bryn was going to be his magnum opus. He told Bryn that being in this movie would be the most significant thing she would ever do in her life, that when she was an old woman, audiences would still be watching her grow and develop."

"But she just wanted to be a kid," Kevin said.

"Exactly," Jill said. "But when Evan weighed Bryn's need to be a kid against his need to make a great work of art, it was no contest."

"Fucker," Kevin said. He glanced towards Jill. "Sorry."

"No need to apologize for the truth," Jill said shortly. "I guess the next order of business is to check with Dan Kasperski to see whether he's had a visit from FedEx."

I glanced at my watch. "Almost ten till. Dan's appointments start on the hour and run fifty minutes. I'll try him."

When he heard my voice, Dan was enthused, "Hey, your boxes arrived."

"If it's all right with you, I'm going to send over a lawyer to go through them," I said.

"The goodies never end."

"You'll like this lawyer. His name is Kevin Hynd. I'm with him right now."

"Can I talk to him?"

When Kevin rang off, he turned to me. "Sounds like a nice guy."

"He is, and he's amazing with kids. Jill, if you'll give him permission to look at some of the footage Evan shot of Bryn, he'll be able to tell you the best way to approach her."

"There's no question that your stepdaughter needs help, Jill," Kevin said. "Might as well pull out all the stops."

"Okay," Jill said. "I'll keep digging around for that binder Evan kept with the information about his works-in-progress."

"You can't find it?"

"No," she said. "And that's weird, because he was never without it."

"Anyway, you guys carry on with what Larissa sent from Toronto." She walked over to Kevin and kissed the top of his head. "I really do appreciate this, Kevin."

He beamed seraphically. "Now that was nice," he said. He glanced over at me. "Be careful," he said. "The universe has a way of repeating itself."

When we left Kevin's, Jill gravitated towards the window of his neighbour. Pinkies was offering Acrylics, UV Acrylics, Gel Nails, and Advanced Nail Art at Rock Bottom Stocking

Stuffer Prices. "How do you think Claudia would feel about a little Advanced Nail Art?" she asked.

In the end, we gave Pinkies a pass and hit the two last refuges of the desperate on the day before Christmas: the bookstore and The Body Shop. Jill shouldered through the crowds at the bookstore with the single-mindedness of a conquering general. Within ten minutes, we were walking out the door with a shiny Santa bag full of travel books for Claudia, who longed for escape, and a poinsettia-patterned bag of self-help books for Tracy, who longed for nirvana. Both outcomes seemed desirable; both seemed unlikely.

Jill's face relaxed as we wandered through The Body Shop, filling her basket with lotions, creams, glosses, blushes, bath beads, mascaras, eyeliners, and conditioners to enhance the beauty of a seventeen-year-old who had no need of enhancement. When the young woman at the counter wrapped the gifts in silver-starred Cellophane and tied them with shimmering bows, Jill turned to me with soft eyes. "It's great to finally have someone of my own to shop for."

"I take it you're not talking about Claudia and Tracy."

"Hardly," Jill said. "For me, Christmas has always been a day to get through. Now, I can't wait till tomorrow morning. I know this sounds bizarre, Jo, but at this moment, I feel incredibly lucky."

"Because of Bryn,"

She nodded. "She's my best gift. You feel that way about your kids too, don't you?"

"I do," I said. I glanced at my watch. "Speaking of, my youngest treasure is waiting to be picked up, so we'd better make tracks."

The fact that I cherished my children didn't stop me from being realistic about them. Twenty minutes later, when Taylor, Jill, and I walked through our front door, I did what

I always did when I came into a zone that had the potential to be hormonally charged – I made a lot of noise.

"Anybody home?" I called.

When there was no answer, Jill shrugged. "I guess they're still at the mall." She tapped Taylor on the shoulder. "I don't know about you, but I'm dying for a cup of hot chocolate with about a ton of marshmallows."

"Jess's mum made us hot chocolate just before I left," Taylor said. "But she uses carob and she doesn't believe in marshmallows."

"Holy Willie Wonka," Jill said. "What an abomination! Let's hit the kitchen and make some real cocoa."

After they left, I went up to the landing and tried again. "Anybody home?" I called. This time I hit paydirt. Angus, the King of Cool, appeared at the head of the staircase. His hair was tousled, his face was burning, and his fly was undone.

"So, how's everything here?" I asked.

From the time he was three, Angus had flagged the fact that he was engaged in dubious behaviour by hitting me with a river of irrelevant details. When I'd heard more than I cared to about this really hilarious old Adam Sandler movie he had chanced upon, I zipped an imaginary fly.

"So what was Bryn up to while you were sitting alone watching *The Wedding Singer*?"

My son lowered his eyes and adjusted his clothing. "I'm a mutt," he said.

"No argument here," I said.

"It didn't go too far," he said.

"Keep it that way," I said. "Angus, you know I try to stay out of your private life. All the time you and Leah were together, I trusted you to handle the situation."

"Be respectful. Be responsible," he said.

"You've got it," I said. "And it still applies."

That night we had enchiladas for dinner because we always had enchiladas for dinner on Christmas Eve. It was a tradition that endured because in the first year of our marriage my husband had decided that eating Mexican food, listening to Mel Torme, and making love in front of the fire was a fine way to usher in the holiday. Now, even though I could only manage two out of three, it still was.

Our church's early service was at 7:00 p.m. At 6:30, I was rummaging through my closet trying to find something that didn't need ironing when there was a tap at my door. It was Bryn. She was wearing a demure black wool jacket, matching pants, and buttery leather boots. Around her neck was a woven gold chain that held a tiny cross. She was the epitome of pious chic, but there was uncertainty in her eyes. "Is this outfit appropriate?" she asked.

"It's perfect," I said.

"We don't go to church," she said. "I didn't want to wear the wrong thing." She hadn't shifted her gaze from my face. Her thick eyelashes were painterly smudges against her pale skin, and her eyes were as warmly liquid as dark honey. "I know I worry too much about how I look," she said.

"We all do." I smiled at her. "Now if I'm going to come up with anything that makes me look one-tenth as attractive as you do, I'm going to have to get back to my closet."

"I can do that for you," Bryn said. She stepped into my walk-in closet and, after a few minutes of silent appraisal, selected a simple black turtleneck and a black silk skirt with a pattern of red poppies. "If you have some mid-calf boots with an interesting heel, this will work," she said.

She was right. Five minutes later as I checked the mirror, I knew I had never looked more pulled together in my life. I was doing a quick makeup repair when the doorbell rang. I walked into the hall, but when I heard the murmur of voices, I shrugged and went back to my lip liner.

Bryn was standing by the front door when I went downstairs. As soon as she spotted me, she slipped something into her purse.

"Who was at the door?" I asked.

"Nobody," she said.

"I was certain I heard voices," I said.

"Well you didn't," she said brightly. "You really didn't." The tilt of her chin defied me to press the point. I let it go, and the phone call I received five minutes later made me glad I'd exercised restraint.

It was Dan Kasperski sounding more agitated than I ever remembered him sounding. Mindful of eavesdroppers, I asked if I could call him back. When I did, he wasted no time on preamble. "Kevin Hynd spent most of the afternoon watching the footage Bryn's father shot of her. He was alarmed enough about what he saw to ask me to review some of the tape and give him a professional opinion."

I felt a coldness in the pit of my stomach. "Is it that bad?"

"Jo, you have to talk to Bryn's stepmother about getting her some help."

"I was hoping you'd volunteer," I said.

"You've got it," he said. "Bring her in tomorrow."

"Christmas Day?" I said.

"Ticking time bombs don't stop for statutory holidays."

When I came downstairs, Jill, Bryn, and my kids were already wrapped up for outdoors, ready for church. Lit by the twinkling lights of Taylor's tree, they looked like carollers on an old-fashioned holiday card. Heart pounding, I hurried into my outdoor clothes and joined them. It was Christmas Eve. Divine Intervention was not out of the question, but I wasn't holding my breath.

Taylor loved the lustrous magic of the Anglican service of Lessons and Carols. At that service, all the elements that

caused her eight-year-old soul to soar were in perfect align-
ment. She loved music, and her favourite was "Once in Royal
David's City," the traditional processional hymn. Every
Christmas Eve, she would sit on the edge of the pew counting
the moments until the boy soprano who sang the opening
verse a cappella was finished so she could raise her strong
clear voice in song. She was an artist who saw the world in
terms of colour and composition. She loved the perfect rosy
Renaissance feet on the doll that lay in the fresh hay of the
crèche on the altar, and the juxtaposition of the tiny haloed
baby with the soaring black cross that hung above it. And
she loved the candles that flickered dangerously in our
hands and the way the incense mixed with the scents of
pine and perfume. Most of all, Taylor loved communion.
She gave me the blankest of gazes when I mentioned tran-
substantiation, but at some deep level, she understood the
thrill of a world in which wafer became flesh and wine,
blood. That Christmas Eve as Father Gary ruminated on
Plato's observation that we live in a time when it often
seems the sheepdogs have become the wolves, Taylor
fidgeted, but when he called us to the communion rail, she
grabbed my hand.

The whole process intrigued her: Father Gary's explanation that our church has open communion, and that visitors
of other faiths were welcome to take part; the promise that
those who needed healing could come to the communion
rail at the last for special prayers and blessing; the choir's
chant asking the Lamb of God who takes away the sins of
the world to grant us peace.

Bryn was rapt too. As Father Gary talked about the sacrament of communion, she listened, lips slightly parted, her
hand on the pew, fingers touching my son's. But when our
turn to go forward came, Bryn stayed in her place. When Jill
whispered to her, she didn't move.

The sacrament of communion has always brought me the kind of comfort suggested by its Latin root *comfortare*, "to strengthen." That night despite the familiar words, the taste of wine, and the stillness of the scented air as we knelt at the altar, the usual sense of slow-blooming peace eluded me. As we walked back to our seats, the knife-edge of panic was sawing away, sharper than ever.

I couldn't shake the memory of Dan Kasperski's words. My mind was racing. I was so immersed in the problem of how Jill could deal with the daughter she adored that I didn't notice that Bryn herself had slipped away. She was already at the altar when I spotted her. Communion was over. She was alone. She moved with fluid grace past the communion rail, knelt under the cross suspended above the altar, then pros-trated herself beneath it. Father Gary was a gentle and sensi-ble man. He knelt beside her, prayed with her, then put his arms around her and helped her to her feet. Bryn walked back down the aisle with her head high. As she slipped back into her place in the pew, the slightest glimmer of a smile passed her lips. "I'm forgiven," she said. "It's all right. I'm forgiven."

CHAPTER

9

Bryn's convenient conversion might have brought her peace, but it did not usher in a period of amazing grace for the rest of us. From the moment we came back from church, the evening grew steadily worse.

I hadn't even taken my coat off before Angus grabbed my arm, pulled me aside, and whispered, "I need to talk to you, Mum."

"Go for it," I said.

"In private."

"Come upstairs, then," I said.

My son didn't beat around the bush. After we walked into my room, he closed the door, threw himself on the bed, and started talking. "We didn't do that much, Mum. It was just – you know – the usual."

"You've lost me already," I said.

He kept his eyes resolutely on the ceiling. "Bryn and I didn't do anything that should have made her flip out like that during communion."

I sat down on the bed. "You think what happened with Bryn tonight was your fault?"

"You're the one who told me there was more to sex than mechanics," he said. "Remember 'always treat the other person responsibly and respectfully.'"

"I remember," I said. "But don't be too quick to don the hair shirt about this one, Angus. Bryn's had a lot to deal with lately. I think everything just caught up with her tonight."

Relief washed over my son's face. "So it wasn't what we did?"

"You're not off the hook," I said. "You're eighteen years old. You know how powerful sexual feelings are."

"That's why I thought it was my fault," he said. "Bryn told me . . ." He flung his arm across his forehead. "I can't talk to you about this."

"Okay," I said. "But, Angus, we're dealing with major problems here. If you know anything that can help, maybe you should reconsider."

"Can you promise to keep this between us unless it's absolutely necessary to tell somebody else?"

"That seems reasonable," I said.

Angus took a deep breath. "This afternoon Bryn told me she was still a virgin, but she didn't want to stay that way."

"So you were about to grant her wish when we came in," I said.

"No." He slammed his fist into his hand. "I wasn't about to do anything. Look, Mum, I'm not going to bullshit you. Bryn is really hot. But she's a sketch . . ." He picked up on my blank look. "You know, off centre. But the big problem is she's just not Leah."

"I thought Leah was over," I said.

"So did I," he said. "But this afternoon . . . fuck, Mum, it's so weird talking to you about this. But with Leah, every-thing, not just – you know – intimacy, everything felt right. This didn't."

"Trust your instincts," I said.

"Back off with Bryn?"

"Yeah," I said. "Be her friend, but don't be alone with her."

Angus gave me a lopsided grin. "Of course, I would have figured this out myself sooner or later."

"Probably later rather than sooner," I said, then I gave him a quick hug.

When Angus pushed open the door to leave, Bryn was standing so close he almost hit her.

I walked over to her. "Are you all right?"

"I was just going to get ready for bed," she said.

Jill came up the stairs, took in the situation, and dropped a protective arm around her stepdaughter. "Wrong door, sweetie. Our room's next door."

Like a weary child, Bryn lay her head against Jill. "I'm tired," she said. "I guess I just got confused."

Five minutes later, Jill was back in my room. "Bryn's asleep. She was so exhausted I had to help her get into her pyjamas."

"It's been a long day," I said.

"They're all long days for Bryn," Jill said. "Jo, what am I going to do?"

It was an opening, and I took it. "You're going to get her some help." Jill's gaze never wavered as I told her about Dan's call. When I finished, she said, "Bryn's run out of options, hasn't she?"

"Dan seems to think so."

"She doesn't trust anybody," Jill said. "How can I get her to talk to Dan?"

"I'd start by telling her that Dan has seen the footage Evan shot and that he believes what her father did to her was heinous. I'm not an expert, but I think Bryn might open up to someone who knows the worst and is still on her side."

Jill leaned towards me. "You're right," she said. "But the person Bryn opens up to should be me. I'm the one who should tell her that I know everything and I still love her. I'm going to call Dan and ask him if I can come over and look at the films tonight."

"Not tonight," I said. "You've had enough. We can slip over there tomorrow afternoon. Barry and Ed have invited the kids and me to their brunch, but Angus and Taylor will have a great time on their own – so will Bryn."

Jill raised an eyebrow. "Why wouldn't they? Barry and Ed give the best parties in Regina. You, of course, have no interest in champagne splits, lobsters flown in from Nova Scotia, and Barry's famous croquembouche."

"We can stop at Tim Hortons on the way home from Dan's," I said. "You can buy us each a box of Timbits."

After I'd showered and put on my most comforting nightie, I settled into bed with *A Christmas Carol*, hoping that the words I had read and loved every Christmas since I was ten years old would work their magic one more time. But even the thrilling resonance of "Old Marley was as dead as a doornail" couldn't banish the memory of Bryn, prostrate beneath the altar. As I pulled up the comforter, I wondered if, like Ebenezer Scrooge, I was destined to carry my own low temperature always with me. My sleep was spectre-ridden, but my spooks weren't guides to enlightenment – just embodiments of scary possibilities. I awoke the next morning heavy-limbed and heavy-spirited. It was a Christmas morning I would gladly have skipped, but Taylor was one of life's celebrants. She burst into my room with a holiday shine. "Time to get up. I thought we could take our stockings into the hall, so we could listen to the new tree while we looked at our stuff."

"Swell," I said.

"I knew you'd love the idea," she said. "Now come on!"

As we huddled in the hall in front of a tree glittering with images of the famous dead, listening to endless tinny repetitions of "The Way We Were," I was not optimistic about my chances of making it through the day. But my spirits improved when we moved into the living room. It's hard to be gloomy when people are ripping open presents, and we had a mound of presents to rip through. We had all collaborated on Angus's gift, the electronic drum kit that Dan Kasperski had assured me was the very thing for a beginner. Because we'd planned to be at Mieka's for the holiday I'd given him the gift early. By Christmas morning, Angus had already been through three sets of sticks and cracked a cymbal, but he had gag gifts to crow over, and he did loudly and lustily.

Taylor's eclectic interests were reflected in her presents: cool clothes from Jill and Bryn; uncool clothes and an art print of *Pegasus* by Frank Stella from me; a Barbie with a homemade dress for every day of the week – all crocheted in the same retina-searing bubble-gum pink – from our friend Bebe Morrissey. A first edition of Noel Streatfield's *Ballet Shoes* and a pair of aqua dance slippers from our old friend Hilda McCourt; a painting of the bears of Churchill from my son Peter, who was working in the north; and a gift pack of glitter nail polish from Angus.

When the pile beneath the tree had diminished, Jill went upstairs and returned with a large flat package. She handed it to me and said, "For you."

"You already gave me that gorgeous sweater."

"Anyone with a wallet full of plastic and impeccable taste could have chosen that. This is something I made myself."

"Since when did you get crafty?"

Jill scowled in mock exasperation. "Just open your present."

I tore off the paper, prepared for a joke, but Jill's gift

touched my heart. It was a collage of photos of the two of us, starting with the days when I had been a young political wife and mother and Jill had been my husband's press officer. In the twenty-five years of our friendship, we'd shared some amazing moments, and Jill had selected photos of both the public and private times with care. There were photos of the nights when we won elections and of the nights when we'd lost; of my kids knee-deep in the gumbo of a prairie barnyard during a campaign when the rain never stopped; of Jill and me at a glittering dinner with a prince; of all of us at a deep-fried turkey potluck in a town that no longer existed; of births and deaths; weddings, funerals, baptisms – in short of all the small ceremonies that make up a life. Across the bottom, spelled out in letters cut from shiny paper, were the words "The Best of Times."

I was fighting back tears when I turned to Jill. "I love this," I said.

"I'm glad," she said. "I was going to call it 'The Best of Times. The Worst of Times.'"

"But you ran out of shiny paper for the lettering," I said.

She grinned. "Nope. I just realized that even the bad times were good because we were together." Jill caught Bryn's gaze. "That's the way it's going to be for us too, baby."

"You're embarrassing me," Bryn said.

"Sorry." Jill knelt and reached far under the tree. "A final present," she said, "and it has your name on it." Bryn took the package and opened it. Inside was a silver bracelet: wide, handsomely designed, and clearly pricey. Bryn balanced the bracelet on her fingertip for a few seconds, then dropped it back in its distinctive David Yurman box. "I don't want it," she said. "I'm not my mother. I have nothing to hide."

Taylor frowned at her. "When you get something you don't like, you're just supposed to take it and say, 'Thank you for thinking of me.'"

Bryn threw the bracelet into the pile of discarded wrapping. "Thank you for thinking of me."

Jill swallowed hard, then retrieved the box and took Bryn's hand. "You're welcome," she said. "Come on, let's get some food into us."

"Then we go tobogganing," Taylor said. "We always do that on Christmas morning, then we come home and everybody's supposed to have a long bath so we're not bouncing off the walls at Mr. Mariani's party."

"Sounds like a plan to me," Jill said.

It was the most glorious morning of the winter: a Grandma Moses landscape with a high blue sky, a round yellow sun, and snow so white it hurt my eyes to look at it. As we walked along the creek path, Taylor took the lead, planting her feet carefully to make footprints that were clean in the snow. As Bouviers do, Willie used his front paws to swim through the drifts along the way. Bryn started out with Jill but fell back to walk with Angus, who was dragging the big toboggan.

When they came to the first and most dangerous of the toboggan runs, she grabbed his hand. "Let's go," she said.

Jill stepped closer to check out the ice-slick slope. "This is your first time, Bryn, maybe you should start with something gentler."

"Jill's right," Angus said. "That slope's a killer."

Bryn wrenched the sled from Angus, ran to the top of the hill, and threw herself on the toboggan. Within seconds, she had bellied down the hill and across the frozen creek where she rammed the bank and was thrown back on the ice. For an agonizing minute, she lay there, then she pushed herself to her feet, dragged the toboggan back across the creek, and climbed the hill. As she stood before us, flushed with triumph, she was lovelier than ever. The cold burnished her beauty, drenching her cheeks with colour, glancing off the sheen of her hair, but there was a wildness in her eyes that was hauntingly familiar. As she pulled the toboggan to the top of the run, I felt a chill that had nothing to do with the weather. The day before she had told my son that she wanted him to take her virginity. Clearly, Annie Lowell's daughter had entered the high-stakes game of reckless hedonism that had killed her mother. Dan Kasperski had called Bryn a time bomb; it seemed that somehow the fuse had been lit.

Jill's mind had obviously hit the same groove as mine. "Evan's death has transformed her," she said. "She was always so careful. Now it's as if she doesn't care what happens to her. I'd think it was grief except that she hated him."

"Whether she hated him or not, her father was the dominant force in her life," I said. "She's lost her moorings."

"How do I get her back?" Jill asked.

"You've already made a start," I said. "Your handling of that business with the bracelet was exactly right – firm but low-key, and this afternoon we're going to find out how to help Bryn deal with what happened in her life before you knew her."

"If the past is prologue, how can we change the future?"

"Angus's football coach always says, 'Never give up. Never give in.'"

Jill grinned. "Thanks," she said. "I'll be sure to write that on our locker room wall."

Dan and Kevin Hynd were waiting for us when we got to the house on Wallace Street. There was a welcoming fire in the stone fireplace and the smell of fresh coffee in the air. Dan's living room was warm with homemade quilts and framed photos of people in happy times. It was a space that spoke of comfort and family, but as Kevin flicked on the video machine, it was clear that the footage Evan MacLeish had shot of his daughter's life was a violation of both.

The tape we were watching was one of a dozen. It was labelled simply "Girl," and it was clearly part of a work-in-progress. While the screen was still black, Evan's voice, intimate, absorbed, read what appeared to be notes to himself about editing and mixing the rough cut, then he announced the date of the edit: December 12 – ten days before his marriage to Jill. I glanced over to catch Jill's reaction; her face was stony.

From the opening frames, "Girl" was a jolt. The films Evan made about his first wives had been conventional in form: roughly chronological, the story of a life. In each case, the power had come from Evan's stark, unwavering focus on a woman in the process of destroying herself. Linn Brokenshire's biography followed the inevitable arc of the life of a saint: religious ecstasy; testing; suffering; death. The film about Annie Lowell had been infused with the hectic, anarchic spirit of a woman who refused to live by the rules her medical condition dictated. Both were stunning emotionally, but technically conservative.

In "Girl," Evan was using form to reveal dysfunction – film as psychopathology. He crosscut present and past to mimic the jagged bursts of memory that imprison even the healthiest among us. He began in the present with Bryn, in black, sitting on a window seat, framed against a grey late-autumn sky. Given her outbursts, I expected that she would be an unwilling subject, hunted down and run to ground, but she had a model's easy relationship with the camera.

As she hugged one leg, she was almost seductive. "He told me to think of her as a mother," she said. "That is such a sick joke. The only thing my mother ever did for me was kill herself." Bryn tilted her head and a mocking smile curved her lip. "Oh right," she said. "Annie did give me the gift of life."

Immediately, Evan cut to a scene that celebrated motherhood so exquisitely that Mary Cassatt could have painted it.

Annie and Tracy Lowell were picnicking on a spring green lawn. Both were in white, both wore daisy chains in their hair. They were identical in every way except that Annie was hugely and triumphantly pregnant. They were grown women and there was something consciously girlish about the way in which they drew together whispering and laughing. Finally, Tracy leaned down and put her face against Annie's belly, and Annie's hand came up and stroked her sister's hair. It was a moment of such astonishing intimacy that I felt like an intruder witnessing it. But I wasn't the intruder. Evan MacLeish was.

Bryn at seventeen was on screen. "I just don't get this whole mother thing. Somebody gets pregnant – that's her trip, not mine. If it's supposed to be about love, then I totally don't get it. From what I hear, Annie never loved anybody but herself." Bryn checked her nail enamel. "That's actually not true. She loved Tracy, and Tracy loved her. At least I think so."

We were back in Bryn's past, excavating her life through footage that showed the astonishing closeness of the sisters. There wasn't a single scene of Annie alone with her daughter. Tracy was always present, and the dynamic between the two women and the child was disturbing. When Annie and Tracy linked arms to form a hammock for the baby, they rocked the child so violently that her small face was contorted with terror. There were other vignettes – all theatrically perfect, all oddly creepy. It took me a moment to pinpoint the source of my unease, then I noticed that as the sisters built a sandcastle on the beach or sang children's songs or played with a little puppet theatre, they were so obsessed with one another, they forgot that Bryn was there. The Lowell sisters' pas de deux allowed no room for a third. When the inevitable scene of the car crash shattered the silence of Dan's living room, my heart ached not just for Bryn but for Tracy and the magnitude of her loss.

On screen, the seventeen-year-old Bryn had half-turned from the camera; against the dark and roiling clouds, her profile was an ivory cameo. "They tell me I didn't talk for a year after it happened. I don't remember. They say I never sat still. I just wandered through the house looking. I don't remember. I don't remember that time at all." She brought her face close to the camera's lens. "Don't worry," she whispered. "Daddy got the footage."

Indeed he had, and it was harrowing. As he followed Bryn through the rooms of the museum in which she lived, Evan kept the camera at her level. The little girl's search became our search; we saw the rooms and the people in them as she saw them: distant and unknowable. Claudia, thirteen years younger, her fair hair in a thick braid, kept reaching out to the child, trying to comfort her. Every time her aunt's fingers touched her, Bryn screamed. A fashionable woman with a wedge of shining silver hair and a curiously unlined face often followed the child, but she made no attempt to either communicate with the little girl or to touch her. Only once did the woman speak, and it was to the camera. "Chesterton says that suicide is a far worse crime than murder, because the murderer kills one person, maybe two or three. The suicide kills everyone." The woman stared thoughtfully at her jewelled hands. "I wonder if Annie knew or cared what she was doing?"

The only person Bryn seemed interested in was Tracy. The little girl would crawl up on Tracy's knee and run her hands over the face that was a duplicate of the face that had disappeared forever. Tracy never responded to the child's touch. She seemed catatonic. Finally, the child exploded, punching her aunt with her small fists. "Where's the other one?" she demanded. "Dead," Tracy said. And that was the end of Bryn's childhood.

By the time she was eleven, Bryn had created inner walls that were high and thick. Seemingly confident that the camera couldn't reach anything that mattered, she ignored it. But like the worm that inches towards the heart of the rose, Bryn's adversary moved inexorably towards her core. The scene in which the camera finally penetrated Bryn's private world was beyond brutish. Evan had caught his daughter at a pivotal moment on the cusp between childhood and adolescence. She was standing naked in front of a full-length mirror. The only light in the shot came from sunshine pouring in through an open window, dappling a body that, in Karl Shapiro's memorable phrase, was "smooth as uncarved ivory." The camera lingered as Bryn's hands tenderly explored the changes in her taut body. Eyes half-closed, dreaming her private dreams, Bryn was slow to pick up on the camera's presence. When, finally, she did, she crumpled: folding her body in on itself, attempting to cover her nakedness, pleading, "Daddy, don't. Please. Just don't. The other kids – their fathers don't do this to them. Please. Please. Just stop." But the camera continued to roll until Bryn fell to the floor, naked and weeping.

There was a final scene, Bryn at seventeen talking to the camera. "I wish he'd die," she said. "He used you on my mother too, you know. And against the wife he had before. He's a parasite. He can't live without us. But my mother and the wife he had before got back at him. They killed themselves and that moved them permanently out of the range of your lens. I could do that too." She tossed her head. "If I took him with me, it might be worth it."

As soon as the film was over, Dan leapt up and turned on the lights. Seemingly, he didn't want to leave us alone in the dark with our thoughts. "There are other tapes," he said, "but this picked up the coping mechanism I wanted Jill to see."

"The way Bryn addresses the camera directly – as if it were separate from her father," Jill said. "She's so . . . seductive with it. What's that about?"

"She's trying to use the only tool she has to bring the camera over to her side against him," Dan said. "I've never seen anything like it. Of course, I've never had a patient who was abused the way Bryn was abused."

"How could they let him do that to her?" Jill said. "They were there – Claudia, Tracy, Caroline – I could fucking kill them all."

Kevin patted Jill's knee. "Chill," he said. "Also, atomize. Break the problem down into manageable parts. What's your first priority?"

"Bryn," Jill said.

"Good choice," Dan said. "We've left it a little late today. My parents are expecting me for dinner. If you can bring her by at eight tomorrow morning, I can see her before I start my regular day."

"You work Boxing Day?" I said.

"My busiest day," Dan said. "For the kids in my practice, Christmas is never a holly-jolly experience."

"And Bryn and I are adding to your workload," Jill said. "I appreciate this, Dan. I honestly don't know where else I'd go." When she stood, she seemed to lose her balance. Kevin's hand shot out and grasped her elbow. "Steady as she goes," he said.

Jill closed her eyes and leaned into him for a moment. "Words to live by," she said.

"Hey, I almost forgot," he said. "Christmas isn't over yet. I have a present."

"For me?" Jill said.

"Nope," he said. "For Joanne's tree." He handed me a Day-Glo painted sunburst. Inside was a photo of Jerry

Garcia. "I noticed you didn't have a tree-topper," Kevin said. "Nothing's going to bring him back, but it's good to have a reminder that his sweetness will live forever."

By the time Taylor and her swooshy dress swished exuberantly past the doorman at the Hotel Saskatchewan, Jill had come up with an agenda for the evening. She had abandoned her plan to kill the people who hadn't protected Bryn in favour of cozying up to them. Dan had convinced her that knowledge was power; the more she knew about her troubled stepdaughter, the more she would be able to help her.

The dining room into which we walked would have warmed Ebenezer's frozen heart. The hotel was celebrating a true Victorian Christmas: dripping candles, real holly, mistletoe balls, fat geese, turkeys, glazed hams, silver tureens of potatoes, turnips, Brussels sprouts, and, for dessert, trifle and flaming plum pudding. Dickens might not have been able to lull me to sleep, but his iconic feast still had the power to set the Ghosts of Christmases Past rattling.

Tracy and Claudia were waiting at our table. A tiny red teddy bear holding an envelope lengthwise between his paws was on the table at the empty place between them. Both women had taken pains to look festive. Tracy was wearing the sequined white shirt she had worn to the rehearsal dinner, but she'd added an armful of silver bangles and a pair of earrings that looked like links of frozen silver teardrops. Claudia was wearing a tailored jacket and slacks in metallic emerald green; her hair was smoothed into a chic chignon, and for the first time since I'd met her, there was mascara on her pale lashes and a flume of shadow on her lids. When they saw us, they rose expectantly.

"You both look beautiful," I said. "I love what you've done with your eyes, Claudia."

"Thanks," she said. "I'm glad my mother didn't hear you say that."

"She doesn't approve of makeup?" I said.

"Au contraire," Claudia said. "From the time I was three years old, Caroline put mascara on me. She said I was so fair that I looked like a lashless chick. She found it painful to look at me."

Her comment sucked the wind out of my conversational sails, but other people's sorrows didn't register with Bryn. "We've had a real family Christmas," she said happily. "Church and stockings and tobogganing and then a really cool holiday party. This is the happiest Christmas I've ever had."

"You had some lovely holidays with us," Claudia said. "Remember when I took you to that matinee of *Peter Pan* and you liked it so much we went again that night."

"I don't remember," Bryn said.

"How can you not remember?" Tracy said. "I gave you that dress Annie wore when she played Wendy." Tracy smiled at her memories. "She was just sixteen, but the audience absolutely ate her up. I can still remember how the applause would roll over her every night when she stepped forward during curtain call."

"You went to see your sister every night?" Jill asked.

"I was in the company," Tracy said. "One of the Lost Boys. How's that for typecasting?" She sipped her espresso. "One night, Annie and I decided to switch roles – just for fun. By the end of the first act, we both knew the audience hated me, so we switched back."

"I always thought changing places with a twin could be a lot of fun," I said. "Did you two do it often?"

Claudia cut Tracy off before she could answer. "Almost never," she said. "Now, let's see if we can find a waiter. It's time for some Christmas cheer."

The waiter appeared and immediately fell under Bryn's spell. We had to repeat our orders three times, and even then, Taylor, who had ordered her Shirley Temple with great precision, ended up with an umbrella-less rye and Coke. When the drinks were finally straightened out, Claudia raised her glass. "To better times," she said. "Speaking of . . . Joanne, we have to thank you for recommending Lauren Ayala. She's one sharp lawyer, not to mention a generous one. Not many lawyers would see a client on Christmas Day."

"Choosing a lawyer on the basis of how she does sun salutations obviously has something to recommend it," I said.

Claudia laughed. "Whatever criterion you used was obviously spot on, because Tracy and I are finally getting out of here tomorrow."

"And Lauren says that's all right?"

"She says Tracy's empty prescription bottle is worrying but hardly conclusive, especially since Tracy and I were together during the period when the police say Evan was murdered."

"I didn't know that," Jill said.

"Well, now you do," Claudia said matter-of-factly.

"That's right," Jill said thoughtfully. "Now I do."

The pause that followed was awkward. Luckily, Taylor, as she frequently does, leapt into the breach. "Do you think we could go to the buffet now? I'm starving."

Angus shot her a glance. "How could you be starving? Three hours ago you ate an entire lobster, a mound of potato salad, and two helpings of croquembouche?"

Taylor shook her head in wonder. "Beats me," she said. "I just know that that turkey smells really good."

"If I were a well-bred host, I'd insist we wait for Felix," Jill said. She glanced at her watch. "But he's twenty minutes late, and Jo and I skipped lunch. Let's eat."

By the time we had made our way through the buffet line twice, it was clear the evening was not working out as Jill had hoped. Her plan to elicit information about Bryn's past had been torpedoed by a choir in full Victorian dress who sang lustily and at great length, and Felix was still a no-show.

When he finally did appear, he looked as if he had stumbled into the wrong party. Felix took pride in his appearance, but as he walked into the glittering dining room, he was wearing his ski jacket and he was tieless and unshaven. He was also agitated. He went straight to Jill. "I checked the phone messages at our office," he said.

"On Christmas Day? Now that's devotion." Jill indicated his empty place at the table. "Sit down and tell me what's going on."

The moment Felix sat down, Bryn's waiter was at his side. Felix ordered a double-vodka and swivelled his chair to face Jill. For all the attention he directed our way, the rest of us might as well have been cardboard cut-outs. "There were a number of calls for Evan," he said. "Urgent calls."

Jill tensed. "Personal or professional?"

"Professional," Felix said. "NBC is picking up the series. Evan signed an agreement with them. The telephone calls that came after his death were nominally condolences, but everybody wanted to talk to the widow. It's clear they're hot for this, Jill. They want to use the material Evan sent them."

"There is no material," Jill said. "All we gave them was a proposal. How can they be hot for a program that doesn't exist?"

"Because," Felix said tightly, "the program does exist. Apparently Evan gave them a fully edited first show for 'The Unblinking Eye.' The network people are over the moon about it."

Jill picked up on the implications immediately. "Evan submitted something he'd already shot," she said.

"It will be about me," Bryn said in a voice dead with resignation.

"I won't let them use it, baby," Jill said.

"You may have to if Evan signed a contract," Felix said.

"Did he?" Jill asked.

"I don't know. I didn't pick up our messages till late yesterday afternoon. By then everyone was gone for the holiday. The only person I could get in touch with was Larissa."

"Our office manager," Jill explained. "So was she able to help?"

Felix shook his head. "Not really. She told me that everything connected with Evan's current projects had been carted off. I said I presumed the Toronto police were acting on orders from the department out here. Larissa said that was a sensible assumption."

The slightest hint of a smile touched Jill's lips. "Good old Larissa," she said.

Felix's head shot up. "What?"

"Nothing," Jill said. "So there's no way to know what Evan sent to the network until the holiday's over?"

"Which could be tomorrow, and could be after the weekend," Felix said, and I was surprised at how fretful he sounded. His lean, boyish face was suited to whimsy, but that night the creases around his mouth had deepened, and he seemed grave and preoccupied. His response seemed excessive for a problem that, by my reckoning, concerned him only tangentially. When his cellphone rang, he started, and despite furious glances from the diners at the next table, he picked up. As soon as heard his caller's voice, he leapt up. "I'll talk to you outside," he said. "There are people around."

Without explanation, he left the dining room. Jill raised an eyebrow, and I followed him. Felix had stopped just outside the maître d's station, and as people do when they're talking on cellphones in public places, he had turned to face the wall. I stopped behind him, pretending to study a menu. He was almost whispering, but I overheard him make a lover's promise. "I'll never let anyone hurt you," he said. "You are my lifeblood."

When I got back from the ladies' room, it was clear the party was over. Felix had already downed his vodka and pulled on his ski jacket. "I'm going up to my room to make some phone calls," he said. "There must be somebody at NBC who's taking care of business."

Claudia followed his lead. "I guess we should go upstairs too. We have to pack." She took Jill's hand. "Thanks," she said. "Given the circumstances, it was a very pleasant dinner. I'll call you before we go to the airport."

Tracy went to Bryn and stroked her hair. "Your mother always wanted the best for you – it wasn't her fault that her life didn't work out."

"There's nothing you can tell me about my mother that I have the slightest interest in hearing," Bryn said, and she jumped up and ran from the room.

Taylor, oblivious, reached over and nabbed a chocolate truffle from Bryn's plate. "Boy, this was some Christmas," she said.

"You've got that right," I said. "And do you know what the best part of this particular Christmas is?"

Taylor popped the truffle in her mouth and shrugged.

"In four hours, it will be over," I said.

After the kids were in bed, Jill and I took a bottle of Hennessey and two snifters into the living room. I turned on the tree lights and lit every candle in sight. Jill handed me my drink.

I took a sip and sighed with contentment. "There's nothing like Hennessey," I said. "And we earned it. We got through the day."

"We did," Jill agreed. "Now there's only the rest of our lives to worry about."

"It'll get better," I said.

Jill gazed at the candelabra blazing on the mantelpiece. "I love candles," she said. "They always make me think of college."

"Stuck in Chianti bottles and lined up along your dorm window to prove you were a woman of the world?"

Jill smiled at the memory. "For me, candles meant Edna St. Vincent Millay – I loved her image of burning the candle at both ends, so you could make a lovely light."

I swirled my brandy, watching the amber waves hit the curved sides of the snifter. "Living at full throttle becomes less appealing as the years tick by," I said.

"Maybe," Jill said. "But a wise man once told me that when it comes to life, 'the bigger the investment, the bigger the payoff.'"

"So was this sage one of your long line of lovers?" I asked.

"No, but he was one of the few men I've ever truly admired. It was Ian, Jo." The candlelight glanced off Jill's diamond solitaire. "Did you ever realize how lucky you both were to get it right the first time?"

"I realized," I said.

Jill stared at the flickering fireplace, mesmerized. "Sometimes watching your life with the kids and each other, I felt like the Little Match Girl pressing my nose against the window. I wanted that life, Jo – I still do. That's why I'm ready to invest everything I have in Bryn."

"Every investment carries the possibility of loss," I said.

"I know. I'm not a complete idiot." She laughed softly. "But hey, I'm the last of the red-hot Edna St. Vincent Millay fans – want to hear the best two lines she ever wrote?"

"Do I have a choice?"

"Of course not." The tone was congruent with our usual easy mockery, but when Jill turned to me her eyes shone with a terrifying hope:

"Safe upon the solid rock the ugly houses stand:
Come and see my shining palace built upon the sand!"

CHAPTER

10

It didn't take long for the sands under Jill's shining palace to shift dangerously. Just after midnight, my son shook me awake. "Come down to my room, Mum." As I fumbled for my slippers, Angus babbled, "I didn't turn the lights on because I heard somewhere they can get violent if you wake them up."

"What are you talking about?"

He lowered his voice. "Bryn's sleepwalking. I was in bed just kind of staring at the wall, and she came in. Her eyes were open, but when I called her name, she didn't hear me." He pointed towards the graceful naked figure in the window. "Look at her. She doesn't even know we're here."

The moon played tenderly on Bryn's flawless body, outlining her slender legs, touching on the gentle curves of her buttocks. As we watched, she pivoted slowly towards us, staring at us from wide, unseeing eyes.

"Get her robe," I said.

"You're not supposed to interfere with them," Angus said.

"This is a special case," I said. "Get the robe."

When Angus came back, I draped Bryn's robe around her shoulders and led her back to her room. As I pulled the covers up, I leaned close. "I know you're faking," I said.

The bud of a smile touched her lips, but she didn't say a word.

Bryn was at the breakfast table watching the birds crowding each other at the feeder when Willie and I came down the next morning. I let Willie outside, plugged in the coffee, and sat down. It was, I suddenly realized, the first time Bryn and I had ever really been alone together.

With her hair tied back in a schoolgirl ponytail and her face innocent of makeup, it was impossible to believe duplicity was even in Bryn's emotional vocabulary.

She didn't waste the moment. "I've been waiting for you," she said.

"Here I am."

"How did you know?" she asked.

"A gorgeous, perfectly groomed, naked girl bathed in moonlight – it was just too much. Why did you do it?"

"To get him on my side," she said.

The memory of Bryn's seductiveness with the camera was fresh. "You don't have to use your sexuality to get someone on your side," I said.

"It's all I have."

"That's not true. There are other ways," I said.

"Not for me," she said. "I'm damaged goods. I've done terrible things." She lowered her gaze. "None of them involved Angus, if that's what you're worried about."

"Angus isn't my only concern."

"That's right," she said angrily. "There's Jill too. Well, I've done things to protect her."

"What kinds of things?"

"I can't talk about it with you."

"Did you call the police and tell them to check the garbage bin out back?"

Bryn froze, tense as a cornered cat. "Why would I do something like that?"

Her antagonism was palpable. I knew I had to disarm her. "I think you did it for Jill," I said. "To protect her. It was a generous impulse, Bryn, but you need to do more. If you knew the pill bottle was there, then you know who put it there. You have to tell someone."

"I'm not telling you," she said.

"Could you tell a psychiatrist?"

"I don't need another psychiatrist," she said.

For a few minutes we sat in an uneasy silence, then I sent up a quick prayer that the words I was about to utter would do more good than harm. "Do you want to end up like your mother?" I asked.

The effect was electric. "What do you know about her?" Bryn said, and the fear in her voice was genuine.

"I've watched *Black Spikes and Slow Waves*. Her future was so filled with promise, Bryn. It was terrible to watch her destroy herself."

"It was her choice," Bryn said coldly.

I leaned towards her. "Yes, and what happens to you next is your choice. I know what your father did to you. Yesterday, I saw part of the film he was making of your life."

Bryn jumped up so suddenly that her leg caught on the edge of the table. Tears of rage and pain filled her eyes. "Damn him," she said. "Even after his throat is slit, he's still hurting me."

I went to her. "Don't let him," I said. "Don't be another woman whose life is destroyed by Evan MacLeish. You have an appointment with the psychiatrist Jill told you about at eight o'clock. Keep the appointment, Bryn. Give the doctor a chance to help you. Give *yourself* a chance."

"Will you take me?"

"Of course, but Jill will want to do it."

Bryn shook her head. "I don't want her to. I want to start fresh with her – whole, like a normal person. That's what I was trying to do in church Christmas Eve. I wanted to be washed of sin, born again – the way those ministers on TV in the middle of the night say people can be." She buried her face in her hands. "I know how crazy that sounds . . ."

"Not crazy at all," I said. "Why don't you grab something to eat and get dressed. Since you're the first appointment, Dan might be able to sneak us in a bit early."

Bryn and I left the house at 7:40 a.m. At 7:43, I checked my rearview mirror and spotted an all-too familiar silver Audi. Alex Kequahtooway was a skilful cop. On the day he'd graduated from the police college, he had known how to tail a car unobtrusively. That morning he didn't make the slightest attempt to disguise his mission. Alex wanted me to know he was there. I wasn't Bruce Willis. I had no special knowledge about how to lose a tail, and I was afraid of car chases. I continued following the route I always took to Wallace Street, observing the speed limit, stopping at lights and school zones, and exercising due caution.

When the Audi pulled up across the road from me at Dan Kasperski's, I ignored it. I walked Bryn briskly into the office at the back of the house, introduced her to Dan, waited till they had established a comfort zone, and beat a hasty retreat. The Audi was still there. Alex was talking on his cell. I strode up to the car and tapped on the door. He turned towards me and rolled down the window. "What can I do for you?" he asked.

"Just wanted to commend you on your vigilance," I said.

"I'm not as vigilant as you are, Jo – visiting Dan Kasperski twice in two days – once with Jill and her lawyer in tow."

"You had someone watching us?"

"*I* was watching you. There's been a lot of activity at your house."

"It's the holiday season," I said. "People come and go."

"True," he said. "And they make telephone calls."

His eyes bored into me, waiting for my reaction. I met his gaze, and when I responded my voice was steady. "So the call about the prescription bottle in the garbage bin did come from my house," I said.

"You know I can't confirm that."

"Then I guess we don't have anything more to talk about."

My hand was resting on the edge of the window. For the briefest of seconds, Alex covered it with his own gloved hand. "Be careful who you trust, Jo," he said.

"I will," I said. "You be careful too."

A fire smouldered in Dan's fireplace. I rifled through the reading material in the magazine rack designated for the parents and caretakers of his young clients. I chose a women's magazine I hadn't picked up since the early days of my marriage. I'd loved the magazine then for its recipes and for its short fiction, gossamer thin plots with spunky romantic heroines. The feature article in the current issue was on sex games that would add zip to my relationship. I soldiered through "Beat the Clock" (no penetration until a pre-set timer goes off), "Spanking the Bad Girl" (no penetration until after paddling), and "The Love that Binds" (no penetration until your partner has tied you to the bedpost), but when I hit "A Close Shave" (no penetration until he's lathered and shaved your pubic area), I knew the world had passed me by. I slid the magazine back in the rack and returned to my thoughts.

They were not comforting. Alex had confirmed my theory that Bryn had called the police, but I didn't know what had motivated her call. She had hinted that she was protecting Jill, but from what? Bryn prided herself on knowing what was going on. She had either witnessed or engineered the deposit of the pill bottle in the dumpster. Which was it? By the time Bryn and Dan emerged from the backyard office, the questions were multiplying exponentially, and I was longing for the uncomplicated pleasures of "A Close Shave."

It was immediately apparent that Bryn had decided to trust Dan Kasperski. As they walked down the snowy path towards the house, their faces were serious, but Bryn's body had lost its supermodel runway rigidity. Their banter as I pulled on my boots and coat was easy and natural. When Dan suggested Bryn meet him at the same time the next morning, she was enthusiastic. "I'll be here," she said. "Early again, if that's okay."

"Early is good," Dan said. "Be strong."

"I will," she said. As we drove home, Bryn sang Dan's praises. "He's so easy to talk to," she said. "My other shrinks didn't talk at all – they just pretended to listen. But Dan really listens, and he cares about what I say. Joanne, he cares about *me*. He's on my side. Dan says seeing those movies my father made about me helped him come to know me."

"Understanding what happened to your mother might give him even more insight."

"What my mother did to herself shows zero insight. You saw how beautiful she was, but you know what she did? She ruined her beauty. She slit her wrist with a razor blade. She didn't die, of course, but she gave herself these huge Frankenstein scars. She always covered them up with a bracelet, but I knew the scars were there."

"That's why you were so upset about the bracelet Jill gave you?"

Bryn didn't answer. We pulled into the driveway, but instead of getting out, Bryn raised her arms towards me so that the cuffs of her coat fell back. The blue tracery of veins in her pale skin was as delicate as a design in fine porcelain.

"See, no scars," she said. "The inside of me may be totally fucked up, but the part people can see is perfect."

Jill was on the telephone when we walked in the door. "All I'm asking is that you handle it till I get things straightened out here. I just got off the phone with the network, and this can be big for us. But I can't do it now. I'm in the middle of two murder investigations and my stepdaughter is having a breakdown."

Bryn grabbed the phone from Jill's hand and slammed down the receiver. "Don't you ever say that again," she said. "I'm not a mental case."

Jill was clearly stricken. "I'm sorry. I should have been more careful about my language. I was trying to make sure I was here to protect you."

"I don't need protecting," Bryn said. "I'm getting help. Joanne took me to see Dan Kasperski this morning."

Jill whirled to face me. "Bryn's my responsibility."

Bryn moved to position herself between us. "I'm seventeen years old, Jill," she said. "I'm responsible for myself." She touched Jill's arm. "Why don't we go somewhere and have a cup of coffee and talk about it."

For a beat, Jill was silent, taking the measure of her newly responsible stepdaughter, then she smiled. "I'd like that," she said.

I walked upstairs thinking how pleasant it would be to open my bedroom door and find a congenial man waiting with a blindfold and some dark designs on my body. What I got was Taylor, Willie, and the cats having a tug-of-war with an old towel.

"This room is supposed to be my oasis of tranquility," I said. "Dogs, cats, and kids are only allowed in here on serious business."

Taylor scrunched her forehead. "Is that one of your jokes?"

"Apparently," I said.

"Good," Taylor said. "Anyway, I am here on serious business. Today's the day you and Julia and Erica and me go to see *The Nutcracker*. It was part of my birthday present, remember?"

"I remember now," I said. "So what time do we pick up the ladies?"

"The ballet doesn't start till two, but Erica says the GAP is having a big sale – butterfly shirts for ten dollars each. She thought it would be neat if we all got shirts the same and wore them this afternoon."

"Sounds good to me," I said. "Let's take everybody to the mall around eleven, battle our way through the crowds, eat at the food court, and come back here so you can get into your butterfly shirts."

Taylor stretched luxuriously. "This day is going to be so great."

"You bet," I said. "Starting right now because I have two whole hours all to myself."

"What are you going to do with them?" Taylor said.

"See where they take me," I said.

Within fifteen minutes I had the house to myself. Taylor was spending the morning in her studio out back painting; Angus and his friends were cross-country skiing, and Jill and Bryn were taking a walk to talk things over. As soon as the door closed behind them, I went into the family room and slipped the tape of *Black Spikes and Slow Waves* into the VCR. I was convinced that the scenes Gabe Leventhal had been so intent upon the night before he died were key, but tense with the awareness that a single frame might illuminate the mystery, I was on the edge of my seat from the opening credits.

If ever I'd needed proof that context is all, revisiting *Black Spikes* offered it. The first time I'd watched the movie I'd been seeking evidence that would nail Evan MacLeish to the wall – prove to Jill conclusively that he was a rotten choice for a marriage partner. That one had been a no-brainer, but as I watched *Black Spikes*, I knew that in my eagerness to indict Evan, I'd missed much that was significant about the film itself.

First was the consummate skill with which the movie had been made. Using only a hand-held camera and available light, Evan had shown how life looked from inside the eye of the hurricane. The view was seductive. Annie might have been hurtling towards death, but there was an antic, reeling joy about her decision to fuel her passage with a high-octane mix of drugs, booze, and sex. Through the eye of Evan's camera, we saw Annie's refusal to capitulate to her illness as somehow heroic, a braver decision than choosing to live a life that would be measured out in careful teaspoonfuls.

Second was the sensitivity with which Evan revealed the primal bond that linked his wife to her twin. The sisters' constant need to reach out to one another as if for tangible reassurance that they were not alone was both powerful and poignant. When Annie had a seizure, it was Tracy who kept her sister's windmilling limbs from damaging themselves; Tracy who touched her lips to the forehead of the blue-tinged face; it was Tracy who threw her own silk scarf over the urine-stained crotch of Annie's expensive pants.

And when Annie gave birth, it was Tracy who held the ice chips to her sister's mouth, smoothed oil onto the mound of her belly, urging her to breathe deeply, and it was Tracy who held out the arms that caught Bryn as she came into the world. It took a moment for the significance of what I was seeing to register. When it did, I stopped the film and rewound it to the birth scene. The characteristic broad bracelet was on the arm of the woman who caught the baby; the arms of the woman giving birth were bare and flawless.

The phrase "my mind swam" has always struck me as a cliché, but in the moment, I could feel my thoughts fin out in a dozen directions. Some things suddenly made sense: Tracy's reference to herself as the third rail in Evan's life on the night of the rehearsal dinner; the fact that she had shared a house with her dead sister's husband and family for seventeen years; her fury when she discovered that Evan and Jill were taking Bryn to New York City; the curiously symbiotic relationship Tracy shared with Claudia MacLeish.

But there were as many questions as answers. For me, the most pointed of them centred on Gabe Leventhal. When he had asked to see the ending of *Black Spikes*, he was searching for a piece that would complete an old puzzle. The realization that Tracy, not Annie, was Bryn's birth mother had been that missing piece. But where had he taken that knowledge? What had happened to him between the time he kissed me goodnight and the moment when the delivery truck drove over his already-dead body? Seemingly, like X in *Last Year at Marienbad*, I had wandered into a world in which there were "always walls, always corridors, always doors – and on the other side, still more walls." Like X, I had no idea how I was going to find my way out.

Watching Taylor and her friends dart in and out of stores, trading news of bargains, giggling over feathery hair clips and necklaces made of plastic flowers, helped combat what my grandmother called the "grabbers," the painful stomach knots that come with the onset of deep-seated fear. By the time we stopped for lunch, I wasn't in fighting trim, but I was up for an Orange Julius and a Nacho Dog. The girls were still savouring their food court options when, tray in hand, I started looking for a table. Space was at a premium, and when a table cleared, I swooped. So did Angus's old girlfriend, Leah Drache.

Her face lit up when she saw me; mine lit up too. Of all the girls my sons had dated, Leah had been my favourite.

"This is serendipitous," she said, placing her tray on the table. She shrugged off her pea jacket and pulled off her stripy knitted hat. "I've been trying to come up with a non-pathetic excuse to call your house."

"Since when did you need an excuse to call our house?"

Leah squeezed mayo onto her poutine. "Since Christmas Eve. I dropped something by for Angus. It was just a compilation tape I'd made for him. The songs weren't 'deeply significant.'" She made air quotes with her fingers. "Just stuff I knew he'd like."

"He didn't call to thank you?" I said.

"Nope, and that's not like him," Leah said. "I wondered if he was angry with me."

The little girls had found a table across the room. Taylor waved. I gave her the thumbs-up and turned back to Leah. "No, in fact, he's said a couple of things lately that made me think he's really missing you."

"Even with the drop-dead gorgeous new girlfriend?"

"Bryn's not his girlfriend," I said.

Leah raised an eyebrow. "That's not what she told me."

I took a sip of Orange Julius and winced.

"Brain freeze?" Leah said sympathetically.

"It'll pass," I said. "When did you meet Bryn?"

"Christmas Eve," Leah said. "I dropped by your house with the tape and asked to see Angus. She said he wasn't in, but she was his new girlfriend and she'd give him his package." Leah leaned towards me. "You're sure they're not a couple."

"Positive," I said.

Leah grinned broadly, then she pulled a paperback from the pocket of her jacket. "So I reread *Madame Bovary* for nothing. When you've been dumped, Flaubert is absolutely perfect. You need to know that one woman has suffered more for love than you have."

"Were you contemplating arsenic and a miserable death?" I asked.

"Not for me," Leah said. She hugged herself. "I am so relieved. I think Angus and I are really good together."

"I agree."

"Did you ever see *The Matrix*?"

"Actually, Angus made me watch it a couple of weeks ago."

"So he's still into it," Leah said. "A good sign, because *The Matrix* was *our* movie. We really connected with the part where the Oracle tells Neo that 'Being the One is like being in love. No one can tell you you're in love. You just know it, through and through, balls to bones.'"

I nodded.

Surprisingly, Leah coloured. "Maybe that's not the kind of thing a mother likes to hear about her son."

"You're wrong," I said, appropriating one of her mayon- naised fries. "That's exactly the kind of thing a mother likes to hear about her son."

I had lost count of the number of times I'd been to a perfor- mance of *The Nutcracker*, but that afternoon, as always, Herr Drosselmeyer's gift to Clara worked its magic. Watching three little girls in matching pastel butterfly shirts discover the lyrical power of ballet and Tchaikovsky soothed my soul. By the time the Sugar Plum Fairy and the Cavalier danced their final pas de deux, I was as rapt as the eight-year- olds beside me.

Julia and Erica's mother had invited Taylor for dinner and a sleepover. The sisters bolted out of the car and were almost into the house before they doubled back and hollered in unison, "Thanks for the neat afternoon." I was smiling as I turned the keys in the ignition and headed home.

Angus was out front drilling Willie in the intricacies of the "Down" command. "Guess who I saw today?" I said.

"A bunch of people in tights and tutus twirling," he said.

"All that, and Leah too," I said.

His face grew soft. "How's she doing?"

"Fine," I said. "But she was puzzled about something. She said she brought you a tape on Christmas Eve. She wondered whether you got it."

Angus scowled. "Taylor! That kid is such a space cadet."

"Leah didn't give the tape to Taylor."

"Who, then?" Recognition dawned. "Bryn," he said furiously. "What's the matter with her?"

"A lot," I said. "But she *is* trying to make some changes. Angus, do me a favour. Don't come down hard on her. Give her a chance to tell you about this herself."

"As long as she *does* tell me," Angus said. "Mum, nobody is doing Bryn any favours by letting her get away with stuff like this."

"I'll go in and introduce the subject diplomatically," I said.

"You're going to have to wait," Angus said. "Bryn and Jill went to the airport to say goodbye to her aunts."

"Later, then," I said. "Thanks for helping Willie with his homework."

Angus shrugged. "Claudia says if Willie does fifty downs a day, in a couple of weeks he'll be a new dog."

"When that happens I'll buy you both a T-bone," I said. "But right now, I'm going inside to get some tea."

I was drawn to Bryn's room like the proverbial moth to the flame. I prided myself on being scrupulous about respecting other people's privacy, but it wasn't difficult to spin out a rationalization for searching for the compilation tape. The day of the wedding, Bryn had stood before the mirror with her inscrutable bud of a smile. "I like to have things that belong to people," she had said. "Not just material things, secrets too." Her words made the unthinkable easy. I needed to find out what else Bryn had considered valuable enough to appropriate.

I checked the drawers in the dresser I'd cleared for her. I had to search carefully. Even Bryn's underthings were folded as meticulously as the stock in a well-run store. As in a well-run store, there was nothing in the drawers that didn't belong. Her suitcase was empty too. I was about to give up when I remembered that among the items Claudia had sent over from the hotel there had been a jaw-droppingly pricey red Hermes Birkin Bag.

I found it at the back of the closet behind some of my son Peter's camping gear.

The bag was heavy, and when I opened it, I realized it was stuffed with items that had struck Bryn's fancy. The compilation tape, still in its bright holiday wrapping, was on top. Beneath it was a manila envelope filled with Polaroid pictures of schoolgirls at a slumber party doing the kinds of things parents didn't want to know their daughters did at slumber parties. There was also a note card of heavy cream vellum with a handwritten note: *For Felix, who turned my bread into roses. C.* There were photos from Evan MacLeish's first two weddings. Linn Brokenshire had been a blissed-out bride with flowers in her hair, a young husband on her arm, and a New Testament close to her breast. Annie Lowell had been wary. Her vintage sleeveless dress and white mantilla were classic, but her expression was mournful, as if she knew that marriage would bring her more misery than joy. There was a roll of undeveloped film, which, after a split second of deliberation, I pocketed. There were a half-dozen pieces of antique jewellery, carefully wrapped in filmy hand-kerchiefs. Finally, there was a small three-ring binder.

One look inside and I knew this was Evan MacLeish's "Bible," the binder that contained the notes for his current works-in-progress. The information explaining tape reports, times, shot descriptions, size and movement, and best shot was neatly annotated on photocopied forms. At the bottom was a space for the director's notes. The alphabet soup of notations: *T, W, C, ZI, ZO, P,* and *F* meant nothing to me; neither did the title of the project to which at least more than half the sheets were devoted. *The Glass Coffin* had not been among the upcoming projects mentioned in the *New York Times* article Jill had e-mailed me, but it was an evocative title. As I closed Bryn's bag, I wondered which of the women in Evan MacLeish's life he had decided to immortalize as a princess waiting under glass to be awakened by a kiss.

I was in the front hall adding water to the tree stand when I heard a car pull up out front. I opened the door and saw Felix Schiff getting out of a red Intrepid.

"Nice wheels," I said.

Felix's face was grave. "Jill's been trying to locate you," he said.

"Here I am," I said. "What's up?"

"Tracy attempted suicide this afternoon," Felix said.

I was glad I had the door to lean on. "Is she going to be all right?"

"Tracy is always all right," he said. "They've taken her to the hospital. Jill's there. I'll drive you over."

"I'll get my purse."

On our way to the car, I stopped to praise Willie and tell Angus I wouldn't be long.

Felix was silent until we pulled onto the expressway that led to the hospital. "That stunt was typical of Tracy," he said furiously. "Narcissistic, melodramatic, and futile."

"Considering the circumstances, that seems harsh," I said.

"You might want to save some of that compassion for the people who have to clean up after her little venture."

"Felix, why don't you just tell me what happened?"

His voice was monotone. "Bryn and Jill went to the airport to see Claudia and Tracy off. Apparently the prospect of returning to the house on Walmer Road without Bryn was too much for Tracy, and she made some dramatic last-minute plea to the girl to go with her."

"And, of course, Bryn refused," I said.

"Why wouldn't she refuse? Tracy has never shown the slightest interest in her. At any rate, there was a scene. Finally, Tracy excused herself to go to the bathroom. When the boarding call came, and Tracy hadn't come out, Claudia went to get her. Tracy was in a stall slitting her wrists."

The image was so vivid the words seemed to form themselves. "Like her sister," I said.

Felix swallowed hard. "How did you know about that?"

"Bryn told me."

"And I suppose when she did, her lovely eyes filled with tears. That girl is a real piece of work." The loathing in his voice caught me off guard.

"Considering what her life has been . . ."

Felix cut in. "You don't know what her life has been," he said. "People have invested their lives in that child."

"Her father certainly did," I said. "Felix, was that film he was making about Bryn called *The Glass Coffin*?"

Felix's intake of breath was audible. His fingers tightened on the steering wheel. "I don't know what you're talking about," he said.

I knew he was lying. "No point talking about it then," I said.

"But I'd like to talk about it," he said, falsely casual. "It's an intriguing title – right out of a tale by the Brothers Grimm."

"It is an attention-grabber," I agreed.

"Where did you hear about it?" Felix asked.

"Actually, I read it. I found Evan's three-ring binder this afternoon – the one where he kept his shot lists and tape reports."

I watched Felix's face. Control was not coming easily. "Those notations are quite technical. Maybe I should have a look."

"I'm sure if Jill needs help, she'll let you know," I said.

"She has a lot on her mind," Felix said. "I could take care of this for her. Just tell me where the binder is."

"I can't," I said. "The truth is I just happened to come across Evan's notes. I'd feel like a rat telling you where they were without checking with the person who has them."

"Stalemate," Felix said.

"Apparently," I said.

When he dropped me at the main entrance of the hospital, he sped away before I even had a chance to say thanks for the ride.

The decorations in the lobby had a dispirited day-after-Christmas droop, so did the woman behind the reception desk where I checked for Tracy's room number. I rode up in the elevator with a young man drenched in Old Spice and a young woman drenched in White Diamonds. In the duel of the holiday colognes, Old Spice proved an easy winner. Tracy's room was in the new wing. I had found the nursing station and was asking directions when I heard Bryn's voice. "She's only allowed one visitor at a time. Claudia's with her now. You can wait with me if you want to."

Bryn led me to a bank of windows that overlooked the hospital's central courtyard. In the gentle seasons, the place was a green and blooming oasis, but on that raw, windy day it was desolate. Despite the bleakness, the weathered picnic benches were dotted with smokers. Most wore scrubs and winter jackets, but there were a few civilians. One of them was Jill.

"I hate that she smokes," Bryn said. "But I told her to go out and have a cigarette. This is all so awful."

"Do you want to talk about it?"

Bryn nodded. Her state seemed almost fugue-like and I wondered if she'd been given some sort of sedation. "It's my fault," she said numbly. "Tracy says she did it for me."

"Did what for you?"

Bryn shrugged. "Everything, I guess. When the ambulance came to get her at the airport, there was blood everywhere. Do you know what Tracy did?"

"No."

"She dipped her fingers in it and held them out to me. 'This is for you,' she said. 'Your blood for you.'"

My shudder was visceral, but Bryn picked up on it. "See, it freaks even you out. What chance do I have?"

"The only chance any of us have," I said. "You have to make yourself strong enough to handle whatever comes your way."

Bryn spoke without self-pity. "There's always so much."

"I know," I said. "But don't underestimate yourself."

Surprisingly, she smiled. "I've made it this far, haven't I?"

"No small accomplishment."

"And now the camera won't be there," Bryn said. She shrugged. "I guess that's what Tracy meant when she said she did it for me. I guess what she did was make sure that fucking camera would never be in my face again."

CHAPTER

11

Ken Dryden once said that the goalie's job is to know what's coming next and insert himself like a stick into the spokes of a bike and stop the action. When I saw Inspector Alex Kequahtooway get out of the elevator and head towards the psychiatric ward, I knew the time had come to be a stick in the spokes. Tracy had passed the point of meltdown. Alex wouldn't need his considerable skills as an interrogator to unearth the fact that Tracy was Bryn's birth mother. The seventeen-year-old girl beside me had already endured a lifetime of assaults. I didn't have the power to deflect the next blow coming her way, but I could defer it.

I turned to Bryn. "Let's go home," I said.

She looked puzzled. "What about Jill? She's still outside finishing her cigarette."

"We'll find her." I went over to the nursing station and left a message for Claudia. Then I punched the elevator button. When Bryn and I stepped out on the main floor, Jill was there.

"I was just coming up," she said.

"Change of plans," I said. I slid my hand under her elbow and steered her towards the door.

During the taxi ride, Bryn talked about how the smell of hospital in her hair and on her clothes was making her sick. As soon as we were through the door, she ran upstairs to shower and change.

After Bryn left, Jill slumped against the wall. "I can't remember ever feeling this tired," she said.

"In need of your java-enabler?" I said.

"Make it strong and keep it coming," Jill said.

I made a pot of Jill's favourite Kona, and we took it into the living room. The coffee seemed to restore her. After a few sips, she sat forward in her chair. "Okay," she said. "I'm fortified. Now tell me why we had to beat such a hasty retreat from the hospital."

My account of Tracy's true relationship with Bryn observed four of the five W's of journalism. I told Jill everything I knew about Who, What, When, and Where, but I didn't venture any guesses about why Bryn's family had hidden the truth from her after Annie died; nor did I speculate about why Gabe Leventhal had died within hours of discovering what I'd discovered.

Like any smart journalist, Jill was a good listener. When I finished my account, she asked, "Is there more?"

I shook my head. "Your turn now. Any questions?"

"Have we heard from that private detective in Toronto?"

"Not that I know of. I'll call Kevin and get him to stir things up a bit."

"Good." She leaned towards me. "Jo, we need to know what the police have found out."

I met her gaze. "Alex doesn't trust me any more. I've made it pretty clear I'm on the other side."

"Just do your best, okay?"

"Okay," I said. "More coffee?"

"Thanks, but I should talk to Bryn. No point in delaying the inevitable." Jill stood and smoothed her leather pants. "Jo, she has so few resources. How do I break this to her?"

"I don't know," I said. "Just take it slow, and see how she reacts. If she's having a hard time, stop and let her decide where to go next. Bryn trusts Dan Kasperski. I'll call him, so he'll be ready if you need him."

After Jill left, I dialled Dan's number and left a message on his machine. Then I sat back and waited for word of trouble upstairs. When there was none, I picked up the phone and called Kevin Hynd.

"Synchronicity," he said. "I was just about to call you."

"If you tell me you have news from the detective in Toronto, I'm going to believe God is Alive and Magic is Afoot."

Kevin chuckled. "He is, and It is. Our man, whose name is Richard Shanks, called tonight. He struck paydirt."

"So soon?"

"It's all in knowing where to dig," Kevin said. "Richard talked to the MacLeish housekeeper. She was a temporary, but she filled him in on her predecessor. The lady's name is Isobel Carruthers. She'd been with the MacLeish family for fifty years, but she was only too willing to talk."

"Fifty years of service and suddenly she's spilling the beans? What happened? Did they fire her?"

"Apparently, she left of her own volition when she heard that Evan was dead."

"She was that attached to him?"

"No. According to Richard, Mrs. Carruthers believes that whoever killed Evan did the world a favour."

"So what was her problem?"

"Moral outrage. Hang on to your toque, Joanne. Mrs. Carruthers told Richard she quit because she couldn't spend another night in a house that had nurtured a murderer."

"Did she name her suspect?"

"Nope, but she did give Richard some interesting nuggets to ponder. She said that Bryn's relationship with her father was unnatural."

"No surprise there."

"Then try this. According to Mrs. Carruthers, Bryn was not the innocent victim. In Mrs. C's words, it was 'tit for tat.'"

"Meaning what?"

"Meaning that Bryn threatened to withhold favours if she didn't get her way."

I felt a coldness in the pit of my stomach. "What kind of favours?"

"Not sexual. For lack of a better word – professional. Remember that bizarre thing Bryn did with the camera – speaking to it directly about what Evan was doing to her?"

"Yes."

"The housekeeper says Bryn used the camera to barter. She'd tell the camera what she wanted, and if Evan didn't come across, she'd screw up the film."

"And our pillar of rectitude, Mrs. Carruthers, did nothing."

"She didn't believe it was her place to interfere. She felt that was up to Bryn's flesh and blood."

"Who, as we know, did nothing."

"And that's the part I don't get," Kevin said. "I'm not exactly a cock-eyed optimist when it comes to my fellow beings, but you would have thought someone in that house would have stopped Evan."

"Maybe everyone just had too much to lose," I said. "Evan was Bryn's father. If someone confronted him, he could have simply taken her and moved away. Claudia devoted years of her life to that girl. She might have convinced herself that as long as she and Bryn were under the same roof, she could exercise some control."

"And Tracy just needed a roof over her head," Kevin said. "Incidentally, Mrs. Carruthers says that particular need has become more pressing. Tracy lost her job on that kids' show."

"No more Broken Wand Fairy?"

Kevin laughed softly. "Hey, losing her wand might not be the worst thing that ever happened to Tracy. Her 'Magictown' gig looked like a dead-ender to me. And they do say that freedom's just another word for nothing left to lose."

"So is 'desperation,'" I said. "Tracy tried to commit suicide this afternoon."

Kevin groaned. "Oh shit."

"My sentiments exactly," I said. "And it gets worse. Tracy is Bryn's birth mother."

"Whoa," Kevin said. "Now *that* is heavy."

"But it explains a lot," I said. "We saw how close the sisters were. I'm assuming Annie's epilepsy made pregnancy too much of a risk, and Tracy volunteered."

"Does Bryn know?"

"Jill's telling her as we speak. And Kevin, I'm certain Gabe Leventhal had put the pieces together the night he died."

"So Tracy had motives for killing both Gabe and Evan."

"For Gabe, yes, but I don't understand what she'd gain by killing Evan after he and Jill were married. The moment Evan slipped the ring on Jill's finger, she was Bryn's stepmother."

"Maybe the laws are different in 'Magictown,'" Kevin said. "Or maybe something about the wedding just ticked Tracy off. In my experience, the motivation for most murders is pretty mundane."

"I guess it doesn't much matter what was going on in Tracy's head," I said. "She had an alibi, remember?"

"Right," Kevin said. "She was with Claudia. Which, of course, means that Claudia also has an alibi."

"You think it's possible they're both lying."

"I think we'd be smart not to rule anything out," he said. "Mrs. Carruthers is no fan of Claudia's. I gather the Rottweilers may have something to do with her distaste, but, apparently, Mrs. Carruthers is of the opinion that an able-bodied woman like Claudia should be able to make her own way in the world and not sponge off her mother."

"I take it that's a direct quote."

"A close paraphrase," Kevin said. "Mrs. C did add one interesting stroke to our portrait of Claudia. Apparently, she'd been having some pretty ugly quarrels with the man in her life lately."

I thought of the heavy vellum card in Bryn's treasure trove of potentially useful memorabilia. "Any chance the boy-friend had a slight German accent?" I asked.

"Was there something going on between Claudia and Felix Schiff?"

"Enough that they had a shoving match in the hotel lobby the morning after Evan died."

"Never a dull moment," Kevin said. "If they're this rambunctious when they're on the road, they must be a real treat when they're back at the old homestead."

"Speaking of," I said. "Did you find out anything about Caroline MacLeish?"

"No, Mrs. Carruthers was very protective of the matriarch."

"And yet she quit when Caroline MacLeish needed her most," I said. "Doesn't that strike you as odd?"

"Face it," Kevin said. "They're an odd bunch. I'll tell Richard to keep digging – see what else the MacLeish clan has buried in the backyard."

I winced at the metaphor, but it did prod a question. "Kevin, do you know anyone here in town who could do some digging?"

"Sure. There's a woman here who's a whiz. What do you want her to look for?"

"Anything that will get us out of the maze."

Kevin laughed. "Hey, Shania's a whiz, not a miracle worker."

"Shania?"

"Shania Moon," Kevin said. "You'd be amazed at how many people can't resist opening up to a woman with a provocative name."

"See if Ms. Moon can get someone to open up about what went on at Gabe's hotel the night he died."

"You've got it," Kevin said.

It took me a few minutes to screw up the courage to call Alex's office. He picked up on the first ring.

"Kequahtooway."

"Alex, it's Joanne. I wondered if we could get together for a few minutes."

There was a pause. "Business or pleasure."

"Business," I said.

"I have a few things to finish up here. I'll meet you in half an hour at Brenners."

"Thanks," I said, but he'd already rung off.

Every failed love affair has its own subtext. It wasn't difficult for me to read volumes into the fact that Alex had chosen Brenners for our meeting. If the owner of Brenners had been an art lover, it would have been tempting to believe he had modelled his café after Edward Hopper's painting *Nighthawks*. But Marv Brenner's decision to illuminate his café with the harsh, unsparing voltage of a police interrogation room had nothing to do with giving the lonely and dispossessed a sanctuary in which to spend the small hours. Marv was famously misanthropic. The archives of the *Leader Post* were full of letters bearing his signature; the ones the paper chose to print revealed a man who believed the world was divided into four categories: pissants, punks, perverts, and people like Marv. The harsh lighting and floor-to-ceiling uncurtained windows were designed to protect people like Marv from the others. Not surprisingly, the pissants, punks, and perverts flocked to Brenners like moths to a porchlight. Everybody likes a clean, well-lit place.

I was five minutes early, so I found a booth by a window that looked onto Broad Street. I ordered coffee and waited for the silver Audi to appear. Alex was right on time. When he slid into the place across the table from me, I tried not to show that I was shaken by his appearance. His complexion was grey, and the skin under his eyes was pouched and dark. Without being summoned, the waitress brought him a coffee with two creams and a sugar. Obviously in the weeks since we'd broken up, Alex had become a Brenners regular.

He opened the cream containers and the sugar package and dumped everything into his cup. "How was Christmas?"

"I've had better," I said. "And yours?"

"I've had better too." He stirred his coffee. "You said this was about business, Jo. What's up?"

My plan was to be brisk, objective, and matter-of-fact. But seated across from this man with whom I had shared every possible intimacy for three years, the words tumbled out. "I'm scared," I said. "Scared and exhausted and confused. I've got a ton of information. I don't know what any of it means. I keep banging into walls and stumbling into dead ends."

Alex gave me the smallest of smiles. "Sounds like we're working the same case," he said.

"Then let's help each other. My concern is Jill. Yours is the truth. There's no conflict of interest here, Alex."

His gaze was assessing. "You're suggesting we share information."

"Not everything," I said quickly. "I know this is irregular, but I thought we could just ask each other a few questions. No obligation to answer unless we wanted to."

I could see him deciding. "So who gets to go first?" he asked.

"You can," I said.

"Okay," he said. "The Toronto police went to Evan MacLeish's office to see who he'd been in contact with before his death. The place had been picked clean. Do you know anything about that?"

"Yes."

"Are you going to fill me in?"

"No."

Alex shook his head. "Off to a great start. Do I get to go again?"

"Absolutely."

"Okay. Here's something current. We have two witnesses who were at the airport today when the EMT people picked up Tracy Lowell. Both our witnesses heard Tracy tell her niece, 'I did it for you.' Do you know what she was talking about?"

"I have a pretty good idea. For starters, Bryn is Tracy's daughter, not her niece. I'm surprised that didn't come out when you interviewed her at the hospital."

Alex blew on his coffee. "She wouldn't talk to us. Clammed up absolutely, but that is interesting – and significant. So you think Tracy was telling her daughter she killed for her."

"Obviously I can't be certain," I said. "But my instincts tell me Tracy didn't kill anybody. I think she was just making sure Bryn knew that she was the cause of her suicide attempt."

"Nice parting gift for your kid," Alex said. "Your turn now."

I took a breath. "How tight are people's alibis for the night of the rehearsal dinner."

"Not tight at all," Alex said. "And I have no problem giving you this information because if you can add anything to the equation, we might finally get a break on the Leventhal case."

"There's no doubt in your mind that Gabe was murdered," I said.

"None," Alex said. "Pathology is still waiting for some tests results, but they have enough to state that Mr. Leventhal did not die of natural causes."

"The night I identified the body, you said there was blood under Gabe's fingernails. Was it Evan MacLeish's?"

"I can't tell you that," Alex said. He leaned across the table and looked into my eyes. "Maybe this would go more smoothly if I suggested a line of questioning that would help us both. Jo, everyone is covering up for everyone else in this case. Claudia says she was with Tracy, except of course when she went out for a few minutes with Bryn, but luckily Felix happened along at just that moment, so he and Tracy were together. Then Felix went back to his room and Claudia spent an hour with him there. We have some corroborative evidence for that particular encounter. Felix and Claudia were making so much noise that the guest in the next room had to knock on their door and ask them to keep it down."

"They were quarrelling."

"Actually, the guest thought they were indulging in a little overly athletic lovemaking. When Felix answered the door, the guest was surprised to see that he was fully dressed." Alex rubbed his eyes. "Bryn, of course, was never alone – not for a second. After Claudia left, Tracy and Bryn spent some quality time together. It's seamless. The weird thing is, I don't think these people even understand why they've dropped into this mutual protection mode. But they've obviously had a lot of practice cooperating with one another, because we can't break their stories."

"So if I could supply an inconsistency, you'd have a wedge."

Alex wiped a small ring of coffee from the table. "Yes, and a wedge is exactly what we need if we're ever going to crack this open. There's another area where we could use a break. After he left the wedding, Jill's partner, Felix Schiff, apparently disappeared off the face of the earth for a period of at least sixteen hours."

"I saw Felix the morning after the wedding," I said. "He looked like hell. He told me he'd been doing the club scene."

"That's what he told us too," Alex said. "The problem is nobody remembers seeing him. Of course, nobody remembers *not* seeing him, but we're dealing with a population whose powers of observation grow dim when a cop walks into the room. Even Mr. Schiff claims to have zero recollection of what happened."

"Do you believe him?" I said.

"Not much you can do when a man says he had a blackout."

"It's so out of character," I said. "I worked with Felix on 'Canada Tonight' for four years. He was the executive producer in Toronto and I was just a political panellist out here, but we talked every week about stories. We weren't close, but I thought I knew him. He always called himself *ein prakiter Mensch* – a practical man."

"Not the kind of man to go out and get blind drunk after his business partner's wedding."

"No," I said. "Especially when that business partner is a friend."

Alex's cellphone rang. He half-turned from me, mumbled a few words, then looked at me apologetically. "I have to get back to work," he said.

I stood up. "I invited you. I'll pay."

"I'll get it next time," he said. He touched my arm. "Jo, I would like there to be a next time. For what it's worth, I never meant to hurt you."

"I know," I said. "That didn't make the hurt any less."

When I went to pay, Marv himself was at the cash register. He scratched his belly and gave me his best smile. "Come again," he said. "And sit in a window booth like you did tonight. I'm working on strategies to bring in a more genteel clientele." He scratched his belly again, then rasped confidentially, "You know, people like yourself and me."

Angus's car was parked halfway down the block from our house. The windows were fogged. I slowed, waited, and finally hit the horn. After a few too many beats, Angus rolled down the window. On the seat beside him, Leah was adjusting her clothing and smoothing her newly blonde choppy bob. When she recognized me, she waved. "Sorry, Mrs. Kilbourn. It's been a while since we were together. We're hungry puppies."

I smiled at her. "Enjoy the moment," I said.

"I am," she said.

Angus leaned out of the window. "So you're okay with this?"

"I'm great with this," I said. "But keep the action away from the house for a while. Bryn is going through some tough times."

"Do you think I'm a lowlife for bailing on her?" Angus asked.

"You're not bailing on her. Be her friend, and save the rest for Leah."

When she heard the door, Jill came downstairs. She moved slowly, as if even the act of putting one foot in front of the other demanded an act of will. Being bludgeoned by crises was taking its toll on us all.

We gravitated towards the kitchen and sat at the table. Outside, a squirrel cleaned out the bird feeder. "How did Bryn handle the news about Tracy?" I asked.

Jill hugged herself as if she were cold. "Pragmatically," she said. "She wanted to know if Tracy could stop us from moving to New York. I called Kevin. He says it's a dicey situation, but the best thing to do would be to sit down and talk it out, just the three of us – no lawyers, no outsiders to put steel in Tracy's spine. He also told me that since Tracy's lost her job on that kids' show, she'd probably be open to discussion of financial compensation. So I guess Bryn's for sale."

"Pay what you have to," I said. "And be generous about visitation rights. Give Tracy something to hang on to. Bryn doesn't need to go through life believing she destroyed another human being."

Jill looked away. "Do you ever have thoughts that are so ugly, they make you wonder what kind of human being you are?"

"Let me guess," I said. "You wish Tracy had finished the job before they found her today," I said.

"God forgive me, I do." Jill's voice caught. "Jo, I don't know how much more of this any of us can take."

"Then stop beating yourself up, and let's get it over with," I said. "I saw Alex tonight. The police are getting nowhere with this investigation. Alex feels that all their prime suspects are lying for one another."

"Because their own stories are shaky?"

"Exactly. The private detective in Toronto has opened some useful veins of information, but he needs to keep digging. Possibilities aren't enough. We need facts. Kevin's hiring someone local to find out what everybody here's been up to. Given his efficiency, I imagine Shania Moon is already on the job."

Jill rolled her eyes. "My fate is in the eyes of a woman named Shania Moon?"

"It is," I said. "And she's going to need all the help we can give her. Time for you do your homework. Alex tells me that the night Gabe died, Felix and Claudia spent an hour together in Felix's hotel room. Is it possible you were wrong about them – that there really is something going on there?"

"I guess anything's possible," Jill said. "They've known each other forever. Felix came here from Germany when he was twenty-five, and he linked up with the MacLeish family right away. Claudia would have been in her early twenties then. Something could have sparked." She frowned. "Logical, except I still don't believe it. From what I've seen, Claudia and Felix's relationship is more like one of those brother-sister rivalries where there's always a subterranean war going on."

"They know how to push each other's buttons," I said.

Jill looked thoughtful. "All four of them do – or did. Evan and Claudia might have been the only blood siblings in the group, but Tracy and Felix had the rivalry thing down pat too."

"Whose love was the prize?" I asked.

"What do you mean?" Jill said.

"It's been a while since I took Psych 100, but isn't sibling rivalry driven by the need for the parent's love?"

"If that's what they were after, they had a tough row to hoe with Carolyn. She doesn't give her love easily. She and Evan were alike in that."

"The night of your wedding rehearsal Evan told me his mother called him 'the snowman' because he was detached from humanity, unable to love."

Jill winced. "Poor Evan. Poor all of them. Imagine what it would be like to want your mother's love so much that even as an adult you couldn't leave her house."

"Do you think that's what kept them all there?" I said.

"I don't know," Jill said. "But it makes sense, doesn't it? Caroline has a crippling illness, yet by the simple device of withholding love she manages to keep everyone around her in her thrall."

"*Thrall* is a dramatic word."

"She's a dramatic woman," Jill shook herself. "What am I talking about? I'm making Caroline sound like a monster, and she's not. She's never been anything other than cordial to me. I'll have to admit, she isn't exactly warm. She didn't haul out Evan's baby pictures or ask me to call her Mum, but Evan and I were hardly starry-eyed youngsters."

"What *were* you?" I asked.

Jill arched an eyebrow. "We were adults making a deal," she said. "Not an answer to inspire a love song, but the truth. I was a good career move for Evan. His films are brilliant, but they're indies – no matter how provocative and smart they were, the number of people who would see them would be numbered in the thousands. The deal Felix and I were putting together with the network would have given Evan access to an audience of millions. That was what he wanted. He didn't need money. He didn't need love. He needed people to see his movies."

"And what did you need?" I asked.

Jill didn't hesitate. "Bryn," she said. "From the moment I met her, I knew I could make a difference in her life. At the beginning, I guess I saw our relationship pretty much in Movie of the Week terms: the lonely woman of a certain age rescues the damaged girl, and they both learn to trust and love." Jill smiled ruefully. "I am now well aware that Bryn's problems aren't going to be solved in ninety minutes, but as far as I'm concerned that's just all the more reason to stick around."

"I'm glad you're realistic about her," I said.

Jill's eyes were searching. "Is there something else I should know?"

I took a deep breath. "I found Evan's binder."

"Where was it?"

"In Bryn's Birkin Bag."

Jill tensed. "Why were you going through her things?"

"Angus's old girlfriend gave Bryn a gift to pass along to Angus. He never got it. Bryn hid it in her bag and stuffed the bag under some camping equipment in the back of the closet."

Jill was clearly shaken. "Why would she do that?"

"I don't know," I said. "But for the moment, let's just deal with the fact that I found the binder. I only had a chance to give it a quick glance, but almost all the notes refer to a project called *The Glass Coffin*."

Jill looked genuinely baffled. "I've never heard of it, but Felix must have suggested the title. He grew up in a town called Marburg – same place that spawned the Brothers Grimm. They were as obsessed by the beautiful Saint Elisabeth in her glass coffin as Felix was."

"And who is the beautiful Saint Elisabeth?" I asked.

Jill rolled her eyes. "The Church may have seared my soul, but at least it gave me a good education. St. Elisabeth of Thuringia was the princess who married her prince at fourteen, died at twenty-four, and spent her short happy life giving alms to the wretched."

"Will there be a quiz on this?"

"Maybe on Judgement Day. Think how grateful you'll be to me then."

"I'm already grateful," I said. "You and I may have had our problems, but at least we didn't have to find our prince by the time we were fourteen."

"True," Jill said. "But we also missed out on the age of miracles. I doubt if either of us will ever have the bread we're carrying to the poor transformed into roses."

I felt a rush. "Now that's *interesting*," I said. "There was a note in Bryn's bag. It said, 'For Felix, who turned my bread into roses.'"

"Who was it from?"

"Someone who signed herself C."

"Claudia?" Jill said.

"Perhaps," I said. "But there is another possibility."

"Caroline," Jill said. "The woman who's spent the past forty years in her own glass coffin. Evan never mentioned that he'd been filming his mother. But if his shot book was filled with notes about *The Glass Coffin*, that has to be the piece he submitted to the network."

"And he submitted it without telling you and Felix. More secrets."

Jill frowned. "I wonder why Evan couldn't let us see it?"

"Maybe because there's something in it you and Felix wouldn't like," I said. "Only one way to find out for sure," I said. I checked my watch. "Why don't I give Dan a call? If he's still up, we could have a private showing of *The Glass Coffin*."

"Best offer I've had all day," Jill said. "Let's go."

CHAPTER

12

As it always did, Bryn's entrance changed the energy in the room. Whatever plans Jill and I had for checking out *The Glass Coffin* receded into the background as Jill helped her stepdaughter off with her coat.

"You look a little pale for someone who just had a walk," Jill said, touching Bryn's cheek.

"I changed my mind about the walk," Bryn said. She stepped in front of the hall mirror, removed her red cashmere beret, and smoothed her hair.

Jill tried a laugh. "At the risk of sounding like a mother hen, where were you?"

"Taking care of business," Bryn said. She frowned at her reflection, leaned forwards, and removed a speck of mascara from the corner of her eye. "We don't have to worry about Tracy any more," she said. "She's out of the picture."

Jill hung up Bryn's coat. "Care to explain?" she asked.

"There's nothing to explain," Bryn said. "Dan says I should start taking responsibility for my own life. Tracy was a problem, and I took care of her. I'm supposed to keep a journal too, and I found the perfect one in the gift shop at the hospital." She opened her purse and removed a notebook splattered with Van Gogh sunflowers. Bryn grazed Jill's cheek with her lips. "Okay if I get into bed and start writing?"

"Absolutely," Jill said, but after Bryn left, she looked bemused. "I seem to have become redundant," she said.

"No more redundant than the parent of any other seventeen-year-old," I said. I peered more closely at her. "Bryn isn't the only one who looks a little pale," I said. "Why don't we make an early night of it too? The movie will still be there tomorrow, and you can have first dibs on the stack of books I got for Christmas."

"All right," Jill said, "but I get the one with the biggest print and the prettiest pictures."

I was soldiering through the pivotal chapter of a novel about coming of age in London, Ontario, when the doorbell rang. I kept reading, hoping that someone else would get the door. No one did. Guessing the identity of the person pressing the button wasn't a stretch. As I pulled on my slippers, I cursed young love and a son so addled by passion that he'd forgotten his keys. But when I opened the door I wasn't faced with a post-tumescent Angus. My caller was Claudia, and she was steaming mad.

She didn't wait to be invited in. "Where's Jill?"

"In bed," I said.

"Get her down here," Claudia said, and her tone made me understand why she could make Willie quake.

"She's sleeping," I said.

"That's more than any of the rest of us will do tonight. Wake her up." Claudia pulled off her boots, threw her coat on top of them, and strode into the living room. Willie, recognizing his mentor, lumbered in and sidled up. When I went to get Jill, she was already at the top of the stairs.

"You've been summoned," I said.

Jill drew her robe around her and tied it. "What's going on?"

"You'll have to ask Claudia," I said.

Claudia didn't wait to be asked. The moment she spied Jill, she attacked. "We kept the facts about Bryn's birth secret for all these years," she sputtered. "What in God's name made you think you could just spring it on her today?"

"I thought she was old enough to handle the truth," Jill said gently.

"Do you know what she did with 'the truth'?" Claudia asked. "She came down to the hospital tonight and told Tracy and me she was starting a new life and there was no place for us in it. You can imagine what that attack did to Tracy. She was so distraught she had to be sedated."

Jill was coldly furious. "Poor Tracy – having to be sedated. What about all the days and nights when Bryn was distraught? Where was your compassion then, Claudia? More to the point, where were you and your sister-in-law?"

"You don't know anything about us," Claudia said. "You breeze in with my brother, have tea with my mother, smile at the rest of us, remove the lynchpin from our lives, waltz out the door, and leave us to cope. You're the one who's going to have to cope now, Jill. That daughter of whom you are *so very proud* has some secrets of her own. Nasty secrets."

"Bryn doesn't have any secrets from me."

"Really," Claudia said. "So you know that just minutes before Evan died, his daughter told him she wished someone would kill him."

Jill's face was bloodless. "No," she breathed.

"There's more," Claudia said. "After Bryn expressed her heart's desire, she picked up that hunting knife of yours and said how good it felt in her hand, how *powerful* it made her feel."

"You're lying," Jill said.

"Other people heard her. Tracy and Felix were there – so was Evan. That's what made him walk out into the snow-storm. He was trying to protect your future as a family. He knew Bryn was hysterical. It wasn't the first time she'd been like that, but he wanted her to have a chance – we all wanted that." Claudia rubbed her temples with her fingertips as if to erase the memory. "It was probably the single unselfish thing my brother ever did and look what it got him."

I could see Jill was badly shaken, but she was fighting for control. "Let's stick to the facts," she said. "There was a scene between Bryn and Evan. Adolescent girls fight with their fathers – that's a fact. And Bryn had more reason than most to be angry with her father. That's another fact. Everything beyond that is speculation. And Claudia, I've learned not to deal in speculation."

"Really," Claudia said. "Then why did you go racing out towards the maze the second I told you Bryn had taken off? Why was there blood all over that cloak of my mother's? And why was the handle of the knife that killed Evan wiped clean? You were doing a little speculating yourself, weren't you, Jill? And you came to exactly the same conclusion I did. You thought Bryn killed Evan, and you were covering her tracks exactly the way the rest of us were."

For an agonizing moment, the two women eyed each other.

When, finally, Jill broke the silence, her voice was a whisper. "What are you going to do?"

The simple question seemed to extinguish Claudia's fire. Her response was as tentative as Jill's. "I was planning to go to the police, but now . . ."

"But now you realize that would be totally destructive." Jill clasped the other woman's hands in her own, pressing her advantage. "Claudia, your duty is the same as it's always been – to put Bryn first. Evan's dead – nothing will change that. But the police don't have anything. If we all stick to our stories, they never will. I'm begging you. Let's salvage what we can. Help me save Bryn."

In all the years I had known her, I'd never seen Jill abase herself. The sight was wrenching, and I turned away, hoping that the worst was over. It wasn't.

"I can talk to her," Jill said, "convince her that the best thing for all of us is to continue to be part of your family. She has her heart set on New York, but there are weekends and holidays. We could get a place near you in Toronto. You and Tracy and Caroline could be there for Bryn – always."

"Will you get me my own two-wheeler too?"

"I don't understand," Jill said.

Claudia looked at her with pity. "That was a joke," she said. "My way of saying I'll do what you want."

Jill's relief was palpable. "You won't regret it."

As Claudia put on her coat and boots, I was frozen, stunned by the enormity of the devil's bargain I had witnessed. But when she put her hand on the doorknob, I moved. "Do you have a cell number?"

"Doesn't everybody?" Claudia asked.

I handed her a pen and paper and she wrote out her name and number. I checked her signature, satisfied myself that it didn't match the handwriting on the note, and bid her good night.

When the door closed behind Claudia, Jill sank onto the cobbler's bench in the hall. "Don't start on me, Jo," she said.

"I wouldn't know where to begin," I said. "And there's nothing I can tell you that you don't already know. Jill, if Bryn really is involved in Evan's death, you can't cover it up. Kevin's a good lawyer. He'll be able to talk to the Crown about what Evan did to his daughter . . ."

Jill put her hands over her ears, like a child shutting out the world. "I don't know what happened between Bryn and Evan. I don't want to know. I just want her to have a life. I want *us* to have a life. Is that too much to ask?" When Jill raised her face to me, the misery in her eyes killed the answer in my throat.

"We can talk in the morning," I said.

She nodded. "I'll phone Kevin and tell him to call off his investigators."

"Why not let them keep working?" I said. "They might find evidence that implicates someone else."

"And they might not," Jill said. "You know the old axiom: a smart lawyer never asks a witness a question to which she doesn't already have the answer. I don't have any answers, so I can't afford to have people running around asking questions."

"What happened to 'And the truth shall set you free'?"

Jill met my gaze. "Will you ever be able to respect me again?"

I put my arms around her – in part because I wanted to reassure her, but also because I didn't know what to say.

The next morning when I came back from taking Willie for his run, there was a note on my plate telling me that Bryn had insisted on keeping her appointment with Dan, and Jill and she had gone to his office in a cab. Clearly, Jill was no more eager than I was for a face-to-face, and I was grateful she had spared us both an encounter that would have been beyond awkward.

I had no idea when Kevin Hynd started his business day, but I was in no mood to wait. I was also in no mood to roll over and play dead while a friend made decisions that could land her in jail. When he answered his phone, Kevin sounded foggy, but my précis of the night's events galvanized him. "We need to talk, Joanne," he said. "I'll put on the coffee pot."

My pulse quickened as I spied Further's multi-coloured, Day-Glo, spray-painted exterior. Like Ken Kesey, the owner of the iconic, iridescent bus from which Kevin's business took its name, I was going into uncharted territory, but Kesey had a garden of pharmaceutical delights to ease his passage, and I was going in straight.

Kevin opened the door immediately. "I saw your car pull up," he said. "Welcome." Mellow in blue jeans and a mohair sweater the colour of a frozen grape, he helped me off with my coat and ushered me into his kitchen.

He handed me a mug of coffee and a plate filled with still-warm biscotti. "Comfort for the body *and* the soul," I said. "I'm a lucky woman."

"We at Further aim to please." He pulled up a chair opposite me. "Your timing couldn't have been better, Joanne. Shania called just after you did. She's on her way over."

"News?"

"Apparently," he said. "But it can wait. Let's enjoy the moment."

The coffee had a chicory bite that conjured up New Orleans and the biscotti were dotted with pistachio nuts and cranberries that made them simultaneously savoury and sweet. Giving myself over to sensual pleasures was easy, but as I reached for a second biscotti, I knew it was time to fill Kevin in. I omitted telling him about Jill's decision to call a halt to the investigations, but even without that information, Kevin was uneasy.

"Her mind is clouded by fear and love," he said. "She's making bad choices."

"My thinking exactly," I said. "So what do we do?"

Kevin shrugged. "Stay the course," he said. "See what Shania comes up with, and keep hoping that neither of us has to remind Jill that mother love is not a justification for condoning murder."

The Shania of my imagining was a woman with big hair, a midriff she was proud to bare, and three navel piercings. The Shania who walked into Kevin's shop had a small, plug-shaped body, a round, flat face, almond eyes, coppery-red hair that was smartly buzzed, and skin the colour of strong tea. She was dressed in layers that she proceeded to strip away: first a pea jacket with wooden toggles, next a heavy satin jacket with a mandarin collar and frog fastenings, then a turquoise silk shirt covered in birds of paradise. When she came to a simple cotton T-shirt with a picture of Jim Morrison, she stopped.

Kevin introduced us, offered her refreshments, and smiled. "Whenever you're ready, Shania."

"I'm always ready." She turned to me and said, "A word about my methods. I have a good brain, and I use it. Kevin has given me photos of the principals and accounts that are as detailed as he can make them. If he was aware of the actual words used by one of the principals, he attempted to relay them accurately. The value of a true verbatim account is beyond rubies, but even close is good. After Kevin and I talked, I went home to contemplate." Her face was split by a slow moon-like smile. "I must thank you, Kevin, for that exquisite box of Thai sticks."

Kevin touched his forehead in a small salute. "I knew you'd appreciate them."

"Oh I did," she said. "And they speeded an epiphany. As I sat in my room, smoking and mulling, one sentence nagged. You reported that Inspector Kequahtooway told Joanne that

Felix Schiff seemed to 'disappear off the face of the earth for sixteen hours.' That action didn't jibe with Joanne's description of Mr. Schiff as a 'go-to-guy.' What, I asked myself, would make a man known as the one to be counted on in a pinch vanish when his friend's need for him was so great?"

"Because his friend asked him to," I said.

Shania nodded. "Of course, that raised another question. What had Mr. Schiff been asked to do during those hours? Here two figures of speech fused in my mind: Inspector Kequahtooway's image of Mr. Schiff 'disappearing off the face of the earth' and the image you used, Kevin, when you paraphrased the inspector's remarks. You told me that Felix Schiff had 'vanished into thin air'?" Shania gazed first at Kevin, then at me. "Are you following my train of thought?" she asked.

The penny dropped. "Felix flew somewhere that night," I said.

Shania nodded approval. "Precisely. I took Mr. Schiff's photo out to the airport and showed it to someone who's been known to share information with Kevin and me. After a little detective work of his own, our contact discovered Felix Schiff had flown to Toronto on the early-evening flight and returned the next morning."

I remembered Felix's appearance when he'd come into the hotel the morning after Evan was murdered. He looked like hell, but it wasn't because he'd been cruising the club scene. He'd travelled three thousand miles in those hours, but except for the time he'd been seated on airplanes, his whereabouts was unaccounted for. "What was he doing in Toronto?" I said.

"That's still to be determined," Shania said. "But as a rule these quick flying trips indicate the need to cover something up or recover something. Kevin, I think your client should give Richard Shanks the go-ahead to hire more people to find out exactly what Felix Schiff was up to that night."

Kevin shot me a look.

"Just tell Richard Shanks to do what he has to do," I said. "If the bills for the detectives get out of line, I'll cash in my pop bottles. And let's make sure the former housekeeper gets special attention." I looked at Kevin. "Does Shania know about the cooperative Mrs. Carruthers?"

Shania answered for him. "I do," she said. "Did Mrs. Carruthers's sudden departure from the household where she's worked for fifty years raise a question in your mind, Joanne?"

"It did," I said. "And there's something else. From all accounts, Caroline MacLeish is incapable of living in that house alone. If Mrs. Carruthers has really moved on to greener pastures, why hasn't Caroline called and asked her daughter to come home?"

Kevin arched an eyebrow. "Are you suggesting that if I were to phone the MacLeish household at this very moment, the mysterious Mrs. Carruthers might answer the phone?"

"My guess is she wouldn't be far away," I said.

Kevin pulled an address book from his pocket, consulted it, then picked up his cell.

The speech he gave to the person who answered the phone in Toronto revealed that, as a prankster, Kevin was canny as well as merry. "This is Jim Morrison," he said.

Shania beamed and glanced fondly at the image on her T-shirt.

"I'm with CHJO Radio," he continued. "We're doing a story on Evan MacLeish. The word out here is that MacLeish's mother is some kind of nutcase. Would anybody at that address be willing to talk to us about her on air?"

I could hear the sputter of outraged denial from where I sat.

"And your name, ma'am."

Kevin listened, then touched his index finger to his thumb in the circle that indicates success. "Thank you, Mrs. Carruthers, we here at CHJO pride ourselves on our accuracy." Kevin hung up and shook his head. "It appears Mrs. C didn't leave her post after all," he said. "We've been had."

Shania rubbed her buzz thoughtfully. "Sometimes 'being had' is instructive. Obviously Mrs. Carruthers didn't come up with the idea for this wild goose chase on her own. She was acting on someone's instructions."

"Whose?" Kevin asked.

"Someone who was willing to throw every member of that household except Caroline to the wolves," I said.

"Or someone who wanted to make it appear that way," Shania said.

"'Always walls, always corridors, always doors – and on the other side, still more walls,'" I said.

Kevin leaned back in his chair and closed his eyes. "*Last Year at Marienbad*," he said. "A truly strange adventure in cinema."

"It was indeed," I agreed. "And I'd like to stay and talk about it, but I have my own adventure in cinema waiting. Do you two need me here?"

"We *like* having you here," Kevin said. "But need is another matter."

"We're cool," Shania said. "We're just going to discuss logistics and personnel. What movie caught your interest?"

"Another film by Evan MacLeish," I said. "All I know is the title. It's called *The Glass Coffin*."

"Evocative," Kevin said. He picked up a biscotti, wrapped it in a paper napkin, and handed it to me. "One for the road," he said. "And don't forget to call me with your movie review."

I drove around Dan's neighbourhood until I was certain Bryn's appointment was over. At this point, my relationship with Jill was too precariously poised to risk confrontation. When my watch indicated that it was five minutes to the hour, I thought I was safe.

Dan was in his backyard scooping sunflower seeds into one of his bird feeders. He acknowledged my presence with a wave of his scoop and kept filling the feeder with seeds. "The house finches love these," he said. "They've just started coming to Saskatchewan, so I want to make them welcome."

"They're lucky they have such a thoughtful provider," I said.

"Works both ways," Dan said. "As soon as the angle of the sun is right, the finches begin to sing. They have the most glorious song, and they begin so early – late February or early March. To hear them when there's still snow on the ground is like a promise from spring."

Dan closed the bag of seeds and faced me. "You have to talk to Jill," he said.

"The session went badly?"

"The session didn't go at all," he said. "Jill refused to leave Bryn alone with me. I don't get it. The whole idea was to give Bryn someone she could open up to, but today it was as if Jill was afraid to let Bryn say anything. Understandably, Bryn was upset at Jill's interference. She'd brought along this journal she'd started, and she was anxious to talk about what she'd written."

"But Jill wouldn't let her?"

"No," he said. "I suggested Jill come into the house to resolve the problem, and as soon as we were alone, she fired me."

"I don't know what to say, Dan – except to apologize. You've gone out of your way to help us." I looked at him carefully. "You are aware that this is no reflection on you."

Dan nodded. "My ego will survive," he said. "It's Bryn I'm concerned about."

"I'm concerned about everybody and everything," I said. "And I haven't a clue about what, if anything, I should do next."

"Do you want to talk about it? I still have a couple more minutes before my next appointment."

"Okay, I guess I should start by saying that Jill would not be happy to see me here."

"She doesn't want you talking to me?"

"She doesn't want anybody talking about Bryn – she wants Kevin to shut down his investigation; she wants you to stop Bryn's therapy; and she's offered Claudia and Tracy pretty much whatever they want if they'll agree to keep spinning stories that will protect Bryn."

"From what?" Dan asked. "The biggest threat to Bryn is herself."

"Jill doesn't see it that way. She thinks that if people start delving too deeply into Evan MacLeish's murder, they might find something that will connect Bryn to it."

"Does Jill really believe Bryn killed her father?" Dan's words formed little clouds in the frigid air.

"I think she doesn't want to risk knowing the truth," I said.

"And she's prepared to build a life on not knowing." Dan said. "That surprises me. Jill struck me as someone who would want to know everything."

"As a rule she does, but she's also a human being, and as you once told me, that means being 'fallible, fucked up, and full of frailty.'"

Dan grinned. "The world according to Albert Ellis," he said.

"There are worse teachers," I said.

"Yeah," Dan agreed. "There are."

A teenaged boy in an army surplus winter jacket came around the corner. "Hey, Dan," he shouted. "Notice that I'm right on time for once."

Dan gave the boy the high sign. "I'm impressed," he said. "Let's get rolling." Dan turned back to me. "I'll keep eight tomorrow open for Bryn. Bring her yourself if you have to."

"I'll do my best," I said. "Dan, I'd like to go inside and check out some of the films that came from Evan's office. I shouldn't be long."

"Stay as long as you like," he said. "You won't be in my way. I have back-to-back appointments all morning."

Even the warmth of Dan's welcoming home couldn't dispel the chill I felt when I contemplated Jill's future. The night of the rehearsal dinner, as Jill stood between Angus's torches, swathed in the soft folds of her timeless velvet cloak, it seemed she had finally gotten it right. In that incandescent moment, everything seemed possible for her. Now it was clear that no matter what Jill did, her story wouldn't end with "happily ever after."

As I came into the living room, I was overwhelmed with despair. For days, I'd been fuelled by adrenaline, responding to the unimaginable, reacting, deciding, hoping against hope. Now the heart had gone out of me. I was sick of tragedy and death. In the words of the old Spirit of the West song, all I wanted was to turn my head and walk, walk away.

But if the last days had taught me anything it was that, wherever I walked, trouble would follow.

I sank to my knees and began hunting through one of the boxes of tapes that had been sent from Evan's office in Toronto. My search was perfunctory, but *The Glass Coffin* wasn't hard to spot. The other tapes were obviously works-in-progress with titles and dates hand-printed on their spines. *The Glass Coffin* was in a paper sleeve with the name and address of a film and video processing company printed on the box and a computerized label describing the box's contents: *The Unblinking Eye: The Glass Coffin, Seamless*

*Master, Length: 44.58 minutes. (Textless @ Tail), Ch1&2:
Stereo Mix.* There were other notations, too cryptic for
me, but I knew at once I'd found the tape Evan had sold to
the network.

I put it in the machine and pressed *play*. In seconds, the
room was filled with the hauntingly elegiac "Pavanne for a
Dead Princess" by Maurice Ravel. On screen, the ruffled
deep-mauve petals of a perfect rose bloomed slowly in the
soft morning light. A woman began to speak. "Even their
names are beautiful," she said. "Shropshire Lad, Abellard,
Cajun Dancer, Gabriel's Fire, Dakota, Black Magic, Callisto,
Natasha Monet, Flamingo, Cachet, Cadenza, Hand in Hand,
Lasting Peace." The camera pulled back, revealing as it
moved a fairy-tale profusion of roses in the extravagantly
gorgeous hues of early summer: deep rose, soft pink, apricot,
lemon, pale peach, cream, burgundy, magenta. As the distance between the camera and the roses increased, the
vibrant life of the garden ebbed, making the petals seem less
a product of nature than of an artist's broken brushwork.

The woman's seductive contralto continued. "It's been
forty years since I felt the sun like a hand on my back as I
bent to the earth; forty years since I knew that numinous
moment when the scent of growing roses perfumes the air.
For forty years, I've watched the world from behind a wall
of glass."

When the camera moved to the woman's face, I was
struck by how young Caroline MacLeish appeared to be.
Evan's lighting of his mother had been benevolent, but
Caroline's agelessness went beyond a filmmaker's trick. Like
the cloistered nuns of my childhood, Caroline had been sheltered from the harsh rays of the world's scrutiny, and, like
them, her complexion retained the faint pearl-like aura of
youth when chronological youth was just a memory.

There were no flashbacks to still photographs of Caroline

as she had been before the postpartum incident that circum-
scribed her life. Evan's interest was clearly less in what had
shaped Caroline than in how Caroline had shaped her world.
The first minutes of the movie followed Caroline through the
small ceremonies of her day: her hour in bed with Indian tea
and the newspapers; her careful coordination of her makeup,
clothing, and accessories; her diligent study of current
medical journals and the Internet for the latest information
about her illness; her supervision of the plantings and prun-
ings in her rose garden. It was impossible not to pity this
woman who hadn't felt the wind on her face or been touched
by a raindrop for four decades. But as Evan enlarged his focus
to include the secondary players in Caroline's drama, sympathy turned to revulsion. One by one, the members of
Caroline's inner circle – Evan, Claudia, Tracy, Bryn – made
their entrances. All approached Caroline with the pitiful
eagerness of beggars seeking alms; all left with nothing more
than scraps of her attention. No matter how often they were
ignored or rejected, they kept coming back – arms out-
stretched, eyes wary but hopeful. Evan's portrait of the power
of the clinical narcissist was devastating. It also raised some
provocative questions about the filmmaker and his subject.
Had Evan been aware of what his film revealed about
Caroline or had years of living with her blinded him to the
truth? And what about Caroline? What had she seen when
she looked at footage of *The Glass Coffin*? A dutiful son's
tribute to his mother or betrayal? One thing was certain. The
film proved that Jill had been wrong about her mother-in-law
– Caroline MacLeish *was* a monster.

When I heard the outside door open, I was so certain it
was Dan, I didn't even turn my glance from the screen. "You
have to see this," I said. "Not just because it will give you
insight into Bryn, but because you could build your career
on this woman."

On screen, Caroline was commiserating with Tracy. "Sometimes the wisest thing is simply to accept the fact that the best part of your life is over. Why fight the truth?

"Acting is for the young, and you're no longer young. From now on, the spotlight will always be on someone else." Caroline placed a finger under Tracy's chin so she could tilt the younger woman's face towards her own. "Let's not have any more talk about you starting a new life," she said in her warm voice. "You have a life, Tracy – here in this house, with us."

"So you found *The Glass Coffin*." Felix Schiff's voice was a shock, but not an unpleasant one.

I glanced over at him. He was still dressed for outdoors. "Take off your jacket and boots and come sit by me," I said. "I could use some company. How did you know where I was?"

"I didn't," he said. "I was looking for Jill. Your son thought she'd brought Bryn over here."

"They left," I said. "They're probably back at my house by now."

Felix removed his coat and boots and threw them in the corner of the living room – it was an uncharacteristically thoughtless move, but given the fact that his eyes hadn't once left the TV screen, an understandable one. "I don't need to see Jill any more," he said. "I found what I was looking for."

"*The Glass Coffin*," I said. "I don't think there's any doubt now that this was the film Evan sold NBC as the pilot."

I handed him the box the tape had come in.

"He's a Judas," Felix spit the epithet. "What kind of man would betray his mother for a handful of silver and a moment of fame?"

"No one betrayed Caroline MacLeish." I pointed at the television screen. "Look at her. She knew she was being filmed."

"Of course she knew she was being filmed," Felix shouted. "But that movie was never intended to be a commercial property. That film was supposed to be a research tool. It was Caroline's gift to the world."

"I don't understand," I said.

"Don't blame yourself," he said. "True altruism is rare. You can be forgiven for not recognizing it. Allowing herself to be the subject of a film was excruciating for Caroline. She's an intensely private person, but she knew the medical community needed to be shown the limitations of its thinking." Felix threw the empty film box on the table in front of us. "Caroline said psychiatry was still a primitive discipline – in its infancy."

"And *The Glass Coffin* was supposed to add to the body of knowledge," I said.

"Exactly. Caroline wanted the doctors who had presented themselves as her saviours to see that she could triumph without them."

On screen Caroline was staring into the camera. Her eyes were startling – the blue of forget-me-nots. "I used to believe that John Milton was right," she said. "That 'the mind is its own place, and in itself/can make a heav'n of hell, a hell of heav'n.' For years I blamed myself for what my life had become. I convinced myself that I had taken heav'n and turned it to hell. The moment I realized that my mind was more complex than anything a seventeenth-century man could have imagined, I was freed – if not into a fully realized life, at least into a life. The mind may be 'its own place,' but the superior mind can make accommodations – ensure that it has what it needs to feed it, to keep it from being conquered."

My stomach clenched. This was beyond hubris; this was insanity.

Felix gripped my hand with excitement. "There," he said. "Now you can see it. Fate wounded Caroline, but she used her intelligence and spirit to heal herself. She's incomparable."

I was dumbfounded. "You're in love with her," I said.

"I've loved her for twenty-five years. We plan to marry, but we have to wait."

"For what?" I said.

"For her family to accept us. The health of the household on Walmer Road means everything to Caroline. She was afraid our marriage would introduce an element of instability that would disturb the balance."

It was an effort to keep my jaw from dropping. "The balance," I repeated.

Felix's eyes were glazed, and there was a sheen of sweat on his upper lip. "Caroline knew how much every member of that household relied on her. Everything she said or did had to be exquisitely calibrated to maintain the equilibrium." There had always been a certain boyish athleticism about Felix, but as he leaned forward to stare at the screen he was a shell, like a building that had been gutted by fire. "Are you beginning to understand now, Joanne?" he asked softly. "We wanted nothing more than to be together, but she was prepared to sacrifice her happiness for her family's sake. And I had to sacrifice too."

"What have you sacrificed, Felix?" I asked.

He looked at me from unseeing eyes. "Self-respect, friendship, honour." He drew his hands together as if in prayer. "And now comes the final sacrifice. She said it might come to this. That's why she gave me the gun."

Felix took the remote control from my hand and pressed *pause*. On screen, Caroline was frozen in the pool of deep gold light cast by the antique lamp behind her chair. Out of nowhere came a memory of a paperweight from my childhood: a chunk of amber that preserved a lifeless but still perfect wasp.

Suddenly, I was numb with fear. "What are you going to do?" I said.

When Felix pulled out his cellphone, I almost laughed with relief. The cell as a lifeline to the real world was a cliché of the film industry. But as Felix tapped in a number and waited for an answer, he was not a comic figure. He was as tightly wound as a man calling to hear medical test results that he knew would spell his doom.

As he listened to the voice on the other end of the line, it seemed the screws were tightening.

"It's over," he said. "People have seen the film. The network is committed to showing it. There's nothing more I can do. Not about *The Glass Coffin* – not about anything. I have the sense that I'm being followed. That can mean only one thing. The police know it was me." As he listened to the response to his words, Felix hung his head, a schoolboy being chastised. "You have nothing to fear," he said finally. "There's no way they can connect you to any of this. They could rip the tongue out of my mouth before I'd tell them anything." He fell silent again, taking in every word. Then for the first time since he walked into the room, the weight seemed to have been lifted from his shoulders. "Yes," he said. "I have it with me. You promise it will be that way? That's more than I could have hoped. A double exit – with our souls leaving our bodies at the same moment." He smiled to himself. "I'll wait for your call."

Felix placed the cell carefully on the table in front of him, then he took a small pistol and two bullets from his jacket pocket. His hands were trembling, but he had no trouble inserting the bullets in their chambers.

"There," he said, looking down at the loaded gun in his hand. "I'm ready. Nothing to do now but wait."

"She's not worth it," I said. Uncensored and unwise, the words tumbled out of my mouth. "Felix, she's using you. Look at the movie. She uses everybody. She's evil and manipulative. She's destroyed so many lives already. Don't let her destroy yours." I moved towards him and reached out to touch his hand. "Listen to me," I said. "You know I'm right."

"You couldn't be more wrong," he said, and his voice was tinged with pity. "My life began the night I met Caroline MacLeish. All I've ever wanted was to share my life with her fully, deeply, completely. Her family kept us from sharing our lives. I cannot allow anyone to keep us from sharing our deaths."

Felix's face was wax-pale, drained, but his eyes had the zealot's glow. The metamorphosis of *ein prakiter Mensch* into madman was mesmerizing. When he changed the position of the gun, it took me a moment to realize that, suddenly, the muzzle was pointing at me.

CHAPTER

13

For a few moments, Felix and I sat in silence – both of us staring stupidly at the gun in his hand. I had no idea what he was thinking, but I was running through my options and there weren't many. Given what I had to work with, even Ken Dryden would have had trouble stopping the action.

For the next twenty minutes, Dan Kasperski would be in his office, in a garage that had studio-quality soundproofing so that he could practise his drums without alienating his neighbours. When he'd advised me to choose an electronic kit for Angus, Dan had demonstrated his acoustic drums. Inside the garage, they were ear-splitting, but outside, even the wildest riff was just a muffled thump. No matter how loud I screamed, there would be no help from that quarter.

And I had no idea how to appeal to the man who was aiming the gun at me. During the time I'd been a political panellist on "Canada Tonight," Felix and I had a good working relationship, but we had never fraternized outside the show. I had no reservoir of warm feelings to draw upon and no real understanding of what made him tick.

"I can't let you go." Felix's voice was too loud, and he flushed with embarrassment. "I apologize. I didn't mean to shout. This is difficult for me. I'm not a cruel man, but I can't take the chance that you'll send someone in here to stop me."

Outside, a car alarm began its rhythmic bray. The sound was an irritating staple of the urban soundscape, but Felix started as if it were a threat. The hand holding the gun moved so that the muzzle was less than six inches away from my breastbone. Fear is a powerful stimulus. Suddenly, everything fell away except the problem at hand. "If you kill me, there'll be no one left to tell your story," I said. "All there will be is Evan's film."

"A distortion," he said.

"Then you've seen it."

Felix looked stricken. "I didn't have to. I know that it's a spiteful, twisted character assassination of a woman who deserves to be venerated. She saved my life, Joanne."

"How?" I asked.

"By loving me," he said.

"That's reason enough for loyalty."

"My feelings for Caroline go beyond loyalty. I worship her."

"Then tell me about her. If I'm to be the keeper of your story, I should know everything."

"The keeper of my story. I like that," he said, but he didn't lower the gun. "I was twenty-five when we met. A very young man from a very small town, who'd made a film about a boy who fell in love with a saint."

"Autobiographical?" I asked.

Felix shrugged, "Aren't all first films? The movie was crude and naïve, but it seemed to lend itself to interpretation, so it enjoyed a certain success."

"Is that how you came to Toronto?" I asked.

"Yes," he said. "And in Toronto, I found Annie Lowell, who introduced me to the concept of life as an extreme sport."

"I saw *Black Spikes and Slow Waves*," I said.

"Then you know that I was self-destructing. I would have died the way Annie did, if Caroline hadn't redeemed me." He fell silent.

"Another saint in your life," I said.

Felix smiled. "There are always patterns," he said. "But Caroline wasn't an ideal. She was a flesh-and-blood woman. The night I met her I was at my lowest point. Annie and I had been at a party and she told me she was tired of having me hang around like a whipped dog. So of course when she left the party, I followed her to the house on Walmer Road."

"She and Evan were still living together when you had your affair?"

Felix's laugh was bitter. "Our affair meant nothing to Annie, but it meant everything to me. That night I was wasted on booze and drugs – a wreck of a human being abasing himself in every possible way. Annie did what people do with whipped dogs. She gave me a couple of verbal kicks and threw me out. I pounded on the door, begging to be taken back. For once, Fate was kind. Caroline answered the door." His eyes shone at the memory. "She invited me in. This exquisite woman had created a closed private world, where no one could follow her, but she chose me to be a part of it. I was the only one, and I stayed."

"You were lovers."

"Lovers, comrades, friends, confidantes – everything. She had no one."

"She had a house full of people, Felix – her own children, her granddaughter, Annie, Tracy."

"None of them measured up. Evan especially was a disappointment."

"In what way?"

"He needed other women."

"Women other than whom?"

"Other than Caroline. She didn't understand it. She said that the only woman Evan ever truly loved was his first wife."

"Linn Brokenshire?"

"My only knowledge of Linn Brokenshire came from Evan's movie," Felix said. "But I understood why Evan was drawn to her. She was a shining presence. After these years Caroline still loathes her."

A psychiatrist would have had no difficulty identifying the source of Caroline's antipathy for the one woman her son ever loved, but I was anxious to know the extent of Felix's illusions. "Why do you think Caroline hates Linn?" I asked.

He answered without hesitation. "Because Caroline is sufficient unto herself. Walt Whitman says that some people have a need for 'something unproved, something in a trance, something escaped from the anchorage and driving free.' Caroline never understood that longing, but Linn did and so did I."

"Evan did too," I said. "Felix, why do you think he always came home to his mother?"

"He wanted her love," Felix said. "He wanted to be the most important person in her life."

"Is that why you introduced Evan to Jill – so he'd be working on a project that would get him out of the way?"

"That was my hope. 'The Unblinking Eye' was going to be an American production that focused on American experiences. Eventually, Evan would have found it impossible to keep his base in Toronto."

"And with Evan out of the way, you'd have your chance," I said.

"What I wanted didn't matter," Felix said. "Caroline was my concern. The time had come for her to be liberated."

"From whom?"

"All of them. That's why when Jill and Evan announced their marriage, I thought my prayers had been answered. Bryn was the lynchpin that kept everyone in place. When she moved out, there'd be no reason for Claudia and Tracy to stay in the house on Walmer Road."

"And the path would be clear for you and Caroline," I said. "What went wrong? I know Claudia didn't object to the marriage. Did Tracy make some kind of threat?"

"She didn't have to," Felix said tightly. "Caroline felt the circumstances weren't right for Bryn to leave."

"I don't understand."

"Neither did I, but Caroline always knows what's best. When it was clear the wedding was inevitable, she sent me out here to convince Evan and Jill to stay in Toronto."

"And that's why you and Jill were quarrelling the night of the rehearsal."

Felix nodded miserably. "I'd assured Caroline that everything would be all right – that Jill and I had become so close, I could make her understand, but Jill had completely bought into Bryn's dream. She refused to listen to reason. So I went to Evan. I was labouring under the misapprehension that, like me, he would sacrifice anything for Caroline."

"But he wouldn't give up his plan to move to New York."

"Even worse, the night before the wedding, I discovered that it was highly likely Evan's ticket to New York was the film he'd made about Caroline."

"How did you find out?"

"A fluke. Remember the luggage mix-up we had at the airport the night we arrived in Regina?"

"Of course, that's why you were late for dinner."

Felix nodded. "I thought I'd straightened everything out. But when I was in my hotel room after the rehearsal dinner, I opened what I thought was my suitcase and discovered Evan's binder. He'd been so secretive about the project he

was working on for 'The Unblinking Eye' that I couldn't
resist checking his notes about works-in-progress. What I
found astounded me. Almost all his notations referred to
The Glass Coffin. There was only one explanation why he
would have been working so intensely on a project that was
supposed to be shown only after Caroline's death."

"He'd already sold the film to the network," I said.

"Right. So I went to his room to confront him." Felix's
laugh was short and bitter. "I had to get in line, Joanne. It
seemed another of Evan's chickens had come home to roost
that night. He and Gabe Leventhal were fighting. When Evan
opened the door, he was rubbing his jaw, and Gabe was
hunched over on the bed. He seemed to be having trouble
catching his breath."

"So Gabe did die from a heart attack," I said.

Felix looked away. "I wish that were so," he said. "Gabe
was a good man, and he deserved a good death."

"But he didn't get one," I said.

"No," Felix said. "He didn't. After I came in, Evan suggested we all have a drink and calm down. Gabe agreed, but
he said an odd thing. 'I'll drink your liquor, but it's still Sam
Waterston time – time finally to stand at moral attention.'
The reference didn't mean anything to me, but clearly it did
to Evan. The room became even more tense. Evan appeared
distracted. He said he'd forgotten he didn't have any Scotch,
and he went down to Claudia's room for a bottle. When he
came back, we had a few drinks, then Gabe slumped in his
chair. I was a little drunk myself. I suggested we order some
coffee and sober up.

"Evan was very cool. He told me Gabe had been determined to tell Jill something she didn't need to hear until
after the wedding and he'd put something in Gabe's drink to
calm him down till he could listen to reason."

I could feel the hysteria rising, but my voice was firm. "Felix, it's important for me to know how Gabe died?"

Felix's gaze was soft. "You cared for him, Joanne?"

"Yes," I said. "We didn't have much time together, but I liked him very much."

"What I'm about to tell you isn't pretty."

"I still want to hear it."

"I respect your decision," Felix said. "The moment we picked Gabe up to carry him to his room, I knew something was wrong. He wasn't moving at all. His jaw had fallen open, and his eyes were glassy." Felix closed his own eyes as if to shut out the image. "I felt for his pulse. There was none. I told Evan we had to call the police."

"And he stopped you."

"He didn't have to. Evan held up his binder and asked if I'd read it. When I admitted I had, he made me an offer. He said he knew I was in love with his mother and that if I helped him cover up Gabe's death, he'd refuse to allow the network to use the film of Caroline. I was in a state of shock. There was a dead man in the room. Everything seemed unreal. I didn't say anything. Evan seemed to interpret my silence as a rejection of his offer. He picked up the phone, handed it to me, and said, 'Call my mother and ask if she'll be able to live with your decision to expose her life.'"

"And Caroline convinced you to change your mind," I said.

Felix nodded. "Evan and I took Gabe's body down in the freight elevator and carried him out into the back alley. It was deserted. It was late, and there was a blizzard – the conditions couldn't have been more perfect. I've had nightmares about what I did every night since I walked away from that alley."

"Felix, I won't lie to you. We both know that what you did was terrible, but you were faced with an impossible choice."

"Since I introduced Jill and Evan, there've been nothing but impossible choices," Felix said. "That's why I've had to rely on Caroline's guidance."

"Were you relying on Caroline's guidance when you killed Evan?"

"She showed me we had no alternative. At the reception, Evan told me the deal was off. He said the network had called earlier that day and they were so high on *The Glass Coffin* they were bumping another program to show it during sweeps week in February."

"But that was your chance to back out and go to the police," I said. "If Evan wasn't going to honour his part of the agreement . . ."

"Honour," Felix repeated the word as if were a vestige of ancient language. "Joanne, Evan and I had left a man's body beside a dumpster behind the hotel. As Evan pointed out when I begged him to reconsider, that made us equally culpable. I was beside myself. Caroline was about to be publicly humiliated, and my stupidity had made it impossible for me to be her champion. I went downstairs and called her. Evan was her son. I thought she might have some insight into how I could appeal to him."

"But she didn't."

Felix shook his head. "She said Evan had never loved her as he should, and that he was a cancer that had to be removed from our lives."

"So Evan was murdered because he didn't love his mother enough?" I said. Even to my own ears, my horror was evident, but Felix didn't pick up on it.

"No, no," he said impatiently. "Caroline was able, as she always is, to take in the larger picture. She had seen Jill's commitment to Bryn. She saw that with Evan out of the way, Jill would be the one making the final decisions . . ."

His eyes searched my face, waiting for me to finish the

sentence. "And Jill would make certain Bryn's grandmother was protected," I said.

Felix relaxed – grateful that no further explanations were necessary. "It was only a question of waiting for the opportune time. Given Evan's family, I didn't have to wait long. When I got back to the party, Bryn and her father were arguing. At one point in their quarrel, she picked up the hunting knife. I suppose she was just being dramatic as the young often are, but unwittingly, she had shown me the way. When Evan left the room, I picked up the knife and followed him." Felix broke. "Do you know what Evan said when he saw the knife? He said, 'My mother sent you.' He was so calm it was as if he'd been waiting for that moment all his life. Then he said, 'In one way or another, she will murder us all.'"

"Evan had come to see the truth about Caroline," I said. "Making the movie must have opened his eyes."

Felix scowled. "If his eyes truly had been open, he would have seen what I saw. A woman of infinite strength. The night Evan . . . died . . . she was magnificent. After I'd done what I had to do, I was utterly spent. All I wanted was to be in Caroline's arms. I went to the hotel, showered and changed, and caught the first flight out. I brought the bloody clothes with me and left them in a locker at Pearson. I was certain she would welcome me."

"But she sent you back," I said.

"She said that by coming to Toronto I'd linked her to Evan's murder. And of course, she was right. She told me that I had to go to Regina, see the murder investigation through, then we could be together forever."

"And you believed her?"

"Why wouldn't I?"

I was exasperated. "Felix, can't you understand what happened? Caroline manipulated you, the way she's manipulated everyone else all these years. But this doesn't have to be the end of it. Your life doesn't have to end in a stranger's living room this morning. We can get people to attest to your character. We can get experts to testify about what she's done to you."

The hand holding the gun relaxed, lowering it so the muzzle pointed at the floor. Relief washed over me.

"And you really would help?" Felix said.

"I would. Jill would. So would everyone. Please. Just put down the gun, and let me get Dan Kasperski in here, so you can talk to a professional."

Our eyes locked, and for a moment I thought I had him. Then, as if to prove that evil is always a force to be reckoned with, the phone rang.

"Don't answer it," I said. "We can work this out. You can have a life."

"What kind of life would I have without her?" he said.

The phone rang again. Felix touched my shoulder. "You will tell people the truth about us, won't you?"

"I'll tell them the truth," I said.

Felix picked up the phone. "I'm ready," he said. "Thank you, Caroline. Thank you for giving even my death beauty and purpose."

When he rested the muzzle against his temple, I closed my eyes. For a moment after he pulled the trigger, I felt as if I'd been shot too. The sound of the gunshot ricocheted around the small room causing something in my brain to vibrate in sympathy. The stench of sudden death filled my nostrils, leaving me breathless and gagging. The force of the shot had driven Felix's head backwards and I noticed, as if from a great distance, that my clothes were covered with blood and something worse than blood. I felt cold – cold as the dead. I don't know how long I sat beside the body before I bent to pick up the cell from the place on the floor where it had fallen. After I called Alex, I chose the softest of Dan's quilts and placed it over Felix. On the television screen, Caroline MacLeish's image remained frozen – a wasp in amber – beyond regret, beyond pain, beyond humanity.

Suddenly I was angrier than I can ever remember being. I grabbed the remote control and hurled it at the screen. "You murdering bitch," I said. "You venomous, murdering bitch."

Only when the remote control bounced impotently to the floor did I begin to weep.

When Alex Kequahtooway arrived on the scene, I wasn't alone. At some point after the shot rang out, I'd run out to the garage and pounded on the door to Dan's office. Dan had reassured his young patient and steered me into his drum room. There among the dazzling display of Zildjian hi-hats, crashes, and earthplates, I told my story.

After I was finished, Dan took my hands in his. "You did everything you could, Joanne," he said. "And it was good that you were with Felix at the end. No man should go to his death alone."

"He didn't think he was going alone," I said. "Caroline promised that she'd die with him – a double exit."

"Do you think she kept her word?" Dan asked.

I remembered Caroline's image frozen on the TV screen. "Not a chance," I said. "Not a chance."

Alex's interview with me was consummately professional. My answers to his questions were factual but not expansive, and when he realized there was nothing more to be gleaned from questioning me, he told me I could go. He didn't chastise me for throwing the quilt over Felix's body and contaminating the suicide scene. Alex was a good cop, and he seemed to understand instinctively that the answers to Felix's suicide would not be found in forensic evidence.

The day after Felix's death, Alex called and invited me for coffee. We met – not in Marv Brenner's window – but in a small and pretty café where we'd often come to drink coffee, eat cinnamon buns, and count the moments until we could be alone. The meeting was not a success. After a few per-functory questions about how I was handling the trauma of witnessing a man's suicide, Alex lapsed into silence. I asked a few questions about Alex's future plans and about how his nephew, Eli, was doing in university, but the responses I got were monosyllabic. The air between us was heavy with the weight of things unsaid, and we left after ten minutes, each carrying an uneaten cinnamon bun in a red-and-white-checked paper bag. On the sidewalk outside the café, Alex kissed my cheek. "I wish this had gone better, Jo," he said.

"Me too," I said. I was the first to turn and walk away.

Jill and Bryn stayed with us till the last day of the old year. Claudia and Tracy had left for Toronto the night before. They were not going back to the house on Walmer Road – not that day, not ever. Their plan was to spend some time with a friend of Claudia's who lived in Garden Hill, a small town east of the city. Claudia was going to look for an acreage where she could raise and board dogs, and Tracy was going to take in the country air until her next big the-atrical break. Jill was financing the move, and she was san-guine about the fact that the investment she was making would be long-term.

Relations between Jill, Bryn, Claudia, and Tracy had been steadily improving since the four of them sat down together and watched *The Glass Coffin*. Jill described the experience as highly affecting, a breaking of the emotional logjam that had trapped the members of Caroline MacLeish's household for years. Jill said the film was the most important and enduring legacy Evan could have left his family.

The members of Evan's family weren't the only ones who gained entry to the private world of Caroline MacLeish that winter. The morning I was to drive Jill and her stepdaughter to the airport, she called me into her bedroom and pointed at the TV. The network ad campaign for *The Glass Coffin* had started. Someone at NBC had unearthed a treasure from Evan's archives of discarded footage: a poignant scene of Caroline alone in her bedroom. She was wearing a silk robe in the forget-me-not blue of her eyes and she approached the camera with a lover's intensity. "My world is smaller than most," she said. "But what my life shows it that even the smallest world can be made to yield everything. I have known loyalty and betrayal, joy and despair, and I have known love." Her fingers caressed the frame of a photograph on the elaborately carved table beside her. The camera moved in for a closeup of the picture in the frame. It was of Felix Schiff. "I have known unimaginable love," Caroline said triumphantly.

The television announcer's voice was breathless. "And Felix Schiff killed for that love – not once, but twice. In time for Valentine's, NBC is proud to present the passion that made headlines: a very special portrait of a very special love."

Beside me, Jill shuddered. "Poor Felix," she said. "Speaking of – I had a call from the funeral home yesterday. They have two boxes for me: Evan's ashes and Felix's. How's that for a going-away present?"

"Unique," I said. "What are you going to do with them?"

"I've already been in touch with Linn Brokenshire's brother about having Evan's ashes buried with her."

"That's a surprise," I said.

"It shouldn't be," Jill replied. "You were the one who told me that Evan really loved Linn, and I didn't have any other ideas. There's only one catch. The brother's a born-again, so there will have to be what he calls 'a truly Jesus-centred service.' " Jill shook her head. "After all these years, Linn is going to get to save Evan's soul."

"We get our rewards on this side of the grave or the next," I said.

"If only . . . ," Jill's eyes filled with tears. She took out a tissue and blew her nose noisily. "Anyway. That leaves Felix. What should I do about his ashes?"

"FedEx them to Caroline," I said. "To the victor go the spoils."

"What a monster she is," Jill said. "Poor Felix. Poor all of us. Do you think we'll ever be happy again?"

"Sure," I said. "It's New Year's Eve – the most hopeful night of the year – 365 days of possibilities ahead."

"And what are you doing New Year's?" Jill asked.

"We're going to Mieka's tomorrow, so I'm taking down our Christmas trees tonight," I said. "Kevin is coming over to give me a hand."

"Speaking of possibilities," Jill said. Suddenly she looked impish. "Hey, here's a plan. Let's crack open a couple of cool ones and listen to Taylor's tree one last time."

"I don't think I can take it," I said.

"Sure you can," Jill said. "It's for auld lang syne."

So my old friend and I went downstairs, opened two bottles of Great Western, and turned on Taylor's tree. We drank a toast to absent loved ones, then we sat on the floor and listened to the world's most painfully tuneless version of "The Way We Were." Above us, Jerry Garcia, once the bard of Songs of Innocence and Experience, now an icon in a Day-Glo sunburst, beamed down warmth and hope on our cold and needy world.

If you enjoyed

THE GLASS COFFIN

treat yourself to all of the
Joanne Kilbourn mysteries,
now available in stunning new
trade paperback editions
and as eBooks

McCLELLAND & STEWART

www.mcclelland.com
www.mysterybooks.ca

DEADLY APPEARANCES

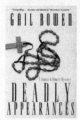

When Andy Boychuk drops dead at a political picnic, the evidence points to his wife. Joanne takes her first "case" as Canada's favourite amateur sleuth as she seeks to clear Eve Boychuk, discovering along the way a Bible college that isn't all it seems . . .

"A compelling novel infused with a subtext that's both inventive and diabolical." – Montreal *Gazette*

Trade Paperback 978-0-7710-1324-9   Ebook 978-0-7710-1322-5

MURDER AT THE MENDEL

Joanne's childhood friend, Sally Love, is an artist who courts controversy. When Sally's former partner turns up dead, Joanne discovers the past they shared was much more complicated, sordid, and deadly than she ever guessed.

"Classic. . . . Enough twists to qualify as a page turner. . . . Bowen and her genteel sleuth are here to stay." – Saskatoon *StarPhoenix*

Trade Paperback 978-0-7710-1321-8   Ebook 978-0-7710-1320-1

THE WANDERING SOUL MURDERS

Joanne's peace is destroyed when her daughter finds a young woman's body near her shop. The next day, her son's girlfriend drowns, an apparent suicide. When it is discovered that the two young women had at least one thing in common, Joanne is drawn into a twilight world where money can buy anything.

"With her rare talent for plumbing emotional pain, Bowen makes you feel the shock of murder." – *Kirkus Reviews*

Trade Paperback 978-0-7710-1319-5   Ebook 978-0-7710-1318-8

A COLDER KIND OF DEATH

When the man convicted of murdering her husband six years earlier is himself shot, Joanne is forced to relive the most horrible time of her life. But it soon gets much worse when the prisoner's menacing wife is found dead a few nights later, strangled with Joanne's own silk scarf . . .

"A terrific story with a slick twist at the end."
– Globe and Mail

Trade Paperback 978-0-7710-1317-1   Ebook 978-0-7710-1316-4

A KILLING SPRING

The head of the School of Journalism at Joanne's university is found in a seedy rooming house wearing only women's lingerie and an electrical cord around his neck. When other events indicate that it was not a case of accidental suicide, Joanne finds herself deep in a world of fear, deceit, and danger.

"A compelling novel as well as a gripping mystery."
– Publishers Weekly

Trade Paperback 978-0-7710-1315-7   Ebook 978-1-5519-9613-4

VERDICT IN BLOOD

The corpse of the respected – and feared – Judge Justine Blackwell is found in a Regina park. Joanne tries to help a good friend involved in a struggle over which of Blackwell's wills is valid, and those who stand to lose the inheritance may well be murderers willing to strike again.

"An entirely satisfying example of why Gail Bowen has become one of the best mystery writers in the country."
– London Free Press

Trade Paperback 978-0-7710-1311-9   Ebook 978-1-5519-9614-1

BURYING ARIEL

Ariel Warren, a young colleague at Joanne's university, is stabbed to death in the library, and two men are under suspicion. The apparently tight-knit academic community is bitterly divided, vengeance is in the air, and Joanne is desperate to keep the wrong person from being punished for Ariel's death.

"Nearly flawless plotting, characterization, and writing." – *London Free Press*

Trade Paperback 978-0-7710-1309-6   Ebook 978-1-5519-9615-8

THE GLASS COFFIN

Joanne's friend Jill is about to marry a celebrated documentary filmmaker, both of whose previous wives committed suicide – after he had made films about them. When the best man's dead body is found just hours before the ceremony, Joanne begins to truly fear for her friend's safety.

"Chilling and unexpected." – *Globe and Mail*

Trade Paperback 978-0-7710-1305-8   Ebook 978-1-5519-9616-5

THE LAST GOOD DAY

Joanne is on holiday at a cottage in an exclusive enclave owned by lawyers from the same prestigious firm. When one of them kills himself the night after a long talk with Joanne, she is pushed into an investigation that has startling – and possibly fatal – consequences.

"A classic whodunit in which everything from setting to plot to character works beautifully. . . . A treat from first page to final paragraph." – *Globe and Mail*

Trade Paperback 978-0-7710-1349-2   Ebook 978-1-5519-9617-2

THE ENDLESS KNOT

After journalist Kathryn Morrissey publishes a tell-all book on the adult children of Canadian celebrities, one of the parents angrily confronts her and as a result is charged with attempted murder. When the parent hires Zack Shreve, the new love in Joanne's life, to defend him, her own understanding of the knot that binds parent and child becomes both personal and very urgent.

"A late-night page turner. . . . A rich and satisfying read." – *Edmonton Journal*

Trade Paperback 978-0-7710-1347-8   Ebook 978-1-5519-9246-4

THE BRUTAL HEART

A local call girl is dead, and her impressive client list includes the name of Joanne's new husband. Shaken that Zack saw the woman regularly before they met, Joanne throws herself into her work and is soon embroiled in a bitter and increasingly strange custody battle of a local MP, who is simultaneously trying to win an election.

"Elegant. . . . Joanne rules the narrative. [*The Brutal Heart*] slips along with grace and style." – *Toronto Star*

Trade Paperback 978-0-7710-0994-5   Ebook 978-1-5519-9233-4

THE NESTING DOLLS

Just before she is murdered, a young woman hands her baby to a perfect stranger and disappears. The stranger is the daughter of lawyer Delia Wainberg, and soon a secret from Delia's youth comes out. Not only is a killer on the loose, but the dead woman's partner is demanding custody of the child, and the battle threatens to tear apart Joanne's own family.

"The underlying human drama of love and good intentions gone very, very bad make the novel a compelling read." – *Vancouver Sun*

Trade Paperback 978-0-7710-1276-1   Ebook 978-0-7710-1277-8

Edward Willet

GAIL BOWEN's first Joanne Kilbourn mystery, *Deadly Appearances* (1990), was nominated for the W.H. Smith/ Books in Canada Best First Novel Award. It was followed by *Murder at the Mendel* (1991), *The Wandering Soul Murders* (1992), *A Colder Kind of Death* (1994) (which won an Arthur Ellis Award for best crime novel), *A Killing Spring* (1996), *Verdict in Blood* (1998), *Burying Ariel* (2000), *The Glass Coffin* (2002), *The Last Good Day* (2004), *The Endless Knot* (2006), *The Brutal Heart* (2008), and *The Nesting Dolls* (2010). In 2008 *Reader's Digest* named Bowen Canada's Best Mystery Novelist; in 2009 she received the Derrick Murdoch Award from the Crime Writers of Canada. Bowen has also written plays that have been produced across Canada and on CBC Radio. Now retired from teaching at First Nations University of Canada, Gail Bowen lives in Regina. Please visit the author at www.gailbowen.com.